Mirror

Michael Koogler

Mirror

By Michael Koogler

ISBN: 978-1-943519-07-1

Book editing by Elizabeth Humphrey
Bookworm Editing, Littleton, Colorado USA

Book cover art, packaging, and design by
Kreative Storm Press, Coralville, Iowa USA

Map illustration by Clayton Chambers. ©2015 Clayton Chambers.
Chambers Studios, LLC. All Rights Reserved.
www.chambersstudios.com

Other works by Michael Koogler:

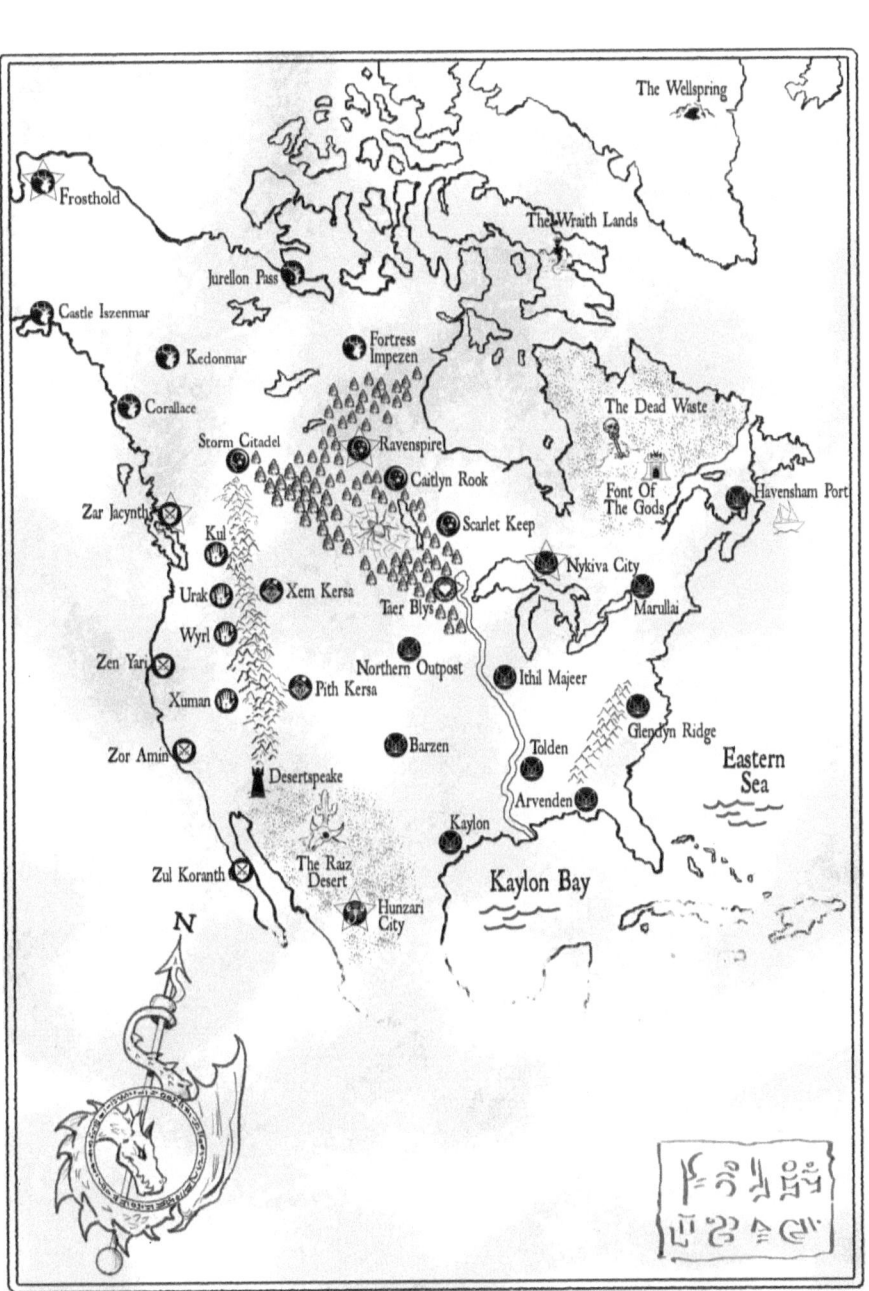

The Wellspring

Frosthold

The Wraith Lands

Jurellon Pass

Castle Iszenmar

Kedonmar

Fortress Impezen

The Dead Waste

Corallace

Storm Citadel

Ravenspire

Caitlyn Rook

Font Of The Gods

Havensham Port

Zar Jacynth

Scarlet Keep

Kul

Nykiva City

Urak

Xem Kersa

Marullai

Wyrl

Taer Blys

Zen Yar

Northern Outpost

Ithil Majeer

Xuman

Pith Kersa

Zor Amin

Barzen

Glendyn Ridge

Eastern Sea

Tolden

Desertspeake

Kaylon

Arvenden

Zul Koranth

The Raiz Desert

Hunzari City

Kaylon Bay

N

For Aaron

Prologue

The tinkling of the tiny bell over the shop's entry door signaled the departure of the last customer of the day. Old Sam Spade shut down the lights. He then shuffled around the edge of the worn counter and walked slowly to the front door to lock up for the night.

Spade was far older than he looked. He looked to be all of 70, his face grizzled and his hair white. But the black short sleeved t-shirt he wore did nothing to hide a powerful physique, and his arms bulged with corded muscle. Still, he was tired and his movements showed it.

He'd been in business for nearly twenty years now, living under the name of one of his favorite Dashiell Hammett characters while running Spade's Pawn and Consignment. While he was certainly a fan of Humphrey Bogart's depiction of the detective in the movie, Spade much preferred the book-written character Hammett created in his 1930 novel, *The Maltese Falcon*.

Name aside, Spade's life as a pawn shop owner was a relaxing one, but one that he knew he was going to have to end soon, like he had ended so many of his past lives. Twenty years—that was about all his kind could hope to get out of any layover during their journey of immortality. Twenty years was about all they could risk before mortals started asking questions.

He would miss it, to be sure. He loved Branson, Missouri, and it loved him back. But for the last few months, he had been laying the groundwork for his new life further north, this time in Little Falls, Minnesota, some ways north of St. Cloud. He'd see a lot more snow up there than here in Branson, but he'd get in a lot more fishing, too, and that was always a good thing. In Little Falls, he'd be able to put in another couple of decades before he would be forced to do it all over again somewhere else. Whether he stayed in the States or ventured to another country again, though, remained to be seen.

Such was the life—and the curse—of the immortal Arcai.

As he threw the deadbolt on the front door and turned back toward the counter, he suddenly felt a presence and he realized that he was not alone. It wasn't just a mortal presence, either. No, it was something far more. Another Arcai had come calling and that was more than a little disturbing, all things considered.

Most of his brothers and sisters steered clear of each other and had for hundreds of years now. Earth had progressed mostly beyond the need or desire for gods or their children—and truthfully, the old gods had only a fraction of the powers they once enjoyed, when the prayers of their faithful rang out strong and loud. Their Arcai offspring had even less strength today, and yet he was one of the strongest that remained. What he felt in the sudden presence in his shop, though, was something from the old days; something that far outstripped his own power, and it left him feeling cold.

"I confess that I'm at a loss," he said aloud, knowing the intruder could hear him clearly. "I haven't seen any of my siblings for well over a hundred years."

Only the silence answered him.

"Still, I know when I feel the presence of another such as I," he went on, reaching under the counter and picking up a worn leather belt that had been coiled up, laying there for years on the outside chance he might need it. "You are neither," he finished, casually strapping the belt about his waist. The artifact came to life and power thrummed through him as he reconnected with it for the first time in ages.

"I sense your companion stirring," a women's voice finally spoke up from the shadows of the darkened store, her voice quietly dangerous. "Where is she?"

"That's an odd question," Spade replied, peering into the darkness.

He still saw nothing. "Show yourself, that I may see who I am speaking with."

He was somewhat surprised to see the figure materialize immediately out of the shadows. She was clad in unadorned robes of black, the silk cloth shimmering in the gloom. A cowl was pulled up high over her head, hiding her features.

"Your companion," the woman said again, an edge to her voice now. "Where is she?"

Spade shook his head. "You speak in riddles," he said plainly. "There is only you and me. I have never taken a companion—well, at least in the past several hundred years."

There was a soft laugh of understanding, but devoid of mirth. "I sense that life follows different rules in this world," she remarked.

"Ah, so now we're getting somewhere," Spade said. "We have established that you're a stranger here, and the fact that I don't know who you are seems to corroborate that. You are not from this world, which means you have found a way to cross over, haven't you."

"An astute observation, Immortal," the woman said, reaching up and pulling back her cowl, revealing her face for the first time. Her skin was pale, almost alabaster. Her dark eyes glittered with a malevolence that Spade had only seen in one of the old gods, long ago, but never in one of their children. He knew immediately that this woman was extremely dangerous and well beyond him. He felt a slight tinge of regret, knowing that this was where it would likely end for him. So much for the fishing in Minnesota he had been looking forward to.

"Your arrival here means the merging is finally upon us, the prophecies coming to pass," Spade said with a knowing nod, strangely at peace with what he knew was going to happen.

"I am not aware of the prophecies of your world," she said. "Enlighten me so that I may know their importance."

"Time is not endless and will ultimately pass, as will the power of the gods and their children," he said, more out of habit than because she requested it. "With their waning, the barrier will weaken. The end draws nigh when one that is your sibling but is not, crosses the barrier."

"I've never known prophecy to be so direct," she said scornfully.

"Well, I'm paraphrasing and it's more of a personal message anyway, father to son."

"Was there any more to it?"

"A little," Spade answered with a shrug, shuffling around the counter again to face the strange woman. "Something about protecting the Nexus, but I don't think that matters here."

"The Nexus?" she questioned, visibly surprised.

"Like I said, it's more of a personal message. You wouldn't be interested."

"Share it anyway," she commanded.

"Naw," Spade countered, moving his feet into a combat stance and bracing himself. "Deal with the disappointment."

"You cannot defeat me, Immortal," she said quietly, a smile of condescension on her face.

"Probably not," Spade shrugged. Even with the belt's power surging through him, he already felt the limits of his strength. If she was as strong as her presence indicated, it would be a short fight and he was going to be on the losing end of it. He wouldn't give her the pleasure of knowing that, though. "That doesn't mean I'm not going to give you a good ass-kicking before I check out," he finished, giving her a look of contempt.

"A colorful threat, if pointless," she said dangerously. "I am Arcai like you, yet I am more than you. Much more."

"You also talk too much, lady," he scoffed. "How 'bout you just shut up and bring it."

Without another word, she did, stepping forward and raising her hands, a sickly green light beginning to gather at her fingertips.

The old pawn shop owner moved so fast, she never even saw him as he covered the ten feet between them as if it were nothing. His fists hit her simultaneously, slamming into her chest with force enough to shatter stone. The strength of the blow smashed her backward through several counters and a rack of clothing, leaving her half buried in a pile of clothes and debris. Shoving the wreckage aside, she got up slowly— not due to pain, but because of surprise and not a little bit of anger.

Standing tall once more, she stepped away from the ruined counters and items and disdainfully brushed a hand across her shoulder as if shooing away a fly. "Impressive strength, Immortal, but not nearly enough to harm me," she said with a wicked smile. "What is your name, so that I may know who you are before I kill you."

"That's really none of your business," Spade said flatly, "but I told you I was going to give you an ass-beating. That much, you can still count on."

He moved forward again with a speed that was nearly a blur, but this time she was ready for him, vanishing from where she stood and reappearing behind him. Before he could reorient himself, she had grabbed him around the neck and spun him to the floor with a strength that was much more than his own.

Spade started to roll back to his feet, but she drove a knee hard into the side of his head, slamming him up against the oaken counter where he conducted all of his business. Before he could recover, she tangled her fingers in his hair and pulled him back to his feet effortlessly. "Did you honestly think," she growled, smashing her forehead into his nose, shattering bone in a spray of blood, "that you could hurt me?"

Spade went slack, his eyes rolling back in his head, still being supported by the single hand that held him up. He had fought many times in his life, his opponents ranging from other Arcai to fantastical monsters to the gods themselves. He had even fought and defeated a titan once. But never, in all his long life, had he been hit as hard as she hit him. And if that wasn't enough, she head-smashed him two more times, fracturing his orbital bone and breaking his jaw.

Just like that, he knew he was beaten. With little hope, he tried to draw strength from his belt, from the one item that had been bequeathed to him by his father, an artifact of the gods themselves. But even as he felt the wave of power begin to flow into his weakened limbs, it vanished. Opening his one good eye, he saw that she was holding the belt in her left hand, having ripped it effortlessly from his waist while she still held him up with her right.

"So this is your companion?" she taunted and, as he watched in a daze, her hand flared with bright blue fire, which ran the length of the belt. In seconds, the belt was little more than a charred strip which quickly fell apart as so much ash.

He felt the sudden weakness associated with the loss of the artifact acutely, but it didn't matter anymore. Even with the strength that it could have given him, augmenting his own godly powers, he would not have been able to beat her. And the fact that she destroyed his artifact so effortlessly told him that not only was she more than a match for him and his brothers and sisters, but she was likely a match for the gods themselves. It left him with little doubt that the end was finally upon them all.

"Pathetic," she went on and then leaned closer. He noticed the change immediately…her eyes had grown darker, a reddish tint growing deep within the widening black of her irises. Her lips curled back from her teeth in a sneer, showing elongated fangs, sharp and lethal. "In my world, our godly parents bestowed the gift of dragons upon us, not cheap trinkets," she finished.

"My father..." Spade mumbled through blood and broken teeth, "said something about those dragons, too." He coughed, blood dribbling down his chin. 'The sibling who is not, is but a pittance,'" he quoted. "'Rather, fear the dragon who would be God.'"

A look of rage passed across the woman's face and without another word, she leaned forward, her mouth opening wide, baring her teeth.

Sam Spade had been known by many names over the millennia that he had lived. The names he took when masquerading as a mortal were varied and colorful, always relating to something important in his life or something that he enjoyed. The original name he had been given by his father, Zeus, however, was Hercules.

The woman tore his throat out.

Shayene returned to New York City the following night, sated on the blood of the Arcai, the first she had confronted in this strange new world. She had killed the demigod outright, draining him dry, as it would not do to have another Arcai with similar powers to her own running loose, even if he was under her control. She would not be challenged. Ever.

As she entered her apartment, she found Grum waiting for her, seated in his customary place on the small stone platform in the middle of the fireplace. The fire burned brightly around him, the flames licking at his scales. But he was wholly unaffected and stepped out of the flames to hop up on the mantle, where he could better see her. He was a small being, no more than three feet in height, thin and gangly with green and black scales and sharp claws and teeth. An imp with exceptional intelligence and a nasty streak of malice that rivaled anything she had encountered before, Shayene had summoned him from the depths of the Nether shortly after arriving in this world. He had turned out to be a capable servant, if a little irritating at times.

"I sense his power on you," Grum said, his voice low and gravelly as he looked closely at her.

"It will pass," she said off-handedly, considering his words. Indeed, when she had taken the blood of the Arcai, she had felt his strength take root within her, adding itself to her own. But as she returned to New York City, the added strength began to ebb away and by the time she had stepped back into her home, it was all but gone. "He was known as Hercules," she went on thoughtfully. "I explored his thoughts as he died. What do you know of him?"

"Son of Zeus," Grum replied immediately, having been studying the tomes of this world since he had arrived, learning all he could about the gods and their Arcai children and the myriad of different names they called themselves. "Great strength he had."

"That's disappointing," she smiled. "He put up little fight."

"Weak are the Arcai of this world," Grum went on. "Science rules here, Mistress, and the Arcai have faded. Elusive they will be, now that one of their own has been killed."

"Indeed," she agreed, "They are already stirring. They feel the void."

"They will hide."

"I will find them."

"Perhaps, but what of the fallen?" the imp changed the subject, and he did nothing to hide the challenge in his voice. "You forget them, Mistress. This displeases me."

"They continue to sleep, awaiting my call," she soothed him. "Have patience, Grum. You will bear witness to their awakening. I have promised you this."

"Call them soon?" Grum asked greedily. "I desire what they will bring to this world."

"Very soon, Grum," Shayene replied, walking toward her bedroom, before stopping and tracing her fingers down the jawline of a man who stood motionless next to her door. He stood where he always stood, guarding her chambers, alert and at attention, but never moving unless she dispatched him on a specific task. "It is a shame they could not all be like this one here," she purred. "But it would not do to be worshipped by a world of mindless automations. I desire their feelings, their emotions, and their fear. The fallen retain all of that."

"I don't like this one," Grum growled, glaring up at the French commando, one of those who had gone through her original gate more than a year ago. "I have never liked this one."

"He will serve his purpose for as long as I consent to let him live," she said seductively. "When I grow tired of him, I will simply dispose of what's left."

"He will be given to me?" Grum asked gleefully. "I should very much like to eat him."

"We will see, Grum," she said lightly, walking into her chambers. "In the meantime, continue studying the Arcai of this world. See what you can discover about their companions." She paused and then turned to look at him. "Oh, and Grum?"

"Yes, Mistress?"

"What do you know of the Nexus?"

The unblinking eyes of Aramis Bonheur watched her enter her chambers, Grum hopping happily along behind her, chattering away in his guttural language. Bonheur was the perfect soldier. He never moved, never slept, and never questioned orders. He did exactly what he was told to do and had done so ever since Shayene had delivered him from death in the Wraithlands at the hands of Rick Branson. On the outside and in his world, he would be called a machine— emotionless, detached, cold.

On the inside, though, his silent screams continued within the never-ending nightmare of his undead life.

Interlude I

The day was sunny and calm, and the ocean waters lapped gently across the fine sands of the beach. The rasping calls of seagulls fishing in the shallows cut through the air and a single figure stood ankle-deep in the surf, deft hands sweeping through the water, plucking small crabs from the ocean and tossing them into a tattered cloth bag that hung from the frayed rope tied around his waist. It was a day like any other day for the old man, safely sequestered on his little island, comfortably away from the misery of man—and Arcai—and without a care in the world.

All that changed when the sky caught fire and thunder exploded overhead, the force of it flinging him into the surf. Shrieking angrily, the gulls took wing and the old man struggled to his knees, wiping water from his face, his eyes wide in shock.

At the far end of the beach was the little hut the old hermit had built years ago from tree branches and woven palm fronds. Behind that was a line of trees, the edge of the thick tract of woodland that comprised more than three quarters of the total island. A short way in, smoke was already beginning to rise above the treetops.

Slowly, the old man climbed back to his feet, eyes on the rising plume, the crabs he was gathering for dinner forgotten. He had been on the island for nearly a decade, eschewing all contact with any other humans, Arcai, or their companions…especially their companions. He embraced his solitude, sharing his home only with the seagulls and the wildlife that lived in the woods. It was a peaceful existence and, beyond weathering the occasional storm or hurricane, nothing unexpected ever happened.

This, however, was altogether new and he did not like what it might portend.

He hurried to his little hut, his bare feet kicking up the sand as he kept his eyes on the rising smoke. Nearest that he could tell, the source couldn't be more than a few minutes by foot into the trees directly behind his shelter and, if it turned out to be something hostile, he wanted to be ready for it. Leaning up against the wall of the hut was his spear, well-kept and crafted of an iron and steel alloy that kept it rust-free, the last reminder of his previous life. He grabbed it, feeling its familiar weight in his hands again. It triggered uncomfortable memories, but he pushed them down, hardened his resolve, and started off toward the trees.

Before he reached the tree line, there was a heavy crashing sound, followed by a grunt of pain and a high-pitched squeal. A strange voice shouted out, cracked and broken. "I have visual on the package! Heading is Valkyrie Niner Niner Two! Request launch permission!"

Silence.

The old hermit braced the spear and waited. He recognized the language as an odd derivative of his own and, while he could understand it, he had no idea what the voice was talking about.

"Repeat, Valkyrie Niner Niner Two!" the voice repeated, nearly a wail now.

The breeze blew off the sands, ruffling the palm fronds, but no words answered back.

"Equipment malfunction," the voice went on, suddenly changing pitch and this time sounding female. "Launch mechanism disabled."

"I'm going to have to ditch!" the wailing voice returned. "Requesting immediate evac!"

The silence returned while the gulls continued to circle, eyeing the ground below them. The old hermit remained frozen, waiting. For some time, there was nothing.

Finally, when it seemed as if nothing more would happen, there was a rustling sound in the trees as if something big and ponderous was moving toward the beach. Moments later, the thing emerged from the tree line, pulling itself laboriously onto the sand. It might have once been a man, but its body had been merged with metal and wire, turning it into what could only be described as a monster.

The hermit stared in horror as the creature moved toward him, its head down, seemingly oblivious to his presence. It pulled itself forward with arms that looked mostly normal—but beneath the shoulders, it was hard to tell where the man ended and the machine began. Its body was a mangled wreck of flesh and metal and, where his legs should be, there were only ragged stumps. There was little blood, far less than the hermit would have believed judging by the injuries, but the thing was in obvious agony. It whimpered in pain as it moved, dragging itself toward the water.

"Who are you?" the old man finally asked, spear still at the ready.

The creature stopped and slowly raised its head, and the hermit had to consciously force himself not to take a shocked step backward. There wasn't much left of the man's face—a forehead and left eye and part of a mouth, pushed to the side where his cheek should be. The rest of his face was a hybrid of metal, wires, and blinking lights, all seeming to have fused with his flesh.

"Help…me," he said, and this time his voice was more a man's, full of agony and fear.

His own fear suddenly gone, the old hermit dropped his spear and knelt in the sand, turning the man over to his back so he could better ascertain his injuries. His body turned out to be much like his face, a ghastly mix of flesh and machinery. "By the gods," he muttered quietly, probing with his hands, trying to understand what lay in the sand before him. It didn't take him long to realize that he was not looking at a wounded man. The metal and wires were not imbedded into his body; they were part of his body. He was looking at a man remade into something else.

"Help…me," the man gasped again.

The old hermit looked down helplessly, having no idea what he could do. Perhaps a healer, maybe, but himself? He had no healing magic. If he had, he might have saved his treasured companion one day long ago and perhaps the last decade would have been vastly different for him. But no, all he could do was try to make the man's last hours as comfortable as possible.

"What's your name, son?" he asked quietly, placing his wrinkled hand on the thing's forehead.

"My…name," it said. "My name…is…"

"Take your time," the hermit said gently.

"I am…Rook," it finally said. "Rook."

"Well, Rook," the old man said softly, "you're safe. Rest now. I will do what I can to help you."

The stranger seemed to relax. His remaining eye closed and the lights blinking on the metal parts of his face and body slowed and dimmed. The hermit sat back on his haunches, watching. There was nothing for him to do but wait for Rook to die. He thought he would not have to wait long.

But Rook did not die that day, or the next, or the next. Lying in the sand where he had collapsed, he awoke time and again, feverish and in agony, shouting strange words and phrases in voices that were not always his own. The old hermit tended to him as best he could right there, afraid to move him. He built a fire next to his body and fed him sips of crab soup and water. In time, the fever broke and the old hermit realized that his mutilated visitor was not going to die. Instead, he began to get stronger. Rook's moments of lucidity were longer and more frequent, but the old man understood nothing of what had happened to bring the man to his little island. He only knew that the man was still grievously wounded and needed help.

Finally, three weeks after Rook arrived, the hermit prepared to depart himself for the mainland. He left Rook in his hut where he had finally moved him, a pot of soup, plenty of dried fish, and containers of water. He hoped it would be enough to last Rook until he returned. It had been ten long years since the old man had been on the mainland and he wasn't looking forward to returning. Doing so meant forsaking his vow to never have contact with the outside world again. But Rook needed help, and there was one individual the hermit thought he could still trust.

That is, if she didn't kill him first.

Mirror

Part 1

Birth

Mirror

Chapter 1

The firelight burned low in the cave as Terion knelt beside the makeshift bed of pine needles and ran the damp cloth across the woman's forehead. She slept fitfully now, her body tensing at regular intervals, and for the first time in what seemed like months, his weapons had been laid aside and he was able to concentrate on the woman and her condition.

It was time.

After the events in the Wraithlands nearly nine months ago, he had mourned his personal losses in ways that had surprised him. To feel the loss of a companion and a friend like Cavanah was one thing; to feel the kind of loss that had struck him when the gate had closed, trapping Cavanah's killer in the Nether, was something he had struggled mightily to reconcile. Her loss had saddened him, and something about that felt supremely wrong. But something else about it also felt very right. Eventually, he realized he could not put it to rest—not until he knew there was truly no hope.

Shortly after the end of the war, he had traveled to Ravenspire under the pretense of accompanying the Dom'Ithi council leader, Myngar, on official business and paying their respects to the Vi'Raaji queen for her aid in helping defend Nykiva in the final battle. But he had also gone for another reason—to ask a question from a renowned Vi'Raaji seer known only as the Revelator, a mysterious and wholly dangerous sorceress that few men in all the land would consider approaching. She was not only well-known for her ability to accurately divine future events, but also for the price she would sometimes exact upon those seeking her guidance.

But because of his actions in helping defeat Shayene in the Wraithlands, and no little bit of input from the Vi'Raaji queen herself, the seer had granted him his one question, requiring nothing in return. She had seemed to know what his question would be and shown him his answering vision almost before he had finished speaking. Then he was off, practically running from Ravenspire and plunging himself into the Spider Forest. He had no idea where he would find her, only that she was alive.

And in grave danger.

He searched every day without fail, traversing the woodland paths and daring even the hunting grounds of the great spiders deep in the center of the forest. He fought often and left a trail of dead arachnids and other dangerous hunting creatures behind him as his search dragged into weeks and then months.

Several times, her trail had become very fresh, and one time he had even caught sight of her. But she vanished immediately upon setting eyes on him. Terion knew why, too. The Vi'Raaji possessed the Star Stone and, although it still pained him how she had come by the artifact, he was able to set that loss aside and continue searching. The war had been brutal and the dead, including friends and companions, were many and buried. What mattered now was what would happen in the future, and that is what drove him.

Winter set in and his searching slowed, hampered by cold and snow that piled higher and higher. Yet he never stopped looking. It was rough going, but at least the spiders were gone, hibernating in burrows and nests throughout the forest. Most of them, anyway. Some still stirred. One found the woman before he did.

She had taken refuge in a cave—the very cave they were in now. She was wounded and ill and being stalked by a monstrous predator that had been pursuing her for weeks. Terion still shivered at his encounter with the creature. It was one of the great forest spiders, easily as large as a horse. It was mottled white and, despite its huge size, it was sleek and fast, blending well with the winter landscape. When Terion found it, it was just beginning to work its bulk into the cave, seeking to finally take its prey. He had caught it from behind and inflicted several nasty wounds to it before it had gotten itself backed out of the cave and turned to face him.

At that point, the warrior found himself in one of the most dangerous fights of his life. Even wounded, the creature was more than a match for him and pursued him relentlessly. Terion knew that the spider only had to catch him once and he was finished. That would only be a matter of time. It seemed that, no matter how many times he was able to get in a cut or a slash, the monster kept coming.

Ultimately, it was sheer luck that saved him. Exhausted from the battle, he had backed up against the trunk of a large tree. The spider had rushed in just as Terion jumped to catch hold of a branch above his head to escape it. But the brittle wood had snapped and he fell back to the ground, the six foot piece of wood in his hands. Unable to stop its momentum, the spider ended up driving nearly half of the branch's length through one of its huge eyes and into its brain.

Terion had still nearly been killed as the frenzied thrashing of the dying monster had almost crushed him against the tree. But eventually, it was over. The huge hunter was dead and Terion had survived.

Bruised and battered, but thankfully not bitten, he stumbled back to the cave, hoping to catch the Vi'Raaji witch before she teleported away. But she was heavy with child now and had been wounded earlier by the spider. She was unconscious and shivering and nearly dead when Terion carried her further into the cave and began to take care of her. He made a bed out of pine needles dug from underneath the snow and dried by a fire he had built near the cave mouth.

At any other time, such a blaze would have drawn other predators from miles around, even if it would have kept them out of the cave itself. But the huge spider he had killed most likely had driven the others far away from its hunting grounds. So Terion counted on that and kept the fire well-tended, which made the cave comfortably warm.

He could not bring himself to butcher the huge arachnid for food, so he had used the Star Stone, returning to Nykiva for supplies as needed. He told only his long-time friend, Notyet, of what was happening, preferring to keep the woman's existence a secret from anyone else for now. Notyet implored him to at least bring her to safety, but Terion knew that she was too ill to be moved, and the Star Stone—the weakest of the set of artifacts—had been created for the use of one person at a time. He could have probably used it to move both of them a very limited distance—a few hundred yards at the most—before needing a day to recharge. But that would have been of no help at all.

So he stayed with her in the cave, taking care of her as best he could, dealing with her wounds as well as her pregnancy. Before he had stumbled upon her, the monstrous spider had gotten a fang into her thigh and, while Terion was able to heal the deep puncture would, it was her own inner strength against poisons that allowed her to ultimately survive the venomous bite.

Two weeks later, she finally awakened.

Terion knew the situation between them was tenuous at best, but instead of keeping the artifact away from her and trying to convince her to stay, he had simply given the Star Stone back to her and allowed her to decide if she would use it to run from him again. It was the ultimate act of trust on his part and for several hours, she held it close, her eyes never leaving his. Neither spoke a word, the silence between them speaking volumes itself.

Finally, she handed the stone back to him, curled up around her swollen belly, and fell asleep without a word. Terion stayed by her side through the night, finally falling asleep himself, his head resting near her own. When he awoke with a start in the morning, she was already awake, tracing a slender finger down his cheek, her eyes intently studying his face.

"Why have you come?" she asked as he opened his eyes, her voice gentle and soft, nothing like the cold voice of the assassin who had nearly killed him in the past.

Terion could only shrug. "I don't know," he stammered. He honestly did not understand what drew him to her, only that something had.

"Did you think that because you saved me in Balgar's mansion, that I would be grateful and fall in love with you when you saved me again?" she asked pointedly, but there was no malice in her voice. Only honesty.

"No," Terion replied, "at least I don't think so."

The Vi'Raaji smiled and said nothing, but her eyes saw the truth in his own.

"Look, Vendetta," he began, but she quickly held up a finger and placed it against his lips.

"No longer," she said quietly, her eyes meeting his. "I prefer my given name."

"But I thought…"

"A friend once told me that I cannot change who I was, but I can decide who I will be," she explained, looking at him intently.

"Of course, I also remember you telling me that if I ever uttered your birth name again, there would be no end to the pain you would inflict upon me," he pointed out.

She offered him a half smile. "Things change," she replied. "People change."

For long minutes, neither spoke, until Terion cleared his throat and looked away, feeling somewhat flustered. "So, uh…what happens next?"

"That depends on you," she answered. "I am grateful to you for saving me again. It seems I am deeper in your debt. But I cannot ask you to stay with me."

"What if I want to?" he asked, a little hastier than he was comfortable with. He had only felt this way one other time in his life, and that had ended in tragedy when his betrothed was killed by the guardian in the Font of the Gods. But now? This woman was an assassin! She had killed a dear friend of his and tried to kill him, as well. How could he be falling for someone like her? But he had. And he had no idea how he should feel about it.

"If you choose to stay," she said softly, her eyes straying away from him as if she, too, was struggling with what was happening between them, "I will be grateful."

"Then I choose to stay," he answered, before finishing with a smile, "Avenrael."

That had been nearly two months ago. The Vi'Raaji had slowly worked on regaining her strength within the confines of the cave, getting her feet back underneath her and stretching out her muscles. Her belly continued to grow and, as winter moved into its final days, they both understood that their situation was still dire. They had only had to defend themselves twice against the arachnid predators, but both those times had happened within the past six days. The weather was warming and the spiders were stirring. In a short time, they would be out hunting in force and ravenous from their long winter slumber. As deep in the heart of the forest as they were, that meant the truly monstrous spiders were nearby.

Then Avenrael had taken sick again, a fever coming upon her suddenly one night. Terion had been awakened as she thrashed next to him and he had spent the rest of the night and most of the next day doing everything he could to cool her body with melting snow. Eventually, the fever had broken, but it had left her weak and helpless.

The first contraction came not long after.

Nearly a day later, Terion was still kneeling beside her, talking softly as he brushed her damp hair away from her face, their eyes meeting again. Her beautiful and exotic face was tight with pain, her dark skin shining with sweat as she endured another contraction. They had been coming stronger and stronger over the past hour and Terion knew the baby was about to be born.

For as bad as their predicament was, he was as prepared as he could be with what he had brought back from Nykiva. He had a couple of blankets folded up nearby and a metal pot that he had melted snow in and brought to a boil over the fire. The fire had burned lower, but it would be enough to keep out any predators, should they stumble upon them. He silently prayed that none would. Helping Avenrael deliver her child while trying to fight off a hungry spider was not something he was anxious to attempt.

Avenrael bore the pain well and did not cry out, but as the moment arrived, she gripped Terion's hand with a strength that left him wincing in pain. Freeing his hand as gently as he could, he positioned himself to deliver the Vi'Raaji's child. The birth itself was quick. Three pushes and the infant crowned, a swirl of dark hair preceding her entrance into the world. Terion gently guided the baby onto the blanket he had prepared, oblivious to the tears gathering at the corners of his eyes.

A baby. The birth of a child! A beautiful baby girl! For the moment, nothing else mattered to him. Not the past. Not even the future. Only this single precious moment that he wished would last forever.

It was at that moment when all hell broke loose.

As the baby's first cry sounded out, a foul stench filled the cave as a portal of dark energy opened up not more than a dozen feet away. It was roughly the size of a man and fluctuated wildly, wavering in the air as it sent out tendrils of purplish sparking electricity. Terion felt the electrical energy twist about him as he gently lifted the newborn baby into his arms. Numbing cold shot through his body, but he fought it off as he laid the baby next to her mother. She was beautiful, pale skin and raven hair, an image in stark contrast to her dark-skinned, light-haired mother.

"Rayne," Avenrael whispered, her eyes closing in exhaustion, a happy smile on her face. She was completely unaware of the otherworldly happening that had followed her daughter into the world.

Kraegor the Black stepped through the portal. In his human form, he looked as he always had, tall and angular and draped in black robes embroidered with silver runes and symbols. But there was something more to him now, an ancient, dark power seeming to surround him.

The human-form dragon drew himself up to his full height and stared at the scene before him—the Vi'Raaji witch who had survived her battle with him by stealing back the Star Stone and leaving him trapped in the Nether, the newborn baby that was even now laying in her arms, and the pitiful human warrior grabbing up his weapons to gallantly defend the woman and child.

The baby stopped crying just as the portal behind him snapped shut and, with a casual wave of his hand, he sent the warrior slamming into the rock wall of the cave, knocking the man senseless.

"Well, well," Kraegor said as he stepped forward and leered down at the helpless witch and her baby—a child he knew with absolute certainty was his. His voice was low and throaty, full of menace. "What an amazing coincidence we have here."

"No…" Avenrael gasped, curling herself protectively around her newborn daughter. But Kraegor raised a hand again and her voice was cut off as an invisible force constricted her throat.

"I suppose I should simply kill you and the baby," he said, drawing nearer, staring down at her, his eyes hungry. "But there is just too much going on here to ignore."

With one hand, Avenrael clawed desperately at her throat. With the other, she cradled her baby closer, desperate to protect her. But she was helpless to stop him, stars beginning to swim before her eyes as she was slowly strangled. Kraegor simply reached down and took the baby from her arms.

"No, I think it far better to let you live," he went on, his voice like ice. "Taking from you again really seems the better decision," he finished with a perfectly depraved smile.

With another wave of his hand, he released the choking force from the Vi'Raaji and then turned away, the newborn tucked under one arm, her cries silent now. He began walking toward the front of the cave, stopping as he drew near the dying flames. He paused to look back at the woman one more time as she choked and gasped for breath. "I admit, I do not fully understand the circumstances that have allowed me to return to our world and claim my daughter from you," he said, "but I will in time." He looked down at the child in his arms. "Rayne you have named her? I like that. I really do." Then he walked past the fire and into the night.

"NO!" Avenrael screamed, as the dragon disappeared into the darkness. Pain roared through her belly as she tried to climb to her feet and she fell back to the bed helplessly.

Terion had regained his senses enough to see the dragon depart and had crawled back to his feet, his sword in hand. He took several shaky steps toward the cave entrance before Avenrael grabbed her belly and moaned in agony. It took him only a moment to realize what was happening and it tore at him like nothing before. Rayne had been taken by the dragon, and he knew he would have given his life to save her. But on the pine needle bed lay Avenrael, in agony and not yet done. There was really only one decision he could make.

Tossing his sword to the floor, he positioned himself once more, this time to deliver Avenrael's second child. Biting back the feelings of failure that threatened to overwhelm him, he spoke quickly and gently to her, talking her through the desperate moments of losing one baby daughter and giving birth to her second.

Fyre came into the world much like her twin sister—with a baby's cry and the opening of another portal that once again threw ribbons of energy throughout the cave. As Terion laid the crying baby beside her mother, he caught one crackling bolt directly in the chest and, for the second time that night, he found himself lying dazed and motionless on the cave floor.

But instead of anyone coming through the second portal, this one began to collapse back in on itself, encompassing mother and baby in a cocoon of energy, before finally vanishing with a pop and the strong smell of ozone.

Of Avenrael and the baby, nothing remained except for the blood-stained blankets and the echoing sound of a baby's cries.

Terion was alone.

Chapter 2

The first thing that Terion realized after the gut-wrenching disappearance of Avenrael and her baby, was that the Star Stone was gone. Frantically, he tore apart the interior of the cave, rifling through their meager belongings and searching through the pine needle bed, but it could not be found. He had no idea if it had disappeared with Avenrael or if Kraegor had taken it when he had abducted Rayne. Whatever the case, it left his options extremely limited. He knew what he had to do and where he had to go—the problem was going to be getting there.

Setting his mind on the monumental task before him, he packed up what he needed and dressed for the journey, taking particular care to roll up the birthing blankets and tuck them into his pack. As morbid as it was, he knew that he would need them if he was going to find Avenrael and Fyre. He was ready to go in less than five minutes. The intelligent thing would have been to wait until the sun rose, but Terion wasn't waiting. Not anymore.

He set out from the cave in the dark of night, loping through the woods as quickly as he could without injuring himself in a collision with a branch or a tree. Thankfully, the moon was full and provided him with enough light so that he made good progress. For nearly three weeks, he ran doggedly on, taking a few hours here and there to rest high in the boughs of trees. He saw the occasional hunting arachnid, but they were of the smaller variety, stalking birds and squirrels and even raccoons. Of the monstrous ones, he thankfully saw no sign. That did nothing to allay his fears, though. He knew they were out there.

He reached Taer Blys on the morning of the twenty-fourth day. The peaceful Taes had reclaimed their city from the Gols after the invading army had been defeated last year. He had hoped to find a horse to finish his journey to Nykiva, but fortune smiled on him when he found out that a powerful arch mage had claimed the Tae tower of magic. An hour later, he had been teleported directly to the arch mage's tower in Nykiva. The first phase of his journey was over.

The residing arch mage of Nykiva was a young man by the name of Aylan, a former companion of Terion and his friends, and one of the heroes of the war with Draven. He was dressed as he normally was, forgoing the traditional robes of a wizard to dress in the desert brown tunic and beige leggings favorable to his people. He looked, to Terion, like he always had and that brought a smile to his face.

The swordmaster had taken on Aylan several years prior when the young lad decided it was time to leave the security of his master's tower, far to the southwest and deep in the Raiz desert. During their travels, Aylan had shown himself to be a true friend, lending his growing magical expertise to a number of their adventures—most successful, some spectacular failures. But through it all, he had grown in stature and in power. When Draven had marched his Gol army eastward last year, Aylan was thrust into the fires of change an apprentice, and he emerged a formidable young wizard. When Draven had been killed and his Gol army finally defeated, Aylan had stepped in and reluctantly accepted the mantel of Nykiva's arch mage at the behest of the Dom council—and with no little bit of urging from his friends. The young wizard had been working tirelessly ever since to help rebuild the might of the Dom people.

Aylan met him immediately as Terion stepped off the stone platform—the safe zone for any tower-to-tower teleportation spell—and the two embraced.

"Well met, my friend," Aylan exclaimed excitedly with a wide smile. "I haven't seen you in months!"

"And for very good reason," Terion replied tiredly. "We have much to discuss."

"You look like you could use some rest. I can have you shown to a room where you can take some time to clean up and sleep beforehand."

"Maybe later." Terion waved off the suggestion. "Can you get word to Notyet to come to the tower immediately?"

"He's in town, so yes," Aylan replied. "Is everything alright?"

"No," was the honest answer and then he asked outright, "How much have your powers grown?"

"Well, I've been busy," the young wizard replied, pushing one of his sleeves up and revealing that the magical glyphs that indicated a mage's power went well past his biceps now. A wizard's power was marked by the appearance of arcane tattoos, starting at the fingertips and working their way up the arms and onto the body as magical power was used. The more the wizard used their power, the more the tattoos grew and changed and a truly formidable arch mage could find themselves completely covered in glyphs during their later years. "Why do you ask?" he added.

"How are you with teleportation?" Terion asked hopefully, although knowing it was probably a long shot.

Aylan shook his head ruefully. "Sorry, but the closest wizard with that kind of power is Valan in Taer Blys. Came up from Glendyn Ridge about three months ago to help rebuild the city. The Taes love him. But I'm sure you already know that, since he just sent you here."

"There is no one else?"

"That spell is one of the most difficult to master. Besides Valan, the only other one that I know of is Loken, and he never leaves DesertSpeake. I'm afraid it'll be some years before I can attempt it myself."

"And Loken is who I need to see—or more specifically, the

gatekeeper who is keeping him company these days." He was referring to Eric "Tuner" Johansson, the stranger from another world who had somehow ended up in the middle of their war last year when he and a number of other soldiers had been brought through a gate by the Arcai sorceress Shayene. The young man had soon found himself the recipient of magical powers, those of an actual gatekeeper, and the fight to possess him for that power had nearly killed him. After Shayene had been defeated and her dragon banished to the Nether, Terion had taken Eric to DesertSpeake and given him over to the care of Loken, a powerful, if perpetually grumpy, arch mage. In the end, all had agreed he would be safest there.

"I have heard nothing of Eric since the war," Aylan said.

"That's not surprising, considering the potential trouble a gatekeeper could get into these days. I'm certain Loken is keeping him under lock and key."

"You are probably right, but you might have been better served having Valan send you directly there instead of here," Aylan replied. "As an aside, what do you need Eric for?"

"It's a long story, my friend," Terion replied, gripping the young man's shoulder. "But I will be in need of his services, unless you or your own apprentice has figured out how to open portals to other worlds." Seeing Aylan's look of surprise, he continued. "Get word to Notyet. I'll explain it all then."

"Very well," Aylan said, before pausing. "You know, there might be another way to get you to DesertSpeake that doesn't entail you walking across the continent."

"How?" Terion asked, cocking an eyebrow expectantly.

"Jayadra has been in Nykiva this past week," the young arch mage replied, talking about the Arcai priestess who had forsaken her oath of non-interference in order to aid the race of man against the depredations of the armies of Draven and Shayene. After the war had been won, she had stayed in the city to help where she could, since so many had been killed or injured. In that time, she and Aylan had become friends. "I saw her and Volsaun just yesterday. Perhaps you can convince the dragon to take you?"

Terion immediately brightened. "That's an excellent idea. Can you see if she will speak with me?"

"I will ask her to come," Aylan replied. "In the meantime, go get yourself cleaned up. I imagine Anthony will want to talk to you. I warn you, though. He's not very happy that you have been gone for so long."

"Well, I hope he'll forgive me after I explain my story. How's he been doing, anyway?" Terion remembered Anthony fondly—the little crippled boy everyone called "Toad" had helped them escape the occupation of Taer Blys and become an invaluable friend and companion to all of them.

"As well as I could have hoped for in any apprentice," Aylan answered. "He is extremely bright and gifted, and his handicap is of no concern to him. As a matter of fact, he's developed some spells of his own that help him get around quite well."

"He's not hopping around on his hands anymore?"

"Oh, he still does that," Aylan smiled as he turned to leave. "He's just a little more acrobatic than before. I'll let him know you're here."

That evening, a small group gathered in Aylan's study. Jayadra, in all her Arcai splendor, along with her dragon companion, Volsaun, who was present in his hulking human barbarian form, were the first to arrive. Shortly after that, Notyet showed up.

The huge warrior was happy to see his closest friend again,

although he was still struggling to come to grips with the fact that Terion was so concerned about the Vi'Raaji witch. This was the very same assassin who had killed their friend, Cavanah, just last year and something about that didn't seem right despite her helping them later against Shayene. For a moment, he wondered what Cavanah would have thought about it had he still been alive, but Notyet quickly realized that their gruff and rotund companion would have been all for it, as long as it made Terion happy. He supposed that would have to do.

Aylan's apprentice was also present in the meeting—Anthony, the little crippled boy who got around better than most acrobats despite withered and useless legs. The boy was no longer the dirty street urchin who had rescued Terion and his companions from Taer Blys. Today, he was dressed in black clothing more befitting of a thief than a magic user. His tunic was sleeveless and the tattoos that marked him as an apprentice mage were already visible on his calloused fingers. His legs were still tied together in a cross-legged position, but he moved with precision and grace, swinging himself up to a table where he could better see the others and then using his magic to levitate himself to an even better vantage point.

Once everyone was gathered, Terion settled in and told his story. He did his best to keep it brief, beginning with his visit to Ravenspire and finishing with his long and dangerous search of the Spider Forest for Vendetta. He did not use her real name or mention their growing closeness, preferring to keep the relationship to himself for the moment. He spent the most time detailing the birth of the twins and the emergence of Kraegor, along with the appearance of the two gates, which caused great concern to all who were gathered. When he finally finished his tale, the room was engulfed in silence, each of them contemplating the meaning of what had happened.

Eventually, it was Jayadra who spoke, the Arcai's voice low and full of uneasiness. "The opening of these gates is what concerns me most," she said. "As much as I wonder who is behind it, I am more concerned with how easily they seemed to be appearing. This would not be the first time I've heard of this happening this year."

"It has to be the convergence," Aylan pointed out. "The barrier between worlds must be weakening quicker than we thought."

"I agree," Jayadra answered, looking at them all in turn to ensure they understand the gravity of the situation. "One of the reasons that earth gates have been so rare in the past is because the barrier between worlds is very strong. Normally, it would take an incredible amount of magical energy to force one open, and that was magic only a gatekeeper could use."

"So a normal elementalist wizard couldn't do it?" Anthony asked, clearly intrigued.

"No," the Arcai replied, "at least not in normal times. When Shayene opened the gate to the Nether last year and made it permanent by using the sentient artifact, Varankyl, that single act began a weakening of the barrier. Opening up additional gates into Eric Johansson's world and bringing Eric and Branson and the rest of his soldiers through accelerated the weakening. What's worse, Eric showed that he had the same abilities as a gatekeeper from our world, when he and his friends were attacked in Nykiva and he accidentally opened a gate himself."

"I heard about that," Anthony said. "Aylan told me that it normally takes a lifetime to become a gatekeeper."

"Which made Eric's ability to accomplish the feat quite alarming," Jayadra nodded. "Since that initial accident, he went from opening portals in this world, to opening portals back to his own world—and he did so in a very short amount of time. If the convergence is truly happening, then that would explain why he is able to do it so easily.”

“Are you saying that Eric’s gatekeeper skills aren’t all that they’re cracked up to be?” Notyet asked in a deep voice, unconsciously signing with his hands while he spoke. It was hard to stop doing something you had done your entire life. Even after nearly a year of having his voice restored by the Tae empath, Arianna, he hadn’t gotten used to the fact that he didn’t have to use sign language anymore.

“Eric’s powers are definitely unique,” the Arcai explained. “Gatekeeper magic is different than any other type of magic, and very few people are born with those abilities to begin with. But it has become much easier for those people to work their magic today.”

“So we know the barrier is definitely weakening,” Notyet said.

“It is,” Aylan added, taking up the explanation. “As more gates are opened up—even small temporary ones like what Terion experienced—the process will continue to weaken the barrier between our world and Eric’s. In some places, it will eventually begin to tear on its own. I think that might be what happened in the cave.”

“That is likely correct,” Jayadra added.

“No,” Terion disagreed, his voice quiet and thoughtful as he reflected on what happened. “It wasn’t random,” he went on. “Those gates were opened by individuals.”

“How can you know this?” Jayadra asked doubtfully. “Kraegor does not have the power of a gatekeeper and even if he did, the coincidence of him opening up a gate directly to you is beyond astronomical.”

“Trust me, it wasn’t a coincidence,” Terion went on, finding strength in his conviction as he spoke. “He was drawn to that spot. He had to have been.”

“But how do you explain the gate?”

“It was the babies,” Terion said quietly.

This brought about stunned silence from all of them.

"Look," he went on, knowing he was right and hoping he could convince them. "I've had a lot of time to think about this and work it out. The babies were the catalyst."

"That's not even remotely possible," Jayadra countered.

"The first gate opened when Rayne was born," Terion pressed on, ignoring the Arcai's comment. "It opened as soon as Rayne started crying. It closed when she stopped. But by that time, Kraegor had already come through it."

"And the other?" Jayadra asked, clearly not convinced.

"When Fyre was born, the other gate opened. When I laid her in her mother's arms and she stopped crying, the gate vanished."

"You're saying that it was their crying?" Aylan asked doubtfully.

"It's stress," he shrugged. "It would seem to be what Eric experienced the first time he did it. Remember the story of what happened when they were attacked? To hear Eric explain it, he still has no idea how it happened. But he was definitely in danger and under stress."

"Even if that's true, how do you explain Kraegor's appearance?" Jayadra pushed.

"Think about it," Terion continued. "He is the father of those girls. Could he not have a mental or psychic connection with them?"

Jayadra turned to look at Volsaun, who had not yet said a word.

"It is conceivable," the human-form dragon finally rumbled slowly, "although it would be impossible to prove. To my knowledge, there has never been a child born of a union between a dragon and a mortal. We are not like the Arcai," he went on, looking at Jayadra. "It has been forbidden to us since we were created, and to break that oath would have meant annihilation by the gods themselves. They were very succinct on this point before we were brought into this world."

"Well, they don't seem to be too worried about you guys anymore," Notyet pointed out. "They haven't exactly seemed to care what's been going on with their pets." When he noticed Volsaun's angry scowl, he quickly added, "No offense intended."

"He's right, though," Terion said, looking at the Arcai. "Is it possible that the gods lack the ability to intervene anymore? Or have they just stopped caring?"

"I don't know," she said slowly. "I haven't spoken to any of them in some time."

"You're an Arcai," he pointed out. "Aren't you supposed to have unlimited access to them?"

"Normally, yes," she answered somberly. "But as of late, they have gone silent."

"Silent?" Aylan asked in alarm. "For how long?"

"Nearly three months now," she replied with a nod. "And on top of that, the font is gone."

"Gone?" Terion repeated. "What do you mean it's gone?"

"It's exactly what she said," Volsaun replied. "After the gods had gone silent, we traveled to the Font of the Gods two months ago to see if she could speak to them directly. We found the temple destroyed."

"Well, that's not good," Notyet said matter-of-factly.

"No, it isn't," Jayadra agreed. "I can still feel their presence somewhere, but it is muted…weak."

"Any idea why?" the big warrior asked.

Jayadra shook her head. "I do not know, but I believe it has something to do with the convergence."

"And the convergence will only grow worse," Aylan added.

"What happens then?" Anthony asked.

"Theoretically, the two worlds will merge and become one."

"You're kidding," Anthony scoffed. "What exactly would that

mean?"

"It would mean that both worlds would suddenly occupy the same space," Aylan replied. "It would be catastrophic to both worlds."

"You're talking everything? People, buildings, cities?"

"Yes," Aylan replied. "Everything."

"So how do we stop it?"

"There is no way to stop a convergence that I know of." Jayadra was the one to answer. "It would be a question to ask of the gods, but...well, you understand the problem."

"I guess that means were totally screwed," Notyet sighed, mimicking an inappropriate motion with his hands. "And we still don't have a clue how Kraegor fits into all of this. But since I'm not one to sit around and wait for the end of the world, what are we going to do? We have to do something, right?"

It was Terion who spoke up, standing as he did. "We are going to rescue the babies," he answered determinedly. "They seem to be the key to all of this."

"How do you propose to do that?" Volsaun asked, his rough voice disapproving. "One is in the company of a dragon, who has been trapped in the Nether for the better part of a year and quite likely unhinged. The other, we have no idea at all of her whereabouts."

Terion cleared his throat before pressing ahead with his request, hoping that it would be received with graciousness and not between the jaws of an angry and offended dragon. "I need to get to DesertSpeake," he said. "Kraegor came back into this world through a portal and we know he's still on our world. Vendetta and Fyre left this world through a similar portal. My guess is that they are on Eric's world."

"How do you know they did not end up in the Nether?" Jayadra asked gravely.

"If they did, then it will be a very short trip for me, won't it," he stated grimly.

"So you're planning on having Eric open a portal so you can go after Vendetta and Fyre?" she questioned, her voice tight. "Do I need to remind you how dangerous opening gates has become? It will hasten the convergence."

"It's already coming, Jayadra," he reasoned. "You know this."

"It could take decades to arrive, Terion. Opening gates needlessly now will only bring it upon us quicker by hastening the weakening of the barrier."

"And yet, you know I have to go. You know that the babies are the key to all of this. You must see the connection!"

For a moment, there was silence in the room, the tension palpable. Then Jayadra blew out a long sigh. "I do," she finally said. "Your points are valid and I cannot see any other explanation. The children do indeed seem to have something to do with all this."

"And how do you propose to get to the Raiz Desert where Loken resides?" Volsaun added, his tone almost accusatory. The dragon sensed what was coming and wanted to make certain Terion knew he wasn't happy with the forthcoming request.

"I would like you to take me, if you would be so kind," Terion said, looking straight at the dragon. "Aylan does not have the power to do it and I'd rather not walk, if it can be avoided. I need your help."

Volsaun did not answer, but simply stared, his jaw set. Terion took that as a good sign.

"What about Rayne?" Notyet asked him. "You can't go after both of them."

"I was getting to that," Terion replied, turning to face his friend. "I need your help, too. I need you to find her."

"I take it that means I'll be going back to the Wraithlands," Notyet mused, pursing his lips. "I didn't really like it the first time I was there, although I did retrieve a wonderful singing voice for myself."

"It's the most logical place that Kraegor will go," Terion replied, ignoring his friend's mirth. He was too keyed up to find the amusement in it.

"Terion is right," Jayadra agreed. "If Kraegor has escaped the Nether, he will most likely reestablish himself in the Wraithlands. But even if we agree that Notyet should go, he cannot face Kraegor alone," she went on. "Kraegor is a dragon, after all."

"Will you come with me?" Notyet asked hopefully. "Having a demigod watching my backside would be much preferable than dying alone in the jaws of a crazy, pissed off dragon."

"Kraegor must be dealt with in any case," she nodded. "That will take an Arcai or another dragon. If Volsaun takes Terion to the Raiz, I am the logical choice to go with you in search of Kraegor."

"There are others," Volsaun pointed out, his voice almost a growl. It was obvious he did not want his companion leaving on such a dangerous journey, regardless of her own powers.

"But none with the experience and knowledge of what has been happening in the world," she pointed out.

"What about Siranschae?" Terion asked, referring to their bronze dragon friend that had aided them throughout their struggles with Shayene and Draven. The death of her companion last year had lessened her strength considerably, but she was still a dragon and a formidable warrior. Her aid could be invaluable to Notyet.

"No one has seen her since she disappeared with Arianna's body after the battle in the Wraithlands," Aylan answered, his voice somewhat sad. He missed the woman. She had been a good friend. He missed Arianna even more, and her death had always weighed heavily on him. "Hard to say what happened with her or where she even is anymore."

"Unfortunately, no other Arcai or their companions have stepped forward to take part in this conflict," Jayadra added. "Their reluctance to involve themselves in the world these days is regrettable, but understandable."

"There's always Zarandrae, but I'm guessing we don't want her help," Notyet said drily. "How is the ol' girl anyway?" he asked, casting a look at Aylan. "Is she still screaming mad?"

"No, she's actually pretty quiet these days," the young arch mage answered. Zarandrae had been Draven's companion and a willing participant in the slaughter that Draven and Shayene had brought upon them all. After Draven had been killed, she had been captured and imprisoned within the sublevels of the very tower they were in. "She's not raving like she was when we first imprisoned her," he went on. "Now, she simply passes the time reading."

"Reading?"

"I procured a small library to keep her occupied," Aylan explained. "I thought it prudent, all things considered. And she's become a lot easier to manage. Sometimes she'll even consent to talk to people."

"Whatever the case, she certainly won't be accompanying anyone," Jayadra pointed out. "So we need…"

"Why not?" Anthony piped up suddenly, interrupting her.

"Why not what?"

"Why can't Zarandrae go with Notyet?"

Notyet's mouth fell open in shock, but Terion perked up. "Sure, why not?"

"Why….what? Notyet sputtered. "Are you crazy?"

"I think the boy might be on to something," Terion replied with a grin. "Let's hear him out."

"It's really pretty simple," Anthony went on, leaning over the table in excitement. "Zarandrae has been in prison for a year, right? And dragons are immortal, right?"

"What's your point, boy?" Volsaun asked, a hard edge to his voice.

"Are we really going to keep her locked up for eternity?"

"If needs be," Jayadra said carefully, her eyes narrowing. "What else would you suggest?"

"Why not give her a chance?" the boy asked, like it was the most logical thing to consider. "Think about it. She's the biggest and nastiest dragon alive. If anyone can face down Kraegor, she could, right?

"You said it yourself, kid," Notyet said. "She's the biggest and nastiest of them all. I'm not sure what kind of crazy has gotten into Kraegor, but I am pretty sure I don't want to rely on someone like Zarandrae to watch my arse when I'm dealing with him."

"All I'm saying is to think about it," the young boy said. "Maybe she would surprise you."

"Maybe she'll eat me."

"You only live once," Anthony shrugged and then smiled mischievously.

"That's the part that worries me."

Again there was a long silence, before Jayadra finally broke it, her voice thoughtful. "It's an interesting suggestion and, while I cannot find fault in Anthony's logic, it is still very dangerous. But this is your quest, so I will leave the final decision to you, Notyet," Jayadra said, looking at the big warrior. "It would be beneficial beyond hope if Zarandrae could be rehabilitated, because Anthony makes a very wise observation. How do you keep a dragon imprisoned forever?"

"Far better than being eaten by one," he grumbled. "I'll be talking to you later, Toad," he finished, narrowing his eyes at the grinning young boy. "This is your fault, you know."

"When will you leave, Terion?" Jayadra asked, turning her

attention back to the swordmaster.

"Tomorrow, if Volsaun agrees to take me," he replied.

"Fine," the dragon puffed out an irritated answer. He might be willing, but he was clearly not happy with it. Dragons, for their part, did not like ferrying people around, no matter the cause.

"Then it's settled," Jayadra said, her voice distant as if something else was on her mind. "If Terion is right and the twins were somehow responsible for the gates, there is far more at stake here than simply rescuing them."

"Is there something more that you can tell us?" Terion asked, noting her distraction and hoping to glean any additional information she might have.

"Nothing I am comfortable speaking about," she replied softly. "Just a hunch, really. There is a lot that I need to study and ponder before I know for certain."

"I suppose that's fair enough," Terion replied, pushing his chair back and standing. "We all know our tasks and can get to them in the morning. I need to get some sleep first before I'm out on my feet."

There was a consensus and everyone eventually departed the room, talking among themselves about what part they would play in the coming days. Only Jayadra remained, staring thoughtfully into the candle. She had lied to Terion; she was already certain of what was happening. As much as she did not want to believe it, Terion's tale had shown her some very difficult truths; truths that could not be ignored. Vendetta's twins were indeed the key. They were the key to everything. And she was certain now that it would be their fate to save the world.

Or destroy it.

Chapter 3

It took several days for Volsaun and Terion to make the flight to the Raiz desert far to the southwest and several more for them to wait out the final stages of a powerful sandstorm before they could approach Loken's tower, known to the world as DesertSpeake, one of the greatest towers of magic in all the land. During the journey, Terion got to know the dragon fairly well over numerous hours sitting astride his back or around a campfire, trading stories.

Volsaun, in his gruff human form, shared his thoughts about the conflict and Terion found him extremely knowledgeable about what was happening in the world, if a bit fatalistic.

"If the convergence happens," Volsaun said one evening around a campfire, as the sandstorm continued to blow itself out, "it will be unlike anything you can imagine. Picture two worlds pressed together into one; two world populations—those that survive the cataclysm—thrown together; people, buildings, cities, nations."

"What about the gods?" Terion wondered. "What happens when they come together?"

"That is the most perplexing question of all," the dragon answered. "That they exist on other worlds is not in question. That they have Arcai children is also a given. We know this when the One takes us from our own home world to place us with them. I can guess that once the convergence has happened, there will be a war unlike anything anyone has ever seen. Person against person, Arcai against Arcai, god against god."

"Hard to believe it could get any worse," Terion sighed, shaking his head at the futility of it all. "Is there any hope for any of us?"

"There is always hope," Volsaun replied quietly. "But what that hope may be, only the gods know for sure. And they're not talking right now."

When the sand storm finally blew itself out a few days later, Terion sat astride Volsaun's back one more time as they soared deep into the desert, flying quickly toward DesertSpeake. They arrived an hour later and both were welcomed—more or less—into the cool confines of the stone tower by the arch mage.

Loken was tall and so thin he was almost skeletal. Despite his age, his ebony skin was smooth and he looked far younger than his nearly ninety years. His hair was cut very short and whether it was white or gray, Terion could not tell. But the wizard was every bit the crotchety old man that he remembered from their meetings in the past.

The arch mage fixed his piercing blue eyes on the two men, a scowl on his face. "Am I to get no peace from visitors? I finally get rid of an apprentice who decides that going off and adventuring is more important than his studies and then I find myself saddled with a gatekeeper. Now you show up with a dragon? Whatever gave you the idea that DesertSpeake was an inn?"

"I am not here to stay," Volsaun rumbled.

"That's what they all say," Loken harrumphed, turning away from them and heading down the hall with long strides. "Come on, come on, the both of you. I'm sure you'll probably want to be eating my food, if Eric and his patchwork friend haven't cleaned out the pantry yet. Will you be eating as a man, Volsaun, or do I need to procure a couple of live cows for you?"

The human-form dragon growled, but Terion only smiled as they followed the old mage. He knew that most of what Loken showed to everyone else was an act. He was condescending and rude and sometimes even crude, but the old wizard was a fierce friend in the end. The fact that they were in his tower put them squarely in that small circle of the man's acquaintances. Had they not been, the wizard would have likely burned them out of the sky.

Besides Loken, the only other permanent resident in the tower was Eric Johansson, or Tuner as he was known to most. Tuner had come through the first portal between their worlds over a year ago with a group of heavily-armed soldiers. Upon arriving, they fell into a terrible nightmare which offered no chance of escape. Over one hundred soldiers from that world had come across at Shayene's behest and she had reduced them down to twenty-five by having them brutally kill each other in a bid to keep only the strongest and smartest. When that number had been reached, she had imprisoned the survivors and then sent a handful of them to Nykiva to begin stirring things up in preparation for Draven's arrival. The remainder had been freed when Shayene had been defeated and most of the displaced outworlders now resided in Nykiva, trying hard to acclimate to a strange new world.

Loken's reference to Eric's patchwork friend meant that at least one of them had come to visit and it could be none other than Rick Branson. Branson was the leader of the outworlders and, during their initial imprisonment, he had been magically torn apart and put back together by Shayene as an object lesson to the others. Consequently, he was covered with so many scars that he resembled a patchwork doll. Knowing what he knew of Branson and of Loken, Terion wondered how the two men had avoided killing each other yet.

"How's Eric doing, anyway?" he asked.

"He's a pain in my ass," Loken snapped. "Always asking questions about the most mundane things. Isn't there anyone else who will take him in?"

"Well, I'm certain he's just curious about our world," Terion replied, knowing full well that Loken would not allow the young gatekeeper to stay anywhere but DesertSpeake. When the wizard had learned of what had happened with Shayene, he was adamant that the young man be sent to stay with him, even if he complained loudly about it. DesertSpeake was a hidden fortress in the dunes of the most inhospitable desert in the world, and under the watchful eye of one of the most dangerous wizards alive. Logically, it was the safest place to keep a gatekeeper—or anyone, for that matter. "Have his powers grown?" he asked.

"How should I know?" the wizard carried on, throwing up his arms in exasperation. "Do you think I'm just going to let him open up gates all over creation in an effort to bring about the convergence in a matter of days instead of years?"

Before Terion could respond, they stepped through an archway into a wide circular room. Eric and Rick Branson were seated at a table, heads bent low in conversation. A couple of empty plates and mugs sat next to them. "See what I mean?" Loken shook his head in disgust. "Always eating! At this rate, I'm going to have to make daily supply runs just so I don't starve."

"You could move to the city," Terion teased.

"Bah, you know I hate people. If I moved to the city, everyone else would have to leave. I don't suppose you'd allow me to transplant fifty thousand desert dwellers to Nykiva?" He didn't wait for Terion to answer. "Eric!"

"Yes sir?" the young man looked up, startled.

"You have visitors," the arch mage said. "I imagine Terion here is going to be asking you to open a gate back to your world, as if the fate of everyone in this world doesn't matter a wit to him."

"How do you know that?" Terion asked, suppressing a smile. He knew the old man was enjoying himself.

"Why else would you be able to convince a dragon to pretend he's a donkey and ferry you here?" Loken asked. "Eric, go fetch some food for your friends, if you have left any. I swear, if you have depleted my stores again, I'm going to send you to Hunzari City on foot to restock."

"No, sir," Eric answered as he stood. "There's plenty. There's always plenty." With that, he hurried out of the room.

"Good to see you again, Terion," Branson said, standing and clasping the swordmaster's hand. "You, too, Volsaun," he went on, repeating the handshake.

"How long have you been here?" Terion asked.

"Couple of days," Branson replied, casting a sideways look at the wizard. "That ol' coot's a mean bastard, but I kinda like him."

"I heard that," Loken grumbled, seating himself at the far end of the table and steepling his fingers in front of him, content to listen.

"So what brings you here?" Branson asked, ignoring the comment.

"Loken was right," Terion replied. "I do need Eric's help."

"What kind of help?" Eric asked as he walked back into the room, a couple of plates of bread and cheese in his hands.

"Start at the beginning, Terion," Loken interrupted, his voice suddenly devoid of condescension. "You have a tale that I undoubtedly want to hear. High time you tell it and leave nothing out."

So Terion told his story, explaining how he went searching for Vendetta and why he thought it was important. He also relayed details about the terrible night of the birth of her twins. He then explained his plan to go after Vendetta and Fyre, while Notyet went looking for Rayne. Everyone ate in silence as they listened and, when he was done, Loken sat back in his chair, his face lined with concern.

"As much as I am against Eric using his powers for obvious reasons, I think it's a wise decision to seek out the Vi'Raaji and her baby," Loken finally said, his voice still calm.

"I'm grateful for that," Terion nodded. "I know what I saw. I know those babies had something to do with what happened in the cave. I also know that we owe it to Vendetta. I know she's done some bad things in the past, but if not for her sacrifice, Shayene and Kraegor would have likely killed us all in the Wraithlands."

"You'll get no argument from me on that," Loken said. He knew the story of the battle very well. "I wonder, though, if you have thought this through to the logical conclusion."

"Meaning what?"

"If Eric sends you back to his world, do you realize that you will not be able to return? He must remain here, safely sequestered from those that would use his powers for ill. I cannot allow him to simply open up gates every day to check on your progress. The barrier is weakening quickly enough as it is."

"I understand that. I guess I've known from the beginning that this is going to be a one-way way trip."

"She means that much to you?" the wizard asked, arching an inquisitive eyebrow.

"I could not live with myself if I didn't try to find her," Terion said evasively, knowing the wizard suspected much more regarding his personal feelings for the woman.

"Admirable, if short-sighted and reckless," the arch mage replied, the arrogance creeping back into his voice. "I assume you have something of hers that Eric can use as a focus? If you do not, I may be forced to have Eric gate you to the middle of the ocean for wasting my time."

"Don't worry," Terion replied with a nod, reaching into the pack he had laid at his feet. "I came prepared."

He retrieved and unrolled a strip of leather. There, the black metal gleaming, were the dragon-forged blades of the assassin. "These are linked to her," he explained. "She will no longer use them, but I have kept them safe."

"That may not be enough, if she has not used them in a while," Loken said. "Their connection to her will be much fainter and Eric may not be able to forge the link he will need to open the portal."

"I also have this," Terion went on, pulling out a tightly-rolled blanket from his pack.

"Would that be the birthing blanket?" the arch mage guessed.

Terion nodded.

"Excellent," Loken said before looking at Eric. "Do you remember how to do it, boy?" he asked, his voice once again crusty.

The young man nodded, reaching out and taking the blanket from Terion. "I can swing it."

"And you?" Loken asked, looking at Volsaun, his eyes hard. "I assume you are not foolish enough to want to accompany him through the portal."

"I have no wish to leave this world," the dragon agreed grimly. "If I have any desire to see what Eric's world looks like, I'll wait and see it after the convergence…if anything survives."

"Let's hope that it doesn't reach that point, dragon."

"I don't share your optimism, wizard," Volsaun replied honestly. "If the gods have forsaken us, I don't see that there is any other outcome."

"Perhaps not," the arch mage agreed. "But I'll take my victories where I can get them. If there is a chance that Terion can find the woman and her child, then he should make the attempt."

"And I agree with you completely," the dragon said gruffly. "Now, if there is no more need for me to stay here, I will take my leave. I wish to return to my companion."

"Thank you, Volsaun," Terion said, standing up and offering his hand. "You cannot know how grateful I am that you brought me here."

"I just hope that you are not too late, Terion," he said quietly as he accepted the man's handshake. "It has been a number of weeks already."

Terion nodded. "I'll know soon enough."

"Farewell," the dragon said. "To all of you."

A few moments later, he was gone.

"Are you certain about this, Terion?" Loken asked after a few moments of silence. "Are you truly committed to possibly never seeing our world again?"

"Without a doubt," the swordmaster answered. It was a question he had asked himself many times already. He was at peace with his answer.

"You realize that your chances of finding Vendetta and the baby are slim," the wizard went on. "And even if you do find them, do you know what you will do?"

"I guess I'll figure that out when the time comes," he shrugged.

"No!" Loken fairly shouted, slamming his hand on the table hard enough to cause everyone to jump. "You are entering a world that is in upheaval and one that has had a powerful Arcai from our world in their midst for nearly a year. If you believe that Shayene will not be aware of the presence of a dragon-sired baby, you are a fool. She may even have already claimed the child."

"How do you know that Shayene is even alive?" Branson spoke up.

"She is an Arcai; a rogue demigod with no ties to the gods themselves," the mage snapped in answer. "She will have grown in power and she has made it clear that she desires to usurp them." Looking back at Terion, he went on. "You will go through the gate and you will find the child, first and foremost. If you rescue the mother, that is your choice, but she is not the important one."

"I don't understand," Terion said, narrowing his eyes. "What are you getting at?"

"Find the child," Loken repeated. "Find her and protect her, at all costs. She must not be allowed to fall into Shayene's hands—and if Shayene has indeed already found her, you must take her back."

"Why? What aren't you telling me, wizard?"

"From what you have shared, the twins are somehow the key to the gateways," Loken said softly. "If Shayene discovers this, and I have no reason to believe she will not, she will exploit the child to bring about the convergence much sooner than later. That must not be allowed to happen."

"If it's going to happen, what's the difference on the timing?" Branson cut in.

"There is always hope for a better future," Loken replied curtly, standing abruptly. "I choose to believe that, given time, we might find a way to prevent the coming cataclysm and save a great many lives." Turning to the young gatekeeper he said, "Eric, do what you need to prepare the portal. Branson, you will go with Terion."

"Say that again?" the marine quipped.

"I will brook no dissent," the arch mage growled at him. "Terion will need a guide in your world and you are the logical choice to accompany him. He will need every chance he can get to be successful."

"Just for the record, I make my own choices," Branson bristled, standing at his full height. "But I was planning on going anyway."

"Whatever makes you feel better," Loken snapped, before turning and striding from the room. "You have two hours, Eric!" he called back. "Be ready then!"

Nearly two hours later, night had fallen and the time had arrived. Eric sat cross-legged on the floor, holding the rolled-up blanket in one hand, while his other hand was outstretched, maintaining the earth gate he had just opened back into his own world. His eyes were closed and his features were strained, but he seemed to be holding up just fine.

Terion looked though the rippling opening, seeing a house in a long row of houses. It was night, but tall thin lamp posts lined the street and cast the area in enough light to see well. Odd steel carriages lined the street and the lawn in front of the house was well manicured with several flowering trees. He could smell the spring blossoms and noted that it seemed rather peaceful.

"Okay, listen up," Branson said quickly, cognizant of the fact that maintaining the portal was difficult for Eric. "Looks like we're going to Minnesota, judging by the license plates on the cars."

"Where?"

"Never mind," Branson went on, not wanting to take the time to explain. He pointed to the house that seemed to be centered in the portal. "I'm guessing that home right there is our target. Eric, can you get us inside?"

Eric did not answer, but seemed to concentrate harder. A moment later, the image shifted and suddenly was showing the inside of a darkened room. They could make out only the dim outlines of furniture in the gloom, but nothing else.

"That's it," Branson said excitedly. "Let's go."

"I remind you one last time," Loken cautioned again, "that once you're through the portal, we can't bring you back. You will likely be lost to us and to our world."

"I know," Terion replied. "If we find them and we're meant to get back, then we'll find a way to return."

"And if not?"

"We'll survive," Terion noted with finality. "One way or another."

Without another word, Terion and Rick Branson stepped through the small portal, stepping from one world into another. As the portal snapped shut behind them, Eric began to scream.

It took a moment for Loken to process what was happening, shocked as he was as the sudden and brazen attack. In his own tower, even! As the portal to Eric's world had closed, another had opened up behind the young man. A figure had stepped out, more of a shadow than anything, and it had fastened itself to Eric, its head bent low, some vague resemblance of a mouth attached to Eric's throat.

Eric's scream died on his lips and Loken could see the young man's skin turning ashen gray. His eyes rolled up and began to sink into their sockets and suddenly, Loken was moving.

Loken was one of the most accomplished wizards in the world and as powerful as any had ever been. Yet, it took all of his considerable power to engage the demon that was feeding on Eric's life. He launched several bolts of bright sun-like energy from his outstretched hands, hitting the demon in its shadowy head and forcing it to release its meal with a scream of rage and pain.

The creature turned to face him, allowing the wizard to unleash the full force of his power, and this time, Loken burnt it from existence. Yet, even as it vanished, another stepped out of the portal and more began to show themselves behind it. Eric had crumpled to the floor, moaning in agony as Loken sent more magic into the invading creatures. They were demons from the Nether, powerful life-stealers that could drain the essence from a living creature in seconds. But individually, they were no match for Loken's magic, and he disintegrated them as they came.

Yet, the gate remained open and, as more began to cluster around the opened gateway, Loken realized what that meant. Eric lay on the floor, unconscious and alive, though likely dying. A thin ribbon of pale glimmering energy connected Eric to the gate, the aura centered on the young man's chest. Loken understood immediately that as long as Eric remained alive and his heart continued beating, the gate would remain in existence, somehow joined to Eric's life-force.

Several more demons entered his tower through the gate and Loken burned them to ash, forcing the gathering demons still in the Nether to consider well what coming across might mean for them.

"Eric," he growled, grabbing the young man's frail shoulder and shaking him. He winced as the young man's body flopped around, like he was made of straw.

Another demon, larger this time, stepped through, roaring its rage at the living. Loken burned it down, leaving it little more than a pile of smoking ash at the base of the gate.

At that moment, he knew what had to be done. He could sit here destroying demons until his strength ran out, or he could close the gate himself. Unfortunately, there was only one way to do that.

"I'm sorry, Eric," he said softly, taking a moment to look down at the young man. Eric's face was white and the consistency of parchment. Even if there was another way to close the gate, Loken doubted Eric would survive the night. He was dying and in agony, his body robbed of most of its life force, fighting to stay alive nevertheless. The human desire to live, Loken thought sadly.

Reaching down, he placed his hand on Eric's chest. His magic flared once, arcane energy flooding into Eric's body like lightning. The jolt shocked the young man, sending his body into one quick convulsion. Then his heart stopped beating. As Eric died, the gate immediately vanished, closing the doorway to the Nether and ending the threat, leaving nothing more than acrid smoke and the smell of death.

Loken, working quickly, hovered over the dead gatekeeper. Much of Eric's life force had been drained by the demon and the young man, who was only twenty years old, looked more like ninety. Loken placed his hand on the boy's chest again and sent another jolt of power into his heart. It fluttered under Loken's fingers before going still again. He tried again with the same result. Muttering under his breath, he modified his magic, sending it creeping into Eric's body instead of with an abrupt shock. Again, his heart fluttered and then died. Again he tried and again he failed. His final attempt caused the heart to flutter to life long enough for Eric to open his white eyes.

"No," Eric whispered as he reached feebly for Loken's hand, his voice dry and cracked. "Let…me…go."

Loken paused and stared into Eric's eyes. In a moment, he understood everything—from the seething pain the boy was in to the acceptance of what had to be. Eric Johansson knew what he was and what he was capable of doing. He also knew what had been done to him, and it wasn't an existence he wanted any part of.

Eric Johansson wanted to die.

With sad resignation, Loken bowed his head and let him.

Eric Johansson closed his eyes for the last time. His body shuddered with one final rattling breath as his heart labored for several more seconds. Then it was silenced forever.

Loken, head bowed in grief, let the tears come.

Chapter 4

Loken stood in his personal chamber high in the tower of DesertSpeake, alone for the first time in months. As loudly as he had complained about having company, Eric's death had hit him profoundly hard, and he had shed a good number of tears for the young man. He had learned long ago that life was never fair, but why was it that the young died young and the old, like himself, continued to linger? Not for the first time in his life, he found himself angry at the gods and at his own long life in general.

He would miss Eric.

He looked out of a window, magically sealed from the blowing sands of the Raiz, and stared at the bright stars of the night, contemplating what he knew and what he suspected. The convergence was coming fast; the appearance of the gateway to the Nether following Eric's opening of the portal to the other world was proof of that. The barrier was weakening quickly. Too quickly. The world was ending or, at the very least, it would be radically changed when the convergence happened and the two worlds collided.

Few people even knew about the convergence or what it meant. Fewer still understood the globe-spanning cataclysm that would follow and what that would mean to the survivors. Oh, there would be survivors and quite possibly a lot of them from both worlds. But it would be those who allied themselves with the right fallen gods who would live to see the end of the cataclysm. Because the gods would fall. And mortals would follow them. The survivors would be the ones to re-forge the world.

Turning away from the window with a weary sigh, he moved slowly to the center of the room and reached out to lay his hand against the smooth facets of a huge cut and polished crystalline stone that stood in an iron tripod before him. His image was reflected multiple times in the smoky crystal and he paused and wondered when he had gotten so old. He envied Terion and Branson and the adventure they had embarked upon, but that envy lasted only for a moment. He had no delusions about how that would likely end. Shayene would be beyond powerful in Eric's world and would know without a doubt about the baby. If she understood the importance of the child, so much the worse for all of them. Either way, he had likely sent Terion and Branson to their deaths.

Loken let his hand slide across the crystal, feeling the sharp edges of the polished facets. The artifact was known as a vision crystal, an immensely powerful relic that allowed a master wizard the ability to watch over those he or she knew, for good or evil, and to converse with them as needed. He had used it to watch over his former apprentice, Aylan, over the past couple of years after the young mage had left his tutelage. During those times, he had silently congratulated the lad for his victories and loudly berated him for his failures, all while watching from afar. He did so because he cared deeply for the young wizard, much like he cared for and grieved for Eric. They were feelings that would remain private, though. He had no wish to have others thinking he wasn't the cantankerous old bastard he portrayed himself to be and, after the events of the evening, he would fully embrace that bitterness with a passion and keep everyone far from him for as long as he lived. He was tired of seeing people that he cared about die.

Loken peered deeper into the relic, letting his eyes wander across its surface as his magic began to hum within him. Invoking the power of the crystal was extremely draining to even the strongest wizard and conversing with an Arcai, as he intended, could put him out of commission for days. He again considered what he might gain by talking with Jayadra. Of all the Arcai who might have insight into the pending cataclysm, she was the logical choice. She had already involved herself in the growing conflict and had been the one to slay Draven in the warrior's challenge before the gates of Nykiva. In doing so, she had made it clear that she would not turn her back on the mortals she had been tasked to watch over.

So, he would contact her and share what had happened with Eric and then listen to whatever counsel she would share with him in return. Despite his extensive life experience and unparalleled knowledge of magic, he knew he was in over his head. They all were, and it might only be an Arcai who could help save them.

He closed his eyes and willed his magic to full strength. Deep within the crystal, the mist began to move, slowly at first and then more rapidly as it morphed into the figure of a man instead of the woman he was attempting to summon. Under his hands, the crystal began to heat up, at first comfortably warm and then hot enough that he had to step backward. As the wavering image began to coalesce into solid reality, Loken dropped to his knees in shock as he recognized that the being that had appeared in the crystal was much more than an Arcai.

A god had come calling.

Benovan, the speaker for the gods of their world, had appeared in the crystal. For a moment, the image wavered and then Benovan himself seemed to step out of the stone to stand before him. "Loken of DesertSpeake," the god said, his voice deep, but quiet and reserved. "Arise and hear me, for my time with you is short."

The wizard looked up, hardly daring to believe what he was seeing. "I am…at a loss," he managed to say, climbing slowly to his feet, his old bones creaking. "I was told the gods had gone silent; the font destroyed."

"All true statements," Benovan replied grimly. "But I stand before you now because these troubling times are graver than anyone can imagine. Humanity must know the truth. The convergence is nearly here, but there is a far greater danger. The Nexus is threatened."

"The Nexus?" the wizard questioned, perplexed. "What is it?"

"The Nexus is the lifeblood of all worlds—the heart, if you will," Benovan explained. "It is what connects every living world to the living universe."

"I don't understand," he said. "Why have I never heard of this?"

"It is not spoken of in any texts, for it is forbidden by the One," Benovan answered gravely. "But now, another has learned of it and seeks to destroy it."

"But how? Why?"

"The barrier between our world and the world of the outworlder is weakening. The cataclysm draws near. This you know."

"Right," the arch mage nodded, an edge to his voice. "But what I don't know is how to stop it,"

"The damage is done, Loken. The barrier will fail. The cataclysm between our two worlds is imminent."

"Are you saying that even the gods cannot stop it?"

"No," Benovan answered, sadness and pain in his tone. "We already struggle with the gods of the other world, as the barrier has weakened enough for us to be thrust into conflict with them. When the barrier is ultimately breached, we will all be cast down to earth, and our struggle will take physical form. That will usher in the cataclysm as the two worlds become one."

"You're saying we have no hope?" Loken asked, his anger rising unbidden, driven by the hopelessness of the situation. "What's the point in finding this Nexus then? We are mortals. We want to believe we have a chance. Otherwise, people like Eric Johansson die needlessly alone in worlds that are not even their own."

"The Nexus is more important than you know," Benovan answered, ignoring Loken's outburst. "It is more important than the life of one mortal."

"I watched him die because he was doing something that he believed was right, hoping to help avert the convergence! Are you telling me that is not important?"

"You misunderstand, because you speak out of anger," Benovan admonished softly. "Eric's sacrifice was valiant, but there is much more at stake than you truly understand."

"Tell me…"

At that, Benovan seemed to grow, his shape suddenly towering over Loken. "Cease speaking and listen, Mortal, for the fate of all is at stake," the god boomed, causing Loken to shrink in horror at the understanding that he had just lost his temper with a god. Probably not his finest moment. "The coming convergence pales in significance to the importance of the Nexus," Benovan went on, his form returning to normal and his voice calming once more, now that he had the wizard's attention. "If the Nexus is destroyed, it will destroy the barrier between all worlds, not just ours and that of the outworlder. All living worlds will become one in a single catastrophic convergence, and all life will cease to exist. Even the gods will not survive."

"Then why destroy it?" Loken dared to ask. "Why would someone seek to destroy every world?"

"Because while the living worlds would be destroyed, one world would survive."

Loken knew the answer in a moment. "The Nether."

"Yes," the god replied. "And hell will have one god."

As the implications became clear to him, Loken slumped down into a nearby chair, the crushing weight of despair washing over him. "So even death will not afford an escape from this," he muttered, shaking his head.

"No," Benovan replied gravely. "If the Nexus is destroyed, all spirits from every world that the One has ever created will be cast into the Nether. Even those pure in heart who have already passed on from life in their worlds will find themselves ripped from their own spirit world of Paradise and cast into hell."

The implication of that statement was beyond overwhelming. Even understanding how anything so catastrophic could happen was fleeting. But he knew it to be true; felt it in his bones. Everything. Everywhere. Everyone.

Gone.

He shook his head and took a deep, shaking breath, letting the more logical part of his mind take over. Not all was lost yet, or Benovan would not have bothered paying him a visit.

"So, this Nexus," he began, his mind still spinning. "Where is it?"

"I cannot reveal the location to you," Benovan answered, his voice again sad, "other than to tell you that it exists in the same place on every world."

"Why can't you give me the specific location?" Loken asked in disbelief. "You claim its importance is beyond anything else and yet you cannot even tell me where it is?"

"Because as much as I have told you already, I have not affected your freedom to choose your path," the god answered. "This is the will of the One and, even in a crisis such as this, I cannot break that oath. I cannot force this task upon you."

"By telling me where it is, you think that would affect my freedom to choose what I should do about it?" he asked incredulously.

"It would," Benovan stated plainly. "If I told you now where it was and tasked you with the quest, would you accept it?"

"Well, yes," Loken snapped impatiently.

"Then you have proven my point," the god went on. "I cannot tell you where the Nexus is, nor can I ask you to accept the task. What I can tell you is that, if you do seek to save the Nexus, your success will be in stopping the one who seeks to destroy it. Then, and only then, can you rebuild the weakening barriers between all the worlds."

"But not this world?"

"Sadly, no," the god replied. "The barrier between this world and the next is too badly damaged. But those of other worlds can be repaired—and must be, if anyone is to survive."

"Then how do we do it? Can you at least tell me that much?"

"Varankyl must be united," Benovan said, his image starting to shimmer. "The mirror must be made whole and the two must become one."

"Varankyl?" the arch mage asked in surprise. "Varankyl was destroyed when it was cast into the Nether. It no longer exists. Surely you know this."

"In that, you are mistaken," Benovan countered. "Varankyl lives, and he has returned from his exile."

"Varankyl is a sentient artifact. It has intelligence, but has no life."

"He has always had life, Loken. It may be different than what you perceive life to be, but it is life just the same, and he has been divided. He must be reunited with himself, as only he can rebuild the barrier. Only his sacrifice can stop what is coming and save everything that ever was or will be."

Benovan flickered again, as if a candle was being blown out in a breeze. This time, only a faint ghost of an image remained.

"Wait!" Loken said, reaching out.

"Find him," Benovan said, his voice nearly indistinct now. "Convince him."

With that, he vanished and the crystal went dark. Loken stared at its polished surface for a long time, mulling over what he had just learned. It wasn't encouraging. The gods were not gone, but already at war with others of their divine kind. The convergence was coming and they could not stop it. But greater still was the threat to this mysterious Nexus, something he had never heard of until now. Yet it was so important that all worlds were doomed if he could not find a chaotic sentient artifact that was actually a living being and convince the thing that it had to sacrifice itself to rebuild the barriers between all worlds.

Not encouraging at all.

He paced his chambers several times before sitting down heavily on his bed and resting his head in his hands. The task before him—before all of humanity—was such a monumental undertaking and, with no idea where to begin, how could they hope to be successful? No one would know of the Nexus, nor would anyone have even the remotest idea where to begin searching. Worse, even if they did find it, it would take an artifact presumed destroyed to repair it. If Varankyl was not destroyed, as Benovan had indicated, then who had possession of it? More importantly, where had they taken it?

And then, with soul-shattering clarity, the answer came to him, as clear as a ringing bell.

He knew.

And he wept.

Interlude II

The old hermit knelt within the trees and sent his thoughts outward again. For three days, he had tried contacting her and, when he wasn't concentrating on having her hear his plea, he was back to futilely attempting to transform himself into his true form. But more than ten years after his companion had been slain, and he had berated the gods for allowing her death and demanding they take his powers from him, that transformation wasn't coming easily. If he wanted to be honest with himself, he was pretty certain it wasn't going to happen at all.

Muttering a curse to himself that he was even getting involved in this foolishness, he began trekking through the woods again and considered the monumental task before him. On foot, it would take him months to reach his destination and he wasn't even certain she would still be in the caves that she called home. Not to mention that Rook would be lucky to last a couple weeks, let alone many months alone on the island. Foolishness did not even begin to describe what he was attempting.

Again he lamented his angry and foolish demands of the gods over a decade ago. It would be so much easier if he were still able to fly. But all he had were the feet of a human. As he walked, his thoughts went back to that day and the weeks following the death of his beloved Jayra.

She was his companion, but more than that. Much more. Of all the Arcai and their companions, he believed his relationship with Jayra was closer than any of the others. He loved her and she loved him back. He would have done anything for her, including giving up his dragon powers if it meant he could be with her. Then the unthinkable had happened. She had been murdered.

Jayra's death at the hands of the Vi'Raaji assassin had devastated him and, in his grief, he had very nearly turned his rage loose on the entirety of the Vi'Raaji race. Had another dragon not intervened, he would have burnt their cities to cinders and killed every last one of them.

He was that angry.

And it took a battle with another of his kind to stop him.

He remembered those days as if they had just happened. The fighting, the arguing—all of it was engrained deeply within him. He would never forget it, nor would he forget standing before Benovan afterwards and requesting—no, demanding—that the god take his life because he could not bear living without Jayra.

However, instead of slaying him, Benovan had granted him mortality, perhaps hoping that one day he would petition the gods to have his powers reinstated. Given the fact that the past decade had mellowed him considerably, the hermit found himself considering if he could indeed return to his former state.

He hiked through the woods for another hour, before stopping again, reflecting on how mortal bodies tired so easily without access to the strength of a dragon's essence. In his decade on the island as a man, he had done little more than fish in the surf and lie on the beach. It had been a peaceful and almost sedentary existence. Now, deep in the forest and with the sun at mid-day, he wiped the sheen of sweat from his wrinkled forehead and wondered if he should have been doing more. Breathing a deep sigh and cognizant of his aching bones, he sank down with his back against a tall oak and pulled out a water skin. He took a long drink and considered turning back, when she finally responded, her voice echoing in his mind.

I am coming for you, Diaman.

Diaman. He realized he had not heard anyone utter his name in years. Not since he had been banished. For some time, he simply considered her challenge. It would not do to answer her quickly, particularly if he was hoping to avoid a fight. Perhaps remaining light-hearted in their banter would help his cause.

"You sound angry," he finally said aloud, knowing that she could hear his voice in her thoughts. Dragons could hold grudges for years, and she would be no different. He had known her since long before they had come to this world. Aside from his lost companion, she was his dearest friend, the operative word being *was*.

Eleven years is not nearly long enough for me to forget your betrayal.

"Bah," he snorted, forgetting his vow to keep things light. "I betrayed no one! It was Jayra who was betrayed by mortals!"

Her reply was immediate. *I mourned for Jayra. And for you! But you betrayed our kind by trying to exact vengeance! You betrayed me by choosing to fight with me, rather than listen to reason! Better for you to have remained hidden and never returned, Diaman.*

"You'll get no argument from me," he growled. He was angry, now, at everything. He was mad at her for holding a grudge and mad at himself for embarking on this foolish quest. He was mad at Rook for showing up on his island and, most of all, he was mad at the gods for allowing everything to happen as it had. "If you are coming for a fight, by the gods, I will give you one! Do you hear me?"

There was no reply.

"Answer me, damn you!" he shouted, pulling himself to his feet and gripping his spear tightly, his knuckles white with rage.

Silence greeted him, causing him to scream her name in frustration.

"Siranschae!"

Part 2

Rayne

Mirror

Chapter 5

Notyet leisurely rowed the small wooden boat across the smooth glass-like surface of the underground lake, the bow pointed toward the tiny island in the middle. He was not in any hurry and common sense told him that what he was doing was foolhardy, but he didn't see any other alternative. He just wasn't sure what the initial confrontation would be like.

The island was a prison of sorts, sporting a magic that long pre-dated the current arch mage of the Tower of Nykiva. It had no walls; it didn't need them. Anyone imprisoned on the slab of rock with a specific incantation was physically bound to the stone, forcing some part of their body to be in contact with the stone at all times. It also had the peculiar property of nullifying any type of magic, which negated any magical attempt at escape. Wizards couldn't cast spells any more than dragons could transform themselves into their true form. For this particular prisoner, the latter was of extreme importance. It did nothing, however, to allay Notyet's concerns.

As the burly warrior pulled the little rowboat up next to the rocky platform, he kept his eyes locked on the island's single prisoner. It was a woman, proud and regal looking as she sat in a chair, one of three pieces of plain furniture on the rock. One of the other items was a table next to her chair. It was currently bare, but the magic of the island would plate it with food and drink twice a day, as needed by the prisoner. Underneath the table was a roll of bedding. Meager as her living space was, she was at least taken care of. The final piece of furniture was a simple wooden stool, placed directly across from the chair, as if waiting for a visitor who would never come.

"Oh look, I have a guest," the woman said in an almost bored tone, her eyes never leaving the book that lay open on her lap. "As you can imagine, I don't get many of those."

"Aye and the reasoning is probably sound," Notyet replied, tying the boat off to a metal pylon imbedded into the rock. He stepped out of the boat and stretched, keeping a wary eye on the woman. He had no weapons; they were not permitted on the rock, for obvious reasons.

"Then why are you here?" Zarandrae, the human-form great blue dragon asked, still refusing to look up. Her voice was calm, but there was the barest hint of anger buried deep in her tone.

"Now that," he said truthfully, "is a question I've been asking myself for a while now."

"You have not discovered your answer?"

"Not entirely," Notyet said, stepping toward her. He went to the stool and paused, looking at her expectantly.

"By all means," she said drily, still having not looked up from her book.

The big warrior seated himself on the stool, facing her. He had no idea how to begin the conversation, and the words that came out of his mouth were not what he would have initially chosen, had he given it more thought. "Tell me about him," he blurted out.

She looked up, her head elevating slowly, her deep blue eyes coming level with his. "Have a care," she said dangerously. "You broach a subject you should not dare to mention."

"Now hold on a second," Notyet replied, holding up a hand to calm her down. "You misunderstand me if you believe I'm trying to hurt or belittle you. I'm aware of what that bond means to your kind."

"Then why ask?" she said, her voice strained.

"Because I want to know," he replied with a shrug. "I fought against Draven," he went on, "or at least his forces. I would have stood against him in battle on the field before Taer Blys, but it was not to be."

"Did you flee?"

"No," he replied, taking no umbrage to the thinly-veiled insult. "It was simply not my destiny."

"Then do you wonder if you could have stood against him?"

"Now that's funny," Notyet snorted. "He was the son of a god; it took the daughter of a god to defeat him. I am a mortal and hold no illusions of what my fate would have been had I fought him."

"Yet you ask about him," she said. "For what purpose?"

"Because I want to know what happened," he answered. "I want to know about you and why you were a part of all this. Why did you let him take the path that he did?"

Zarandrae was silent. For several long minutes, she stared at Notyet, her features betraying nothing. The big warrior waited patiently, returning her gaze, refusing to look away. Time passed slowly around them before she finally answered, her voice contemplative. "He was my companion," she replied. "But he was more than that."

"As I said, I'm aware of the bond your kind shares with your companion and I'm not prying into your personal feelings," Notyet went on, surprised at how easily the words were coming now. "From what I know of Draven, he seemed to covet honor. So I don't understand why he would follow his sister. There was never any honor in what she was doing."

"You do not understand the bond between Arcai siblings," she answered, and Notyet detected the bite of anger in her reply.

"Maybe not," he answered indifferently. "But the fact is that he did follow her and it led to ruin for him, for you, and for a great many others."

"So you would come to gloat over your victory?" she snapped, her face coloring with anger. "Is that why you're here?"

"No," he said, remaining calm. He was afraid of her, but he kept his fear hidden. "I came to forgive."

For the second time during their conversation, Zarandrae was taken aback. Once more, she could only stare at him, trying to fathom his true purpose.

"Look," he said, leaning forward on the stool and resting his elbows on his knees. "I am sorry for the loss of your companion. I truly am. I can understand how difficult that would be for you. Losing a companion or a loved one is never easy."

Zarandrae said nothing.

"But I am not sorry that Draven was defeated," Notyet went on, deciding that only the truth was acceptable if he was going to obtain what he came seeking. "The actions of Draven and his sister led to the deaths of tens of thousands in a pointless war. Innocents were killed, Zarandrae. Companions were lost. Hearts were broken."

"I did what was asked of me," she said, her voice soft again, almost a whisper. "It is our way. It was war."

"It was an unjust war."

"To you."

"To everyone!" Notyet shouted angrily, his voice rising as he got to his feet and gestured angrily. "Shayene wished to rule the world as a god, and she caused uncounted deaths to achieve it! Draven aided her and, by proxy, so did you and Kraegor."

"And all are beyond this world now," she replied defiantly, looking up at him, "leaving only me. Am I to be tried for their crimes, then?"

"No," Notyet answered, his voice softer. He settled back on the stool. "I'm not here to try you for anything."

"Then why have you come?" she snapped.

"Has anyone told you what happened in the Wraithlands?" he asked, deciding to try a different track.

"Only that Kraegor was claimed by the Nether and Shayene

escaped to another world with the help of her pet gatekeeper," she replied with a shrug. "As you might expect, I am not told much."

"What you were told is pretty much all we know," Notyet said. "We do not know where Shayene is, only that she is no longer part of this world. That much Jayadra knows for certain. Kraegor was indeed exiled to the Nether through the very gate Shayene created, which was then destroyed and should have trapped him there."

"Then what do you wish of me, warrior?" she asked impatiently. "I am imprisoned. Justly? Perhaps. But this is a greater burden to one of my kind than you could ever know. I have lost my companion, perhaps for eternity. I am stripped of what remains of my powers and caged in solitude deep beneath the earth. It would have been better had I perished in the battle before the gates of this city."

"But you didn't," Notyet countered, his voice kind and understanding. "Perhaps there is a reason for that."

Zarandrae knew then what Notyet was about. "This is not simply a visit, is it," she said, leaning back in her chair and contemplating the big warrior. "You wish something of me."

"I do," he replied. "I wish to offer you a chance."

"A chance for what?"

"Redemption."

Zarandrae threw back her head and laughed, a rich, boisterous sound calling to mind times much less dire. "Truly you jest," she said, still smiling. But it was a sour smile and it was obvious to Notyet that the dragon did not believe him.

"Let me ask you a question," he said. "How much do you know of what happened between the Vi'Raaji witch and Kraegor?"

"Little," she answered. "I'm told she ultimately sided with you in the Wraithlands and sacrificed herself by taking Kraegor into the Nether."

"That much is true," Notyet said. "But do you know why?"

She shook her head.

"Before the Wraithlands, Kraegor captured Vendetta here in Nykiva," Notyet explained, his eyes never leaving Zarandrae's. "He took it upon himself to rape her in his human form." Ignoring the sudden look of shock and revulsion on her face, he went on. "Terion found her, bound by Kraegor in Balgar's mansion and left to die. He saved her and, because of that, she pledged to aid him; to aid us."

"That is difficult to believe, human," Zarandrae said, but her voice was clearly unsettled. "That is simply not the way of our kind."

"I have no reason to lie to you," Notyet replied evenly.

"How do you know this to be true?" she pressed. "Surely you would not simply accept the word of a now-dead Vi'Raaji that she was assaulted by a dragon, would you? Kraegor was many things, but that is something I cannot believe to be true."

"Why?"

"Because such an act would be an abomination to all that was bequeathed to us by the gods."

"And yet, it happened," he stated quietly.

"How do you know?"

Notyet leaned back, his features tight. "Because Vendetta is not dead," he answered slowly. "She escaped the Nether."

"That is highly unlikely," Zarandrae scoffed.

"And yet, just as true," he countered. "She did escape, and Terion found her again, this time deep within the Spider Forest and heavy with child."

"I don't know whether to be disgusted or insulted," she replied bitterly. "You expect me to believe that Kraegor assaulted the witch and fathered her child?"

"Children," Notyet corrected. "Vendetta gave birth to twins."

"My question still stands, human. Do you expect me to believe this was Kraegor's doing? That a dragon raped a human and produced offspring?"

"The birth happened deep in the forest," Notyet went on, ignoring the question. "The first child to be born, a daughter, was named Rayne."

"And this proves what?"

"Vendetta named the baby right before Kraegor appeared and abducted her."

"And now you are saying that he escaped the Nether, as well?" Zarandrae sneered in disbelief.

"Vendetta did," Notyet answered. "And while I don't know how, Kraegor came through a gate that suddenly appeared as soon as the child was born. He could have killed them, but for some reason, he spared Terion and Vendetta and took the child, instead."

"You said a gate opened?" she asked incredulously.

"One did," Notyet nodded. "One of two gates, actually." Before she could ask, he continued. "The second child was born and her mother named her Fyre just as a second gate opened. This one claimed mother and child moments later."

"What do you mean?"

"The gate opened and then closed and when it collapsed, it took Vendetta and Fyre with it."

Zarandrae turned away, her features paling as she began to realize what these events meant. "It is the coming cataclysm," she said quietly. "The barrier is giving way."

"That is our thought as well," Notyet agreed, his features grave. "What happened to Vendetta and Fyre, we do not know, but we believe them to be on the same world that Shayene took the outworlders from. Terion is hoping to follow them and find them there."

"And of the other?" she asked, looking up. Her sullenness was gone. She looked frightened now.

"I pledged an oath to my friend," he answered. "I promised him I would find Rayne. And I know that Kraegor has her."

"You weave a fantastic tale," she admitted shakily. "Can you prove yourself?"

"Search your senses," he said. "Surely you can feel the presence of Kraegor."

"Unless he was very near, I could not; not in human form, anyway, and I am greatly weakened," she responded. "As my true self, I could feel his presence much further away, but only by miles, not by lands or continents. And as you can see, that's not a possibility."

"What if I offered you the chance?"

"Explain yourself," she commanded, her eyes narrowing.

"It's really quite simple," he said, standing up and stretching. "I am offering you the chance at freedom, if you agree to help me."

"Help you?" she asked skeptically. "As your servant?"

"As my companion," he corrected, before turning and walking back toward the tiny boat that had brought him here. "And perhaps in time, as my friend."

Notyet said nothing more. The big warrior hopped into the boat and cast one more look at her. Their eyes met and held momentarily, before Notyet seated himself and rowed away from the little island.

He returned to her the next evening, rowing back to the island and disembarking as before. Zarandrae was standing before the stool this time, watching him intently all the way. He walked up and stood before her, their eyes nearly level. Zarandrae towered over normal humans when she took their shape, but Notyet was nearly as tall as her in human form. As he looked into her eyes, he knew that she had agreed to his proposal.

"You will extract a vow from me, no?" she asked.

"Only that you hold fast to your honor," he replied. "I am willing to wager that because of what happened, you would want an opportunity to clean the slate. I know dragons prefer their companions and, when that is not available, they prefer their solitude. I also know that dragons are very near immortal, but as with all things, life eventually fades and they eventually find themselves kneeling before the One, to make a reckoning of their life."

She took in a deep breath, but said nothing.

"Help me find Rayne," he asked plainly. "You are the only chance I have of finding and confronting Kraegor. Help me do this and earn your freedom."

"And if we are successful?"

"Then, at least in the mortal realm, we will consider your debt paid and allow you to go in peace," he replied. "You will be free."

"Then I agree, Notyet," she answered solemnly. "I give you my word that I will help you find the child."

"Excellent," Notyet said with a wide smile. "Then we will leave on the morrow. The spell imprisoning you here is now lifted, though I have been asked to request that you do not revert to your dragon form until we are well away from the city proper and civilized lands."

"Agreed," Zarandrae replied. "But I wonder what your friend Terion would say."

"To what?" Notyet asked, stepping toward the boat and holding out his hand to help her into it.

"To the arrangement we just made," she replied, accepting his offered hand and sliding gracefully into the boat. "I am a dragon and was your enemy at one time, and could still be again."

"I don't know," Notyet answered truthfully. "Perhaps one day we'll find Terion and then you can ask him yourself."

"Given what you explained to me, that's highly doubtful," she said. "Our own chance of success is only marginally greater than Terion's, and that's not saying much."

"Then why agree to accompany me?"

"Because as little hope as there is that we will succeed, it is still more than I have now."

"Almost like the faintest of hopes that a dragon and a human would agree to become companions on a noble quest, right?" Notyet asked with a grin.

Zarandrae did not answer, instead looking forward as the boat slid across the water to the far bank and freedom.

Chapter 6

Not everyone was a fan of the unlikely companionship, except for Anthony, who thought it was a perfectly splendid idea. Most of the rest would only grudgingly accept it, with narrowed eyes and distrustful looks. Jayadra was distressed enough at the dragon's release that she voiced it to the others. "I am still not at all convinced that this is the right decision," the Arcai priestess said, looking at the dragon pointedly.

"I don't know that we have a choice," Aylan replied. He wasn't overly fond of the decision, either, and he had gotten to know Zarandrae better than most over the time she was imprisoned beneath his tower.

"You don't," Notyet spoke up, his voice firm. "No offense, but that choice was mine and I made it. Besides, she is the only one that can get me through the Wraithlands safely and the only one that even remotely has a chance against Kraegor."

"Do you trust her?" Jayadra pressed.

"She gave me her word," he shrugged. "I trust that she will uphold her vow."

"If she does not?" Aylan asked, looking hard at the big warrior and then at Zarandrae.

"Then we will hunt her down and exact swift and proper retribution," Jayadra answered softly before Notyet could reply. "Her freedom today is based on her service. If she breaks her promise…"

"I gave my word," Zarandrae said easily as she buckled on a wide leather belt that held her great sword's scabbard. Her twin long swords were already strapped to her back, clinking against her gleaming blue chain mail as she moved. She was a magnificent figure and her very presence was nearly overwhelming to the gathered group, save the

Arcai. "I will not betray it," she finished as she looked up, her ice blue eyes locking with those of Jayadra.

"Everyone is simply concerned, Zarandrae," Aylan interrupted, attempting to alleviate the tension while still seated at his desk. "We are putting our trust in you, Notyet most of all, and even you must admit that it is unprecedented."

"I could go with you and keep an eye on her if you want," Anthony said hopefully, levitating himself up to sit on the edge of Aylan's desk. "Besides, this was my idea, remember?"

"I'll be fine," Notyet grinned, reaching out and ruffling the little mage's shaggy hair. "I trust Zarandrae. We will manage."

"Very well," Jayadra sighed. "The decision, for good or ill, is made and we will not try to talk you out of it."

"Thank you," Notyet said with a smile.

"Your horses are ready for you outside the west gates," she went on. "I am certain I don't need to remind you, Zarandrae, that the wounds of the war are still raw and unhealed. Travel at night as much as possible and keep your true form hidden. Even your human form will surely be recognized by some, so avoid habitations and travelers as much as possible."

"I am well aware of the situation," the dragon replied coldly. "Your reminders are unnecessary."

"But relevant all the same," the Arcai priestess said, refusing to back down. "You understand our concerns?"

Zarandrae brushed a strand of silver hair out of her face and looked hard at Jayadra. "I understand more than you could know," she replied softly. "Notyet trusts me. More importantly to me, I trust him. I will not break that trust. I swear it."

Notyet patted her on the shoulder and smiled. "Then trust me when I say, let's be on our way."

"Safe travels," Jayadra said grimly, speaking for all of them, "to both of you."

They rode out from the gate shortly after midnight, and for nearly an hour they travelled in silence, both astride great gray stallions, horses large enough to carry the two riders and their gear. They rode easily and, if Zarandrae's mount was nervous that a dragon sat astride its back, it showed no signs.

"I would think that a dragon would have little need to ever ride a horse," Notyet finally broke the silence as they trotted their horses side-by-side in darkness brightened considerably by the full moon directly overhead. "Yet you seem to be an accomplished rider."

"I have lived for a great many centuries," Zarandrae answered distantly. "You learn a lot when you are long-lived and spend most of your time in the guise of a human."

"So things weren't always the way they turned out, eh?"

"No," she replied sadly.

"What happened?" he asked. "Care to talk about it?"

She was silent for some time, still cautious about sharing too much, even with a man who had placed his ultimate trust in her. Finally, she spoke, her voice soft and longing. "For the longest time, we simply enjoyed being about the land," she began, a small smile turning up her lips as she remembered the good times. "Draven's greatest love was just seeing the world. He kept his distance from mortals, but held no animosity toward them. He accepted his charge of being their protector when they needed him, which was seldom. That allowed us to spend a great deal of time together, exploring and seeing the world."

"So what changed?" he asked gently. He could hear the ache in her voice. She was truly heartbroken at what had happened.

Zarandrae gazed up into the star-filled sky before answering. "It would be easy to blame it on the gods, I suppose," she said quietly. "Long before any of this ever happened, Draven's sister, Shayene, was in an accident and her body died."

"She died?" he asked in surprise. "An Arcai?"

"It happens," she nodded. "It is rare, but it can happen. And while it might be difficult for you to believe, she was much like her brother in that time—inquisitive, sensitive, and loving life. She stayed far from humans and would never have done what she did. However, after she died, her mother, Karasika, did not see the need to rebirth her for a great many years. During all that time, she wandered as a spirit, separated from Kraegor and everything else. It gave her a lot of time to come to loath the gods, and even more time to find a way around them. Ultimately, I believe it drove them both mad with hate."

"So why did Draven agree to help her?"

"He was her brother," Zarandrae replied. "He missed her terribly while she was gone. When she finally returned, he vowed never to lose her again, and that made it easy for her to convince him to follow her."

"So when Shayene decided to take over the world, he went along with it," Notyet finished the tale.

"He was never the same after she died," Zarandrae pointed out. "Her death and his guilt at believing he had not protected his sister; Shayene's return and her plans to become a god—all of this hardened him, made him bitter. He came to hate mortals and hate the gods even more. So he began to challenge humans to martial combat, knowing it would anger the gods when he killed them. But he did not care."

"How did he end up leading the Gol'Athi in the war?"

"The Gols revered him," she answered. "He fought through their ranks and slew some of their greatest warriors before they realized that he should be their warrior."

"So he decided to just up and lead them?"

"He was already far down that path when Shayene finally returned. When she did, and shared her plans with him, everything was already laid out perfectly. He pledged to serve her cause as leader of the Gols, war was declared, and they marched against the Doms. The rest you know."

"Sadly, yes," Notyet agreed. He was silent for a bit as they rode, before asking his next question. "What about Kraegor?"

"Kraegor has always had a dark soul, made much worse during Shayene's long absence," she replied, and Notyet thought he detected a hint of anger in her tone. "It would not surprise me if he had much to do with her becoming what she did once she had been rebirthed. He fully backed her plans, even expanded them and goaded her on. Kraegor has always longed to see the gods thrown down, but more to win his own release than to see Shayene elevated to that status."

"Win his release? What do you mean by that?"

"We are dragons," she responded. "We are near immortal beings, created by the One on a faraway world, given over to the Arcai through the gods of other worlds to act as their companions and their confidants. Kraegor grew weary of that arrangement; angry that he should suffer because of Shayene's long absence."

"You said you were created by the One," Notyet questioned. "I thought Benovan and the rest created the dragons."

"That is a common misconception," she went on, her voice becoming distant. "In truth, we come from a world all our own, created by the One. We are here at His behest as well as our own desire."

"How many of your kind actually exist then?"

"Our numbers are beyond count."

Notyet was shocked into silence as he tried to reconcile this new information. He had always thought there were sixteen dragons in the world, one for each of the Arcai. Now Zarandrae was telling him there were a whole lot more, and they weren't even from this world. "How is it that no one knows this?" he finally asked tentatively.

"When we are pledged to our Arcai companion, we are given a secondary form that the gods of that world have agreed upon. On this world, we have been given human form, a certain rarity given the potential issues that can arise," she replied evenly, again sending the big warrior spiraling into contemplative silence. "Consequently, few people, if any, have had the discussion that you and I are now having."

They rode for another hour, speaking of nothing more, Notyet thinking about the implications of what Zarandrae's words meant, while the dragon was lost in her own thoughts. In time, Zarandrae broke the silence to mention that dawn was coming and they should make camp. They did so, dismounting and guiding their horses deep into the trees, where they set their camp. Notyet started a small fire and cooked up some of the fresh venison they had brought to sustain them through the first couple days on the road, enjoying it because he knew that dried meat and hard biscuits would take its place when the road got longer. He was somewhat surprised when Zarandrae ate her meal cooked, enjoying it as he did.

"Can I ask you something?" he broke the silence as they ate.

She nodded, tearing off a chunk of steak and chewing slowly.

"Why did you leave your world for this one?"

Zarandrae did not answer right away, instead savoring her meat while she contemplated the answer. "It is complicated," she finally replied. "On our world, our kind rule exclusively. There are no humans; no other thinking creatures of any kind. Only us. We live in absolute peace, but we yearn for more. We seek to further our knowledge and experience; we seek adventure. But that is not something to be found on our world anymore."

"How do you end up here? Or on any world, for that matter?"

"We petition the One," she answered. "We ask to transition ourselves to another world, so that we may obtain that which is no longer possible on our world."

"So you petition the One true God?"

"It is the only way," she said with a nod. "If our hearts are true, He will grant us our wish."

"So you mean you can speak to the One right now and go to another world?"

"Were it that easy," she lamented sadly. "While the One affords us this incredible experience, we do make concessions. We are given over to a world, usually a new one or one remade by some calamity or cataclysm. We are promised to an Arcai, or whatever passes for an Arcai in that world. The gods of that world decide our form and our duty and we are matched, to live out the remainder of our lives as companions."

"When do you go back to your own world?"

"We don't," she replied, her voice again distant. "When we leave, it is forever."

"You mean you give up your friends and families?"

"In this life, yes," she answered. "But it is a chance for personal growth we cannot attain on our own world, so many of us choose to pursue it."

"But it's forever," Notyet remarked. "I don't know how you can stand being away from your loved ones like that."

"Dragons are long-lived, Notyet, beyond anything you can comprehend. But we are not immortal. We do eventually die and we can be killed."

"And then?"

"Then, we pass on to the next life, same as you," she said with a shrug.

"What is the next life?"

"I am only a dragon, Notyet," she laughed softly, smiling for the first time that he had seen. "I am not the One. I would hope we are reunited with our loved ones, but I cannot say for certain. No one can."

"So you don't know."

"I don't," she affirmed.

There was silence between them again, Notyet almost reeling from what he was learning on this, the very first night they were together. No human on the planet knew what he now did about the race of dragons. It certainly changed his perception of them, especially of Zarandrae.

"I think I begin to understand more about your kind," he finally said after finishing off the remainder of his venison. "Not to be hurtful or anything, but if you are so wise when you come to a new world, why would you follow something you must know to be wrong?"

"It is part of the plan," she answered sadly. "We forge bonds with our Arcai companions that are, in many ways, stronger than we forge with those of our own world. We become close to them; feel as they do; bond with them soul-to-soul and desire to make them happy. In my case, I served Draven out of love and loyalty. I wished to see him attain his dreams. I wished to see him happy once more after so many years of despair." She trailed off and turned away so that Notyet would not see the single silver tear that ran down her cheek.

"What about Kraegor?" the big warrior pressed, giving her something else to consider; something that would bring about a different reaction. "With all due respect, he raped a human. Surely that is far beneath a dragon."

"It is," she agreed. "As I said, Kraegor is different, not like me. Our kind are much like you mortals in that we each have that which makes us who we are. Some of us are happy, some loyal, some carefree, some dark and brooding. His was a dark soul on our world and he became darker still on this one, particularly when Shayene died."

"Do you think it's possible that Fyre and Rayne are really his daughters?"

A shadow passed across Zarandrae's face and she did not immediately answer.

"You believe it, don't you," Notyet guessed, reading her expression.

"When we leave our world," the dragon responded, her voice low, "the ability to reproduce is taken from us. It is one of the concessions we make."

"I imagine that's so you don't overrun your new world with your kind," he replied. "With all due respect, there's not much that would keep you in check, at least on this world. But what about in human form?"

"That is what troubles me," she replied. "The restrictions placed on us cover whatever form we are given beyond our true form."

"Then you're saying Kraegor cannot be the father."

"I'm not saying that at all," she countered. "He very well could be and probably is, if the tale you told me of his appearance through a gate is true."

"Then how?"

"The power of the gods of this world are fading and have been for some time," she said after a long while. "As that happens, the restrictions placed on our kind can be overcome."

"That would mean that you will grow stronger if you are no longer constrained by them," Notyet said thoughtfully.

She shook her head. "Actually, just the opposite," she corrected him. "Our powers will fade. The One sent us, but we exist at the behest of the gods of this world. If their power disappears and they are thrown down, we will lose our powers as well. We would become as mortal as you."

"But Kraegor?"

"He was imprisoned within the Nether," she replied darkly. "The Nether is hell for all worlds, not just this one. If he has overcome hell and returned to this world, then his power has grown, not diminished. It means he has truly separated himself from the gods. He is his own being."

"What would that mean for us?"

"The more important question is, what that would mean for all worlds?"

Notyet fell silent and thoughtful. If Kraegor was indeed stronger today than he was before his imprisonment, then what chance did Zarandrae have against him, with her companion slain and her own power fading with that of the gods? It wasn't a pleasant thought and he found himself wondering if there was anything more they could do to prepare themselves for what lay ahead.

They would speak no more that night, lost deep within their own thoughts. In the morning, they were off again, pushing on toward a confrontation that neither was confident they would survive.

Chapter 7

They traveled for many days on horseback, eventually passing north of the Vi'Raaji cities of Scarlet Keep and Caitlyn Rook. They would stay near the massive inland sea for another day or two, before going to the air and striking hard for the Wraithlands. Once clear of human habitation, the road became more of a path than anything else and they rode openly, less concerned about encounters with others who might recognize Zarandrae.

It was one such evening under the light of a full moon when Zarandrae suddenly brought her horse to a halt and smoothly swung off her mount, motioning quickly for Notyet to do the same. No sooner did her feet hit the ground when the audible click of a crossbow launch preceded the fleshy smack of the bolt driving deep into her horse's chest. The horse immediately reared up in shock and pain as Zarandrae skipped back several steps to avoid getting kicked.

"Bandits," she hissed as Notyet dismounted behind her and pulled his sword.

Another bolt shot out of the darkness, this one penetrating the links of Zarandrae's chain mail and finding the mark in her shoulder. With a growl of anger, she grabbed the reigns of her skittish horse and worked to keep it between her and the direction the attack had come from.

"Throw down your weapons!" a voice shouted out from the darkness. "Do as I say and no harm will come to you!"

"A little late for that," Zarandrae replied angrily under her breath as she used her free hand to wrench the bolt from her shoulder and toss it to the ground. Her armor had slowed the bolt enough that it did not penetrate very deep, but that did nothing to allay her irritation.

"Voice sounds young," Notyet whispered back. Then loudly, he asked "Who are you? Show yourselves."

"I only want your money," the voice answered back.

"Only one?" Zarandrae questioned.

"Sounds like it," the big warrior replied. "Some lone highwayman looking for a quick bit of luck most likely."

"That's too bad. No one will be around to learn the lesson I am about to teach him."

"I'll shoot you if I have to," the voice went on, clearly nervous now.

"It's just a kid," Notyet whispered.

"He shot my horse."

"Well…"

"He shot me," she reminded him.

"You're a dragon," he chuckled. "That's not even a mosquito bite to you."

"I don't care," she growled. "I'm going to eat him."

"Now hold on a minute," he soothed, suppressing a smile. Calling out to their attacker, he continued, "Look, we know you're alone and you're in a world of trouble right now. Honestly, son, you can't even imagine how much."

Silence.

"If I'm guessing right, you likely have a pair of crossbows, neither of which is currently loaded. You may have a blade, but we have several each. Not good odds, I would say."

"Just drop it, I said!" the voice repeated, the fear evident now.

"I am going to count to three," Notyet went on, ignoring the plea. "If you don't come out right now, it's going to go very badly for you."

There was silence again, followed by a rustling in the bushes and then what sounded like someone fleeing away from them.

Before Notyet could object, Zarandrae leapt into the brush, giving chase.

"Don't eat him!" Notyet called out loudly enough for the attacker to hear. Laughing to himself, he pulled a torch from his pack and quickly had it alight before walking into the woods in the direction Zarandrae had gone. He found where their ambusher had been hidden and noted the presence of two battered crossbows, just as he had presumed, both lying discarded on the ground. A few crude wooden quarrels lay next to one of them.

In the near distance, he heard a short scream of pain and terror as he bent and gathered up the equipment. Then, he took it all back to the path and tossed it in a pile. While he waited for Zarandrae to return with her prisoner, he stuck the torch in the ground and examined the crossbow bolt in Zarandrae's horse. It had penetrated the beast's chest, but it was not barbed and he easily withdrew it while speaking softly to the nickering stallion.

He was cleaning the wound when Zarandrae came out of the brush, a body thrown over her left shoulder.

"You didn't kill him, did you?" Notyet asked as she unceremoniously dumped the limp form on the path in front of them. It was a young man, barely just a teenager, and he had a nasty gash over his left eye.

"No, I never even touched him," she grumbled, turning toward her horse. "He ran into a tree."

Notyet chuckled and knelt beside the kid as Zarandrae took over caring for her horse. "Oy!" he said loudly, reaching down and slapping the boy lightly on the cheek. "Wakey, wakey!"

Their prisoner began to stir and Notyet reached down and tore a small strip of cloth from the boy's already tattered shirt. As his eyes opened, the big warrior pressed the cloth to the young man's wounded forehead and leaned closer. "Not having a very good night, are you?"

he said lightly.

"Pl…please don't kill me," he whined, his eyes darting about fearfully.

"Well, that depends," Notyet replied, guiding the kid's hand to the cloth pressed to his forehead. "Here, hold this so you don't bleed all over the place." When the boy obeyed, Notyet sat back on his haunches and looked hard at the young man. "What's your name?"

"P…P…Sh…Shadow," he stammered, struggling to sit up.

"That's a stupid name," Notyet said evenly. "What's your real name?"

"Uh…Percy."

"So, Percy, would you mind telling me what you think you were doing?"

"I just…" he began, then trailed off, looking down.

"You know, we're well within our rights to kill you here and now."

"And hang your body from a tree as a warning to other highwaymen," Zarandrae added grimly.

"I'm not…I'm not a highwayman!"

"What do you call your actions tonight?" Notyet pressed. "You wounded my companion and her horse. I should gut you right now," he said in feigned anger, reaching down and pulling a dagger from his boot.

"No! No, please!" the boy pleaded, crying openly now. "Please don't kill me! I don't want to die!"

"Oh, shut him up," Zarandrae growled, "before I do eat him."

"She's not kidding, you know," Notyet went on, waving the dagger before him. At this, the young man collapsed, sobbing uncontrollably, his face pressed to the ground. Notyet looked up at his companion and winked. She shook her head and looked away, but not before the big man caught a glimpse of a grin on her face. That was something at least.

Reaching down, he tapped the kid on the back of the head with the flat of his dagger. "Sit up and stop acting like a baby," he went on, keeping his voice firm. "If you're going to play at being a bandit, you better be ready to accept the consequences when you get caught."

The young man looked up, his face streaked with dirt and tears. "I swear, I've never…I've never done this before," he sniffed, his spirit truly broken. "You were the first."

"And I'm sure the last," Notyet added, fingering the blade and sending the boy into fits of hysterics again. "So tell me, Percy. What prompted you to try your hand at thieving? You really are terrible at it, you know," he added.

The lad took longer to compose himself this time and, when he finally looked up, Notyet realized suddenly that robbery might have been all he had left. His story would confirm it.

"My ma and pa have a home a couple miles back in the woods," he began slowly, pausing occasionally to wipe his eyes and nose on his tattered sleeve. "Pa had a hidden mine that he worked. Wasn't worth much, but he dug up enough chunks of silver to keep us in supplies when we needed it. Everything else, the forest provided."

"What happened?"

"Mine caved in last fall," Percy said, his lip starting to quiver again. "Suddenly, no more Pa."

"Did you ever find him?"

The young man shook his head. "Couldn't get through the cave-in. Too much rock."

"Why not move back to the city?"

"Ma didn't want to," Percy shrugged. "Said we could make it on what we had. Then she got sick over the winter and died, and I was all that was left. Supplies ran out on me a couple weeks ago."

"So you decided to become a highwayman?" Zarandrae asked.

"I didn't see any other option," he replied.

"You seem to be intelligent enough," Notyet pointed out. "You even sound educated."

"Ma grew up in Nykiva and studied magic and history. Met and married my pa and they moved out here about ten years ago with me. Ma was always making me read and study; said my studies were more important than digging rocks."

"Was she a wizard?"

"Nah, not a very good one, anyway. But she was smart."

"So what were you going to do with the money, if you had successfully robbed us?"

"Buy supplies," he answered with a sigh. "My pa taught me a lot about mining, so I'd like to try and get it back up and running again. At the very least, I could maybe find his body and properly bury him beside my ma."

Notyet felt no deception from the boy, only remorse. The lad was alone in the woods and had been away from civilization for pretty much all his life. Going back to the city was likely the worst thing he could do. With a sigh of his own, he slid the dagger back into his boot sheath and stood up.

"Well, I think we've come as far we can on horseback, Zarandrae," he said.

"You have other means of transportation, do you?" she asked with a sideways look at the would-be bandit.

"We'll have to hoof it," he answered. "Besides, your horse isn't going to be able to bear a rider for a while." Turning to Percy, he offered a hand and helped the young man to his feet. "Your actions tonight could easily warrant a hangman's noose, but I'm going to offer you a deal instead."

"You're not…going to kill me?"

"Not today anyway," Notyet shook his head, but smiled warmly. "No, I'm going to turn our horses over to your care."

"You're…what?" Percy asked, not daring to believe what was happening.

"Once my friend's horse is healed, I expect you to take the horses to the nearest town or settlement. These are fine steeds, so find the stable master for the lord or lady of the town. They should fetch a very fine price, more than enough for supplies and a mule, which you'll need to have, living this far beyond civilization. It will make your supply runs in the future a lot easier."

"I don't…understand," Percy stammered.

"What's to understand?"

"I tried to rob you and you're giving me your horses?"

"Call it a successful robbery," Notyet shrugged. "But I warn you," he continued, a heavy scowl crossing his face. "If I ever hear tales of a bandit on these roads, I will come searching for you and when I find you, I will offer no quarter."

"No, no!" Percy said, holding up a hand. "I completely understand! No thievery of any kind! I swear!"

Notyet nodded and unloaded his packs from his horse, while Zarandrae did the same. Once they were done, he took the reins of both and handed them to Percy. "Remember my warning," he said gruffly.

"I will," the young man replied. "I don't know how to thank you enough, but…thank you."

"Just don't make me come hunt you down," he said, reaching down and pulling the torch back out of the ground. He handed it to Percy. "Not get out of here. Go home."

Amid a flurry of continued thanks, the young man carefully guided his new horses into the brush, talking softly to them as he did.

As the sound of the happy young man began to fade, Notyet turned to Zarandrae, who stood staring at him with an odd look on her face. "Not how you would have handled it?" he guessed with a smile.

"Hardly," she replied. "The generosity of humans continues to surprise me."

"He's just a boy."

"He tried to rob us; could have killed us."

"Okay, so he's just a boy that had an amazing moment of severe stupidity."

At that, Zarandrae laughed softly.

"Here, you should let me take a look at your shoulder," Notyet changed the subject, moving to light another torch. "Those weren't iron bolts. No telling what got into the wound."

"It's nothing," she objected.

"Look, I would like nothing more than to believe you, but I don't relish the slim chance of being in the presence of a dragon companion with an infection and a fever. Now take your armor off."

She looked at him, her face unreadable.

"Trust me," he said gently.

After a few moments, she sighed and turned her back on him, before sliding off her blue chain mail and letting it fall to the ground. She wore a thin leather tunic underneath the mail, and there was a bloody hole in her right shoulder. As Notyet moved behind her, she slipped the tunic from her shoulders, letting it gather down around her waist, exposing the wound to him. Her skin was pale, slightly bluish, and Notyet gulped in spite of himself. In later days, he would consider how terrified he was of that moment, but he knew that right now, it was a moment of trust building for both of them.

"What would happen to this if you changed?" he asked, gingerly pressing his fingers alongside the bloody hole, forcing the silvery blood to well up, hoping to push out any splinters or debris that might be stuck in the flesh. The wound wasn't that deep, but she had done more damage to the tissue when she had ripped the bolt out in anger.

"The wound would still be there, but on a bigger scale," she answered. "However, it would still be just a scratch to me."

"Well, this needs a couple stitches," he countered.

"I heal quickly. Stitches will not be necessary."

"Maybe you're afraid of the needle."

"I beg your pardon," she snapped, whirling around to face him, her hands coming up quickly to cover her naked breasts.

Notyet took an involuntary step backward, as much because she was a dragon and could literally eat him in her true form, as from his sudden recognition that she was truly beautiful in human form. As his face flushed with embarrassment, he noted her eyes were fiercely bright, almost glowing in the moonlight. Swallowing his apprehension and pushing back feelings that were wholly uncomfortable, he stepped forward and placed his hands lightly on her bare shoulders. She stared at him in silence, her face unreadable.

"I was kidding," he chuckled and then slowly turned her back around. He swept her long hair back over her other shoulder and inspected the wound again, trying to ignore what he had seen, before picking up a water skin and pouring water into the wound. With a clean cloth, he dabbed at the gash, doing his best to clean it.

"Do I make you nervous?" she asked quietly after some moments of silence.

"Downright terrified," he replied truthfully, with no hesitation. "Is it obvious?"

"Somewhat."

Folding a strip of cloth, he pressed it to the torn flesh, making sure it would stay in place before pulling her tunic up and back over her shoulders. "I'm in unknown territory," he admitted, brushing her hair back into place so that it cascaded down her back. "I would be lying if I told you that I don't get scared when I think about who you really are."

"As you have seen, I'm as human as any woman in this form," she smiled, turning around and reaching out to gently touch his cheek.

"With all due respect, it's your other form that frightens me."

"And yet, you sent our horses away," she said with an actual grin, putting him at ease.

"Well, I haven't always made the best decisions in life."

She laughed again, the sound almost musical to the big warrior. "You certainly have a gift, Notyet," she said with a smile, reaching down and retrieving her armor. She slipped it over her head and let it settle back in place, then rotated her arm a couple of times, testing the wound. Satisfied it would cause her no further issues, she went on, the hardened warrior in her returning as the tender woman retreated. "Tell me, do you trust me?"

"If I didn't, this is probably not the time to mention it."

She smiled at his wit and Notyet felt somewhat better. When they had left Nykiva, she had been mostly withdrawn and quiet and he had asked himself many times if he was deluding himself to put his trust in a dragon. After that first night and the hours they spoke together, she had loosened up some and, as the days passed and they got to know each other better and better, she had become an enjoyable companion, sharing stories with him of her world and listening with surprising attention as he related tales of his own life, most of them adventures with Terion and Cavanah. He found it somewhat odd that a dragon would be interested in the life of a human, but he had begun to understand the insatiable quest for knowledge and experience that her kind sought. It was almost as if she was living his adventures herself as he told them.

"If it would make you feel better, I will hunt down a deer and eat after I take my true form," she said with a knowing smile.

"That does not instill me with a lot of confidence, Zarandrae," he said, shivering in spite of himself.

She smiled and placed a hand on his shoulder, which greatly surprised him. "I gave you my word," she said easily. "Besides, you are much more valuable to me as a companion than as a meal."

Notyet looked at Zarandrae in the darkness, her form seeming to shimmer in the starlight. "So, what happens now?" he asked with some embarrassment, clearly uncertain. "Do I need to turn around or something?"

"Why?" Zarandrae laughed knowingly as she turned away. "You've already seen more of me than any man alive."

As he blushed fiercely in the darkness, she began to walk away from him and as she walked, her form wavered in the moonlight. Suddenly mesmerized, Notyet watched in awe as her transformation took place. It was nothing like he expected as it was almost fluid, every part of her body expanding and shifting at the same time so that one moment she was human and then the next, she was crouching before him in her true form.

Notyet had seen her in flight before when they fled Draven's armies in Taer Blys and, back then, he was thoroughly impressed at her size. Up close, she was absolutely enormous, and he thought he might simply pass out with fright. The very presence of a dragon projected an aura of fear on those around them, and he had experienced that firsthand in the past. But this time, because of the bond they had forged, the fear was not present, or at least not in the way it would be for others. It had been replaced wholly with wonder and amazement.

"This will go smoothly if you follow my directions," Zarandrae said in a voice that was hers and yet not. She dipped her head close toward him, her blue scales glittering in the night, and he flinched, taking an involuntary step backward. Notyet realized that she could quite easily swallow him whole.

"Hoh, boy," he breathed, his eyes wide.

"Touch my face," she rumbled, bringing her huge maw within inches of his face. Her mouth was partially open and the teeth within were the size of daggers. Her breath was hot on his face and smelled of ozone and fresh rain, the same scent one would get after a thunderstorm had passed. For Notyet, he found that strangely settling. Trembling, he reached out a tentative hand, finally placing it on the hard-armored scales of her long snout. It was cool to the touch, but his fingers buzzed and tingled gently, smalls sparks flashing in the darkness.

"I swore an oath," she said, her dragon voice low. "More importantly, you have become my friend where I have no other. I swear no harm will come to you."

He moved in closer, letting his hand run along her scales and underneath her huge ice-blue eye. "I believe you," he finally breathed.

Minutes later, they were off, winging their way northward.

Chapter 8

Two days later, Zarandrae set down in the courtyard before the main gates of Shayene's keep. It was dawn, but in the Wraithlands, even without Shayene's dark influence, it was difficult to tell. The sky was still nearly black, with only a slight increase in light to the west where the sun was coming up. But they both knew it would get little lighter than it already was.

Zarandrae's transformation back into her human form took only seconds, going from the huge blue dragon back to her armored human form as Notyet gazed upon the tower before them. Nothing moved near or around the castle. No light burned in any window. It appeared completely deserted.

"Are you certain you sense nothing?" the big warrior asked, having asked her earlier if she could feel his presence as they drew nearer.

"Nothing at all," Zarandrae affirmed, shaking her silver-haired head. She was as puzzled as he was. "I sense no trace of him anywhere."

"Is it possible that he can mask it?"

"Not to me," she sounded confident.

"What about his time in the Nether? How would that affect him?"

"To that, I have no answer," she replied honestly. "But I believe I would still be able to sense his presence, even if he was in a corrupted state."

"Well," Notyet said, reaching down and picking up his pack. "I suppose there is no sense in waiting for a welcoming committee. We might as well go see what we can find."

Together, they moved along the cracked road toward the main gate of the keep. It was clear along both sides of it, but they knew that the undead moved in the dead forest beyond, remnants of Shayene's army of creatures from the Nether. Zarandrae had seen signs of them as they flew over the Wraithlands, but none in any great numbers. They were scattered and lost, wandering the bleak lands aimlessly. Here, before the keep, it was no different. A few creatures roamed the darkness nearby, but they appeared unwilling to approach to two warriors, which was just as well. Notyet had no desire to get caught up in a fight that might draw more toward them.

The entrance to the keep was open, the heavy wooden gate hanging in disrepair on rusted hinges. Beyond the huge doors lay the darkness of the main hall, shrouded in silence. Still, they saw nothing. They crept onward into the keep, weapons at the ready, moving silently in the direction that Zarandrae indicated. While Zarandrae could see well enough in the dark, Notyet had been forced to light a torch. As they moved down the different halls, he swept it back and forth, seeing everything the flames illuminated.

In numerous places, they had to step carefully around piles of bones, likely those of undead creatures that had been destroyed a year ago when the keep had fallen and Shayene and Kraegor had been defeated. They finally worked their way into the main chamber, where the final battle had taken place—and so much loss had befallen Notyet and his friends.

The warrior's hand went to his throat as he stood in the entry way, thinking back on the battle. He had died in here—or at least, he should have died. His throat had been torn out by a monstrous reaver before the young Tae empath, Arianna, had saved him. She had done so at the cost of her own life.

"This is a place of difficult memories, isn't it?" Zarandrae asked softly, moving to stand beside him. Her fingers entwined with his and she gave his hand a reassuring squeeze.

Notyet nodded, but said nothing. During their travels, he had related the story of the epic battle to her. She was their enemy at that time, fighting before the gates of Nykiva. The story had been new to her and he had seen the pain in her eyes as he told it. She had been on the wrong side of the conflict and, as the days and weeks passed between them, it continued to become clearer to her.

"There is no life here at all," Zarandrae finally said, releasing his hand and moving into the huge chamber. "There is only deadness."

"The gate was set in the far wall," Notyet said, his voice sounding small. "It was through there that Vendetta took Kraegor, moments before Branson destroyed the gate by throwing Varankyl through it."

Zarandrae nodded thoughtfully as she reached the far end of the chamber and laid her hand against the stone. It was cold to the dragon, colder than normal, but nothing that concerned her. The keep was dead, devoid of all life. Nothing existed within its catacombs. Nothing at all. "He was never here," she finally ventured, turning to face Notyet who was looking down at some scattered bones that lay at his feet.

"I don't understand," Notyet said. "Where else would he go?"

"It's a big world," she offered.

"But would he not pick someplace familiar to be his lair?"

"Perhaps," she said with a shrug. "Dragons do tend to prefer familiar places. But perhaps the Nether has changed Kraegor in ways we do not yet know."

"Or maybe he just doesn't want to be found," Notyet said as he knelt by the bones and looked more closely at them. They did not appear to be the bones of the defeated undead. Worse, some of them were smaller, more like those of children. A glint caught his eye and he moved the torch closer to better see. A little skull lay atop a thin gold chain and he reverently moved it aside, then reached down and picked up the necklace. It was a small thing, something a child would wear, and bore a tiny silver pendant in the shape of a world—their world. He looked at it closely, letting it swing in the air before his eyes.

"Memories of the innocent," Zarandrae said softly from behind him, noting the necklace he held.

"Not something a creature from the Nether would wear," he said, looking up at her.

"It wasn't," she replied sadly. This part of the tale she did know. "Draven once spoke of the gatekeeper that Shayene used to open up the gate to the Nether. She tortured his family to force him to obey."

"Here?"

"Yes," she nodded and Notyet saw a flash of grief cross her face. He knew this was difficult for her, a reminder of who she had served and how many had suffered.

"It was only a year ago," Notyet said thoughtfully, holding the necklace up. "The one who owned this necklace would have been a child." He stood up and pulled his sword, then gently wrapped the thin chain around the guard and pommel, making certain it was snug. The little globe charm hung at the center.

"Why?" the dragon questioned, watching him carefully.

"To remind me of what I fight for," Notyet said grimly. "This child perished, and there was nothing we could do to help her. I don't want to see that happen with Rayne."

Zarandrae nodded and placed her hand on his shoulder. "A noble reminder," she agreed softly. "We'll find her."

They spent nearly two days searching Shayene's former keep for signs of Kraegor and the baby, but found nothing. As the time passed, it became obvious that Kraegor had never returned to the keep after abducting Vendetta's child. It was a setback that Notyet found thoroughly frustrating.

He sat back with a sigh into a high-backed chair, looking tiredly at a mirror set into the wall before him. They were in Shayene's personal quarters. It was a large room high in the tallest tower, with several windows and a walk-out balcony, although what pleasure the Arcai would have gotten from looking out over the Wraithlands was beyond Notyet's ability to understand. They had already searched the room carefully, trying to find something, anything that might lead them to Kraegor, but nothing presented itself. Zarandrae had torn the bed apart, seeking things that might be hidden within the musty down-stuffed mattress. They had rifled through chests and bureaus, even searched for hidden doors, and had still come up empty.

"Blasted Arcai," Notyet grumbled, kicking his feet up on a dresser and looking at his growling reflection in the old mirror.

"You knew this would not come easy," Zarandrae said from across the room as she pulled a chest of drawers out from the wall to look behind it.

"Still," he grumbled, leaning forward to rest his chin in his hands. "A hint would have been nice."

And that's when he saw it. It was purely a stroke of luck that he was even in the right position to notice it, but it was there, plain as day. Situated at the very base of the mirror was a tiny protrusion. Reaching out, he ran his finger across it and was rewarded with an audible "click." Before him, what was once a mirror, split down the middle and opened up like a pair of small doors, revealing a large cupboard-like area beyond.

"Zarandrae," he said excitedly, looking inside.

The dragon hurried over to him, her eyes drawn to the contents as well. "It's an extra-dimensional space," she observed, peering closer. Inside were several small chests, numerous rolled up scrolls, a few baubles, and a large leather-bound book. Notyet began reaching inside, but Zarandrae grabbed his wrist. "Careful," she warned. "This is an Arcai's personal belongings. They are likely far beyond a mortal's understanding and very dangerous."

Notyet turned disbelieving eyes on her. "What Arcai worries about common thieves?" he scoffed.

"Shayene was very secretive after her rebirth, even as Arcai go," she explained. "The items here radiate powerful magic."

"How can you tell that?"

"I'm a dragon, my friend," she smiled. "Magic is something I can sense quite easily." She mumbled a string of words that Notyet did not understand, then reached in and took hold of the large book. She gently pulled it out and laid it on the vanity before him. "This is what we want."

"What is it?"

"A journey of life," she replied. "All Arcai keep one. It is one of their most cherished possessions, and they guard them fiercely."

"Strange that she didn't take it with her."

"Not so strange, considering what she had become," Zarandrae countered sadly. "I doubt she cares about it anymore."

"Not many pages," Notyet pointed out, opening the huge binding carefully. There were only a few dozen pages, all of them covered with neat and flowing script in a language Notyet had never seen.

Zarandrae reached out and flipped several pages over in succession. Each time she did, it seemed like the book added more pages behind, so that one could never reach the end. "It is a magical tome," she explained as she noted his astonishment. "It will hold as many pages as the Arcai wishes it to hold."

"That's convenient," he replied in wonder. "Now if we could only read it."

"I can," she said, picking it up and paging back to the first page.

Notyet sat down on the edge of the shredded bed and Zarandrae sat next to him, opening the book so that it spread across both of their laps. She read softly, sometimes to herself, sometimes translating passages for Notyet. It was exactly what Zarandrae had said it was—a chronicling of Shayene's life, written by the Arcai herself. They stayed that way for hours, alternating between her reading and both of them talking about what Shayene had written, trying to find some clue that might lead them to her companion. They paused briefly to eat a late supper of dried venison and hard cheese, before Zarandrae went back to reading. The dragon read through the night and deep into the next day before finally finding what they had been looking for. She translated passage aloud as Notyet listened carefully.

Solitude. I crave it, even as much as I enjoy my limited time with mortals, Shayene had written. But their lives are so very brief, gone in the blink of an eye for someone who will live through all the ages. It grows wearisome, like trying to catch a breath of wind. And so we are here and here is where we will stay. Here, I may pursue my studies. Here, Kraegor may take to the sky without concerning himself with the watching eyes of mortals. Here, we have peace.

Zarandrae looked up excitedly. "This is it," she whispered.
"Keep reading," he urged.

The heights are wondrous. The cold will ensure we get few, if any, visitors. And oh, what a magnificent view, being able to look down and see the world laid out before us.

"Does that mean anything to you?" Notyet interrupted.

"It does," she nodded. "She speaks of her home before the accident that ended her previous life."

"Would Kraegor return there?" Notyet guessed, feeling hopeful for the first time in their long search.

"I think it's highly probable," she said.

"Do you know where it is?"

"Not specifically," Zarandrae answered, "only that it is far to the north. But we should have no problem finding it. It will be on the highest peak and, if Kraegor is indeed there, I should be able to sense him, even from miles away."

"You will go as a dragon?" he asked, wondering if that was safe.

"As close as I can get without him becoming aware of me. Besides, if it is where I think it is, that's the only way we will get to it," she replied. "Come, let us rest and then depart in the morning. We will go to Iszenmar, where we can get suitable equipment and supplies to continue. It is very cold where we will be going."

"It's cold down here," he reminded her.

"Not like this, my friend," she smiled knowingly.

He grumbled and sighed, then began searching for something for them to eat. The next morning, he was astride Zarandrae's back as they finally winged away from the tower in the Wraithlands, heading west into the unknown.

Chapter 9

They hiked the last few miles into Iszenmar after Zarandrae had set down behind a low-lying mountain in the early morning hours, well out of sight of the guards that would surely be manning the walls. Iszenmar was a bustling city, housing tens of thousands of ice-bound Zents, cold-weather barbarians well known for their hardiness and ferocity. Numerous traders could also be found in the city, at least during the spring and summer months, trading tools and grains for furs and other goods. Lucrative trade routes between Iszenmar and cities of the Doms, Gols, and Vi'Raaji made the dangerous journey well worth the risk for traders who stood to earn a lot of gold if they survived the trek.

With the sun just coming up in the east, the two travelers approached the city, and Notyet noted that the huge wooden gates were closed. He could also make out several figures manning the battlements on either side.

"Have you ever been here before?" he asked, walking alongside Zarandrae on a road that was still mostly covered with snow.

"Several times over the years," she replied, her eyes scanning the city walls, "but not recently."

"The gates are closed," he pointed out. "Will they let us in?"

"They usually don't leave open the gates until the land has thawed, since traders will not be arriving for some time yet," she answered. "Before the start of the trading season, the gates stay closed because predators this time of year are likely starving and bold enough to venture into town looking for a meal. But do not worry; the guards will let us in."

The gates did open us as they approached, but it was to let out a dozen armed soldiers, who met them on the road before the entrance to the city.

"It be early in the season for traders," the lead warrior called out, a huge and heavily-armored man who stood even with the nearly seven-foot frames of both Zarandrae and Notyet. The soldiers with him were all nearly as large. "Who are ye?"

"Just travelers," Zarandrae replied gruffly. "We won't be here long. We need to purchase cold weather gear before we continue on with our journey."

"And just where might that be?"

"North."

"Where in the north?" he asked suspiciously, his eyes narrowing. "There be nothin' beyond Iszenmar. Everyone knows that."

"Just north," Zarandrae repeated, staring hard at the man and refusing to give any ground.

"It's a big world," Notyet put in, hoping to diffuse the tension bit. "Lot of unexplored country beyond the city. We just want to see it, that's all."

"Minin' rights belong to the king," the guard warned. "Ye wouldna be tryin' to start a dig now, would ye?"

"If I buy a pick-axe, I'll be sure to let you know," Notyet said with a wink.

"We are just traveling through," Zarandrae added warily. "Our destination is our own business. We will purchase our supplies, partake of the good food and ale Iszenmar is known for, and be on our way in a couple of days."

For some seconds, the huge guard held his ground. Then without a word, he waved a hand in the air and headed back into the city, the other guards falling in behind. The gates remained open, allowing Notyet and Zarandrae entrance as well, before finally slamming shut behind them as they followed.

They found themselves on a road paved with roughhewn stones and surprisingly clear of snow, most of which had been pushed up against the sides of buildings. The street led deep into the city, crawling up the slope of the mountain and cumulating in a large castle high above all the other buildings, home to King Grath, lord over all the Zents. All around them, the city itself was already bustling with activity, even in the early morning light.

"They don't waste any time getting the day started, do they," Notyet stated, noting how all the city residents were dressed in similar fashion—heavy furs, boots, and, in some cases, hats. Nearly all of them were armed, wearing swords and hammers openly on their belts or strapped to their backs.

"During most months, nights here are very cold," Zarandrae replied. "They use as much of the day as they can before locking up their homes and businesses as night falls. Even the inns and pubs lock up. If you're there after dark, you are usually there all night."

"What about in the summer?"

"It's one big celebration," she answered. "They work and play without end, day and night, until the nights get cold again and they are forced to hide themselves from the bitter winter."

"Do you think we'll have any issues, being visitors and all?"

"Spring is close, so their minds will be on other things beyond a couple of strangers showing up in town before the traders roll in," she replied. "As long as we do not bring any attention to ourselves, we should be fine."

They continued walking up the road, noting as they did how quickly the people were going about their business. Eventually, Zarandrae led them down a secondary road that supported a string of shops lining both sides of the stone street. Notyet read the signs as they went, noting stores selling everything from mining gear to equipment to food, even one selling chocolate, a rarity in most parts of the world. After a few minutes of walking, Zarandrae selected one that she seemed to be familiar with and the two of them entered, a tiny bell tinkling in the door frame as the door opened.

"Good day be to you," an ancient-sounding voice called out, before the speaker appeared from around a huge pile of tanned skins and furs stacked on a low table. He might have once been as tall as any of the other barbarians they had seen in town, but now he was old and stooped and as wrinkled as any person Notyet had ever seen.

Zarandrae smiled in recognition. "Well met, Link," she said warmly.

"Zara, my good friend," he greeted loudly, his eyes sparkling. He moved to embrace her, a happy smile on his face as he spoke rapidly. "Why, I haven't seen ye in several years! So good of ye to come back! Come in, come in! And I see you have company. Who be yer friend?"

"This is Notyet," she replied, holding out her hand toward the big warrior. "We are traveling to the north together."

"Beyond the city?" Link questioned, surprised. "Why on earth would ye want to go any further than Iszenmar? There be nothin' north of here but ice and death."

"There are treasures to be found by one who knows where to look," she replied with a knowing smile.

"I hope ye not be planning on openin' up a mine anywhere," he warned her. "Ye know how King Grath feels about that."

"Aye," she replied. "I am well aware of that, and we have already been duly reminded. But I assure you, we are not looking to mine. There are ancient ruins all over this world from before the Earth Storm."

"Oh," he looked surprised. "And ye believe that ye may have found one?"

"I had some time to do a lot of reading recently, until someone convinced me to get out and stretch my wings, so to speak," she said, with a sideways smile at Notyet.

"Any of those ruins that be in this part of the world, they'll be long buried under ice and snow," Link said.

"Perhaps," she replied cryptically.

"Ye wouldn't be lookin' for the dead god's castle now, would ye?" he pressed, narrowing his eyes.

"The dead god's castle?" she repeated, her voice neutral, careful not to look at Notyet. "Are you speaking of Frosthold?"

"Aye, and a very old place it be. Been empty for hundreds of years, I'm told. An Arcai used to live there, but she disappeared long ago."

"Can't say that I'm aware of that story," Notyet spoke up, playing his part. Frosthold was exactly where they were going, but despite the fact that Zarandrae obviously trusted Link, he felt it best to simply play at being ignorant. "Sounds interesting, though. Think it's worth investigating?"

"Hard to say," Link shrugged. "Never known anyone to go lookin' for it. Don't even know exactly where it be located, other than way up north. Ye would need a dragon to reach it anyway, which was probably why it was constructed there."

"Know where we could find one?" Notyet chuckled.

"Aye, I do, but not sure ye would want to be meetin' one of those cursed beasts," Link answered darkly and then turned away and changed the subject. "So what supplies can I round up for ye?"

"Standard snow shoes and sleeping gear," Zarandrae replied in a neutral voice, casting a concerned glance at her companion. She knew better than to mention aloud Link's acknowledgment that he knew of a dragon, and that he had referred to it as a cursed beast. Her first thought was that it had to be Kraegor. It could be none other. They were on the right track.

They spent the better part of an hour in Link's store, gathering up the equipment and supplies they would need and putting their packs together. Link agreed to keep their gear in the store until they were prepared to depart. The rest of their conversation centered around possible ruins from the old world and what treasures someone might be able to find, but that did nothing to allay Zarandrae's rising concern. Something was wrong about the whole situation and she felt it keenly.

Once they had departed, she voiced her worries to Notyet. "He knows something," she explained quietly. "Kraegor has been here."

"How could you know that?"

"The way he answered your question," she answered. "The Zents are very accustomed to Volsaun and they know him well. He spends a great deal of his time here among the people and they are very aware of his true form. They revere him."

"And calling him a cursed beast isn't something Link would likely do, correct?"

"He would never speak of Volsaun that way," she answered. "Link knows him personally. They are friends."

"Does he know who you really are?"

"No," she replied. "I have never revealed my true form to him or any of his people. I find it makes my visits here much more enjoyable."

"So, if Kraegor has really been here, what does that mean for us?"

"Well, he likely would have passed through here anyway," she replied. "The fact that Link is aware of it points to Kraegor's appearance being something of a spectacle."

"So, Kraegor didn't hide his true form from them," Notyet reasoned.

"No, and it sounds like it didn't go well, either."

"Should we ask around and see what happened?"

"No, we are better off not showing any interest at all," Zarandrae said cautiously. "We do not want to draw any undue attention to ourselves, especially if Kraegor has stirred them up."

"Do you think he knows we are coming for him?"

"Kraegor is supremely intelligent. He knows someone will be coming for him," she said. "With luck, he just doesn't know who."

They fell silent, deciding it was best not to speak too openly of their suspicions around the people of the city. They spent the rest of the day browsing shops and inns, making it obvious they were not trying to keep a low profile and that they truly were a couple of explorers, looking to find an ancient ruin in the frozen lands around Iszenmar. Zarandrae reasoned that if Kraegor had placed spies in the city, those agents were already aware of their arrival and skulking about would do nothing but alert those spies that they were someone to be interested in. Best to keep them thinking that the two of them were harmless and not worth watching.

Later that evening, they settled into a small inn far off the main thoroughfare. After stowing their gear in their room, they retired to the commons area to eat a hot meal and relax. There were only a few other patrons in the place, making it easier for them to notice anyone suspicious lurking around. They saw no one beyond a few locals just enjoying their dinner, and a couple of them enjoying more than a little too much to drink.

"You think we're safe?" Notyet asked after a pleasantly plump serving maid took their order and left them with a couple of frothy pints and a cheerful promise that dinner would be brought out to them quickly.

"I see no reason to be concerned," she replied thoughtfully. "Nevertheless, we should remain vigilant and depart as soon as we can. The less time we are in town, the better our chances are that suspicion will not fall upon us."

"You seem distracted," Notyet pointed out after a bit, eying his friend.

"It's nothing," Zarandrae replied. "I'm just wondering what could have happened to cause Link to answer the way he did."

"You're convinced he was talking about Kraegor and that Kraegor did something to get the Zents riled up?"

She nodded but said nothing more. If she wanted to share further, Notyet was content to let her do so when she wished to.

He took a long drink of his ale, savoring the strong taste. It had a unique flavor, but then again, he had never been this far north, so had never tried the barbarian's brews, something they were very well known for. Zarandrae drank with him, turning the topic of their conversations to imagined ruins of the First Born and what they might find if they found such a place. If people were listening to them, the more people would suspect that was their true purpose.

Their time in the commons room was uneventful, and they spent a relatively short dinner, eating a very good meal and enjoying each other's company. The Zents definitely knew how to cook and they both ate and drank well. Finally, feeling more at ease about remaining inconspicuous, they decided to retire to their room, both feeling very tired after a long day.

The poison in their bodies did the rest.

Chapter 10

When Notyet opened his eyes more than a day later, the first thing he realized was that his head hurt so badly that opening his eyes sent waves of agony blasting through his brain. He immediately closed them and lay still, calming his breathing and his heart, which slightly lessened the pounding behind his eyes. He wondered if they had really drank that much the night before, but he honestly didn't think so—and worse, he couldn't quite remember. He wondered if Zarandrae was feeling as bad as he was, but then he realized something else. He was in chains.

Taking a deep breath, he forced his eyes open, doing his best to ignore the pain. Wincing, he fought through it and looked around. He was in a small stone cell furnished with a sleeping pallet—which he was laying on—and an old wooden stool, as well as a bucket for waste. Sunlight streamed in from an opening high above him in the ceiling. It didn't matter that the opening did not have an iron grate over it, as it was nearly thirty feet up and the walls of his cell were as smooth as ice. After a quick glance, he realized the walls actually *were* coated with ice, a thick layer that had probably built up over the years. His cell was very cold, but he had been wrapped in a thick fur blanket. Apparently, they wanted him alive, at least for the moment.

His biggest concern, though—despite his bleak accommodations— were the manacles that were shackling his wrists. Thick chains were attached to the cold iron restraints and fastened securely to a stanchion that had been drilled into the wall next to his bed. The chains afforded him enough room to move around the cell as needed, but little else. Shaking his head in irritation, he pulled the fur blanket back around him and closed his eyes, silently willing his headache to go away.

Roughly an hour later, and with only a slight decrease in his headache, he heard footsteps outside the huge wooden door of his cell, which were followed by voices. Two men argued briefly, before a key was turned in the lock and his door opened.

"Be quick," a deep voice commanded from the hall and then the door swung shut again as a man entered. Surprisingly, Notyet found himself staring into the wrinkled visage of Link, the old shopkeeper.

The old man pulled the stool closer to the bed and sat down facing him, his back to the door. "Ye didn't come to pick up yer gear," he began easily enough, his hands moving in front of him as he spoke. It took Notyet a moment to realize that the man was signing to him while he spoke, a completely different conversation than the one he was voicing. *Zara told me you were once a mute,* he signed. *Taking a chance you can read this.*

"Someone hit me on the head, I think," Notyet said slowly, deliberately slurring his speech. He didn't have to pretend much, though. He was certainly feeling the effects of whatever had been used to knock him out. *I can,* he signed back.

"Were ye fightin'? What on earth would make ye want to mix it up with anyone here?" *You were poisoned. Both of you. Easier to handle.*

"I don't even…remember what happened," Notyet replied. *Zara okay?* he signed back, remembering that's what Link called her when they visited his shop.

"Haven't heard myself, either. Magistrate isn't sayin' much. Maybe you had too much to drink?" *She's fine, being held in another cell under magical restraints so she can't transform.*

"Like I said, I don't remember." *You know who she is then?* He replied with his fingers, feeling a moment of panic. If the Zents knew she was a dragon, then Kraegor would know they were here.

"Well, the magistrate isn't saying what he's goin' to fine ye, but I imagine yer gonna be out in a day or two, if everything goes well." *I do now, thanks to some talk that is going around. I also know that Kraegor only wants Zarandrae. They mean to just execute you.*

"I hope so," Notyet said, trying to remain upbeat despite the grim pronouncement. "Otherwise, I'm going to get really bored." *How long do I have?*

"Well, I'll hold yer gear until they release ya. Ye can pick it up in the shop when you get out," Link said, pushing the stool back and standing up "I won't charge ye anything extra, if it'll only be a couple more days." *Dawn, if I can't break Zara out tonight.*

"Thanks," he said. "Much appreciated." *I'll be ready.*

"Get some rest," Link finished offhandedly. "And try to stay warm. It gets mighty cold in these cells." With that, the old shopkeeper turned away and shuffled back to the door. He wrapped his knuckles on it several times, before the guard opened it up.

"Yer done?" the guard stated gruffly.

"Aye," Link replied. "They already paid me for the gear. Just wanted to make sure they came back and got it."

"Be seein' a bit of profit off that one," the guard smirked, looking at Notyet. "I don't reckon he'll be comin' back at all."

"Oh?"

"Executioner will be taken 'is head at dawn," the guard finished almost gleefully.

"Hmph," Link mumbled and then shuffled past the guard. "A bit of a shame, there, I reckon. He seems a nice enough chap."

The door closed and the footsteps faded back down the hall, leaving Notyet to his thoughts.

Notyet decided that it must be well past midnight when he finally heard movement in the hall beyond his cell door. No one had come to speak with him since Link had left. The guards had not even brought him any food, and his stomach rumbled with hunger. Now, a key was turning in the lock and the door finally swung open.

Link was the first one through, a nasty cut along his cheek under his left eye. A steel warhammer, streaked with blood, was in one hand and a crystalline vial filled with a pale blue liquid was in his other. He looked grimly determined as he stepped into the cell.

Zarandrae followed him, her own face set in anger. She looked relatively unscathed, but was only wearing her leather tunic and breeches. She held a battered steel sword, apparently taken from a guard. She knelt beside Notyet and took the vial from Link.

"Are you all right?" she asked, concern in her voice.

"Yeah, just cold and I've got a screaming headache," Notyet answered. "But I'll live."

"Hurry," Link whispered, going back to the door to watch. "They'll be along quickly."

"What's that?" Notyet asked as Zarandrae pulled the stopper from the vial with her teeth.

"It will freeze the metal so it can be broken," she answered, grabbing his wrists and holding them up. "Have a care. You do not want to get any of this on you."

Notyet held perfectly still as his friend poured a small amount of the potion on the areas where the links of chain attached to the manacles on his wrists. The metal immediately frosted over and he could hear it crack with cold. His wrists grew colder—painfully so—as Zarandrae recapped the vial and then gave the chain a hard yank. The frozen links, along with the shackles themselves, shattered easily and he was free. With a yelp of pain, he quickly shook the freezing metal shards from his skin.

"Can you fly us out of here?" he asked, climbing slowly to his feet with her help.

"No," she shook her hand. "There is magic covering the dungeons and beyond, much like what my prison was like in Nykiva. It prevents me from taking my true form."

"Come, we must go," Link said quickly, interrupting them. "They are coming." He ducked through the door and into the hall.

The two companions hurried after Link, who moved surprisingly fast for his age. He was much more than simply fast on his feet, and Notyet witnessed that first hand as they turned a corner and practically ran into one of the prison's guards. The soldier reacted predictably, bringing his hammer down, looking to crush the old man to the floor. Link quickly swung his own hammer out, intercepting the blow and sending it wide. He followed it up with a hard shot back the other way, scoring a solid hit on the soldier's leather-protected side. The man grunted in pain as his ribs shattered and Link shouldered him aside and rushed past him.

Notyet swept up the man's weapon as he hurried by, feeling better now that he was armed, even if it was with an unwieldy hammer. They hurried down several sets of tunnels, following Link closely, until eventually the tunnel opened onto a slender bridge that arched over a large chasm. There were no rails on either side and on the far end, the span opened up onto a landing that faced an iron door. It made for an effective choke point, and the presence of three guards all but ensured they were trapped. Notyet quickly looked up and down, seeing only the cavern roof overhead and nothing but darkness below.

"Ye might as well give up now," one of the guards called out as he stepped forward, walking to the midpoint of the bridge.

"I think not, Corgan," Link said, stepping out onto the arch and walking forward confidently, his hammer swinging easily in his hand.

"Stand aside and let us pass."

"Ye forget, I don't take orders from the likes of you anymore, old man," Corgan replied, hefting his own hammer easily. "Ye have been gone from the guard for some twenty years now."

"Ye cannot hold these two as prisoners," Link went on, not stopping. "This will be the ruin of us all. Ye have to believe me."

"Yer daft, old man," Corgan spat. "Now stand down."

"I'll not be standin' down," Link said, unruffled. "I'm either comin' over ye or through ye, and if ye've consented to follow the likes of Kraegor, then perhaps through ye is the better option."

Corgan growled in answer and set himself, his hammer held out behind him, prepared to attack. Link launched himself toward the soldier, leading with his weapon. Corgan countered, matching Link's strike with one of this own, and the hammers smashed together in a shower of sparks, the ringing metal echoing throughout the cavern.

Corgan held fast, but Link stumbled, losing his footing on the thin bridge. Corgan took advantage and swept his hammer low, taking Link's legs out from under him and sending the old man tumbling over the edge. With a shout of alarm, Zarandrae dove forward, catching Link's arm as he fell and keeping him from falling away into the darkness. But that left her completely helpless, and Corgan flashed a nasty grin as he raised his weapon high, prepared to finish them both off.

But before the blow could fall, Notyet threw his hammer with every bit of strength he had, sending it end-over-end across the span. It caught Corgan directly in the chest with a crack of bone, sending him screaming into the darkness below.

Zarandrae used the reprieve to haul Link back up. With Notyet helping, the old man was once again standing with them on the catwalk, gasping his thanks, his face white.

"Forget it," Notyet replied, clapping Link on the shoulder. "Whatever happens, we're already square." He looked down into the darkness and grimaced. "Too bad about Corgan, though."

"He was a rat bastard," the old man said, shaking his head in anger, his color coming back. "Never knew him to be anything more."

"He may be gone, but we are not safe yet," Zarandrae said, pointing to the other side of the bridge. Two soldiers remained on the landing, but instead of waiting, they moved back through the door and closed it behind them, followed by the distinct sound of a lock clicking.

The three fugitives hurried forward and Zarandrae wasted no time, pulling the vial of blue liquid from her tunic and shattering it against the metal door. The potion splashed across much of the metal, turning it white with frost. As the metal began to crack, Zarandrae delivered a kick to the center of the door, blasting it to pieces, the shards flying back down the hall. The shrapnel cut down the two soldiers who had been hiding behind it, leaving them dazed and bleeding on the floor.

She stepped over their writhing forms and hurried on. Notyet followed, helping Link along as they went. The short fight with Corgan had winded the old man.

They moved on through the complex, Link occasionally calling out directions. While they heard shouts and hurrying feet echoing in the tunnels, they only ran into another single guard who foolishly tried to stand against Zarandrae. She left him bleeding and leaning up against a wall, wounded but alive.

Link finally directed them along another tunnel sloping downward and toward stairs that wound down into darkness. "We part here," he panted, doubling over to catch his breath. "The stairs will take ye down to the main sewer. There be a grate protectin' it." He pulled another vial of the blue liquid from his belt. "This be the last of me stock," he went on, looking hard at Zarandrae. "Use it sparingly."

Zarandrae took it from his grasp and clasped him on the shoulder. "Are you certain this is the best way to handle this?"

"It be the only way," he nodded. "They will do nothing more to me other than confine me back to me shop."

"They won't punish you for helping us?" Notyet inquired.

"Nah," Link replied with a tired grin. "I have enough secrets on everyone, including King Grath, that they wouldn't dare."

"What about those that died?"

"Warriors, one and all," he replied proudly. "They died doing their duty. Corgan, in particular, will be honored for his sacrifice, even if I think he's always been a prat." Changing the subject, he went on, pointing down the stairs. "Your weapons and armor and the gear ye bought from me is stowed in the rocks about a mile east of the city. Knowin' what I know of yer kind, I placed a magical gem with it that will act as a beacon for ye. As ye get closer, ye should be able to sense it, Zara."

"Thank you," she said, embracing him. "How can I repay you?"

"Ye never told me ye were a dragon," he answered, feigning hurt feelings. Then he smiled and kissed her on the cheek. "Ye can repay me by comin' back one day and sharin' yer tales of adventure over several pints."

"I will," she grinned.

"I'll hold ye to that," the old man said and then looked serious again. "Now, listen close. Yer both facin' a cold trek through the sewer, but as long as ye keep movin', ye should have no issues."

"No other guards, I take it?" Notyet asked.

"None this far down," Link shook his head. "You'll be safe enough." He turned to Zarandrae. "Stay out of yer true form until ye be well away from the city, Zara. Remember, Kraegor knows yer here."

"Understood," she answered solemnly.

"Thank you, Link," Notyet added, reaching out and grasping the old man's shoulder. "I wish there was more we could do."

"Get rid of Kraegor," Link replied grimly. "I already feel the hold he has on our people, and it's a darker day by far."

"We'll do what we can," Notyet promised.

"That be the most I can expect," Link said. "Now go! You'll find a stack of torches at the bottom of the stairs. Once yer in the sewer, stay on an easterly course. And ignore the side tunnels. This will bring ye out north of the main gate and out of sight of the guards. East from there, ye will find yer gear."

After some final words of thanks, Link departed back the way they had come and Zarandrae and Notyet descended the stairs into darkness. True to Link's word, they found a bundle of torches at the bottom, along with a piece of flint. Notyet struck a torch alight and lit another, handing it to Zarandrae. Then they hurried deeper into the sewers. A cold, if uneventful, hour later they were well away from the city, with Zarandrae following the magical beacon that Link had provided her. She led them unerringly to the spot where the old man had stowed their gear behind a pile of broken stone, and they set about strapping on their armor and weapons.

"Do you think he'll be okay?" Notyet asked as he buckled on his weapon belt.

"Zents value honor above all," she answered. "Link has earned enough honor in his lifetime that most will be willing to overlook his helping us, providing Kraegor does not involve himself."

"And if he does?" Notyet pressed. She shrugged, doing nothing to allay his concern. "That's all the more reason to find him," he added.

"I agree," Zarandrae replied, before suddenly freezing, her eyes going to the stars above.

"What is it?" Notyet whispered, following her gaze. But she

quickly held up a hand, silencing him as she stared upward. For several long moments, she was as still as a statue, hardly even breathing. Then she turned to him, her eyes glittering in the darkness.

"It is him," she said softly. "Kraegor has arrived in Iszenmar."

"Can he sense you?" Notyet asked in rising alarm.

"I don't believe so," she answered. "I doubt he knows we have escaped, so he would have no reason to try and sense me outside the city."

"Still think Link is going to be safe?"

Zarandrae looked at him, her features pained. "I can only pray that he is. But for the moment, there's nothing we can do here. Let's get on the road. The quicker we can get away from Iszenmar, the quicker I can transform. I don't dare do it while he's nearby or he would most assuredly find us."

Notyet nodded his agreement. "Right. I don't think announcing our presence to Kraegor just yet would be in our best interest."

"You do realize that he will know of our arrival once we have found Frosthold," she pointed out. "There will be no avoiding it then."

"We can deal with that when we get there," he replied. "Right now, let's concentrate on making sure he doesn't find us before we're ready."

Zarandrae nodded and they began the final leg of their journey. Frosthold. and whatever fate was in store for them, awaited.

Chapter 11

It took them the better part of three weeks to reach the base of the mountain they sought, far to the north of Iszenmar, in large part because Zarandrae often sensed Kraegor in the night skies above as he searched for them. So she had remained in human form much of the time, flying only short stretches here and there when she knew he was gone, while masking herself from his searching senses when he was nearby.

The mountain path they had finally reached was long and treacherous and, in many places, deeply overgrown or missing altogether due to rock slides that had occurred over the centuries. But enough of it remained that they were able to slowly make their way up the mountainside toward a stone keep settled deeply into the cliff near the top.

As darkness descended for their second night on the trail, they could see that the castle was alit, flames flickering in many of the wide windows. They had finally reached Frosthold.

"We need to dig in before it gets too dark," Zarandrae said, leaning on Notyet as they both plodded gingerly through the knee-deep snow. This far north, winter had not yet released its icy hold on the land and travel was treacherous and difficult.

"Tell me again why it was such a good idea to hike the trail?" he asked in jest, breathing hard in the thin air. "If we make it, I'm going to be too tired to fight anything."

"Kraegor knows we are coming," she replied, not really needing to explain herself again. "At least in human form, he may not sense me until we have arrived." She paused and looked up. "As it is, we should reach the summit tomorrow around mid-day."

"Unless we fall off."

"I will not let you fall," she said with a smile as she came to a halt near a stone outcropping and pulled a roll of canvas off her pack.

"Easy for you to say," he grumbled.

Still smiling, Zarandrae pointed ahead to a small cut in the cliff wall as she shook open the canvas. "We can take shelter here for the night."

They found the alcove more than adequate for their needs. They worked quickly, anchoring the tarp with rocks to create a small shelter that would keep the wind out. Ducking under the canvas flap, they began unstrapping their armor and weapons and tossing them aside. Starting a fire this close to Kraegor's castle was out of the question, so the quicker they were huddled in close together, the better off they would be. As both of them began shivering, Notyet grabbed their dinner from his pack, took the tent he had used earlier in their journey, and pulled Zarandrae close, wrapping them together in the material. It was too windy and rocky now to set the tent up properly and that lent itself to situations that were equally inviting and frightening for both of them.

Within the valleys that they had hiked through, the air had been cold, but mostly calm, and they had been able to sleep side-by-side in the pitched tent without freezing to death, even without a fire to warm them. Once they had reached the mountain trail, the icy wind bit deep into their bones and necessity forced them into a much cozier sleeping arrangement. They had slept that way on the first night on the trail and Notyet had been surprised how at peace he had been, nestled closely together, sharing their body heat while talking long into the night. He thought it would not be such a bad thing to spend a lot of time with her like that in the future. He had spent a good portion of his life with Terion as his friend, and the two of them were as close as brothers. But this was entirely different.

"Have you considered what we will face once we reach the keep?" Zarandrae asked after they had both stopped shivering, her breath hot on his cheek.

Notyet tore off a hunk of dried venison and handed it to her as he took a thoughtful bite of his own dinner. The dried meat was salty and tough, but it was filling and did the job. Link had stocked them with plenty of provisions for their journey out of Iszenmar and they were in no danger of running out of food, as long as one was not averse to eating jerky every meal. "You would probably have a better idea about that than I would," he replied between bites.

"He is a dragon," she shrugged, the movement drawing them even closer together. "Normally, a dragon would command no one. But he has been trapped in the Nether for nearly a year. Chances are he has brought demons into this realm to serve him."

"That's a cheery thought," Notyet said off-handedly.

"The point is, we will have to be careful," she went on. "Kraegor was cautious and calculating before any of this ever happened. If he has the baby, he has her for a reason and will have taken precautions to protect her. Additionally, as a dragon, he will not be without servants to help him deal with her."

"What can a baby do that would worry him?"

"You are forgetting that Kraegor is a dragon, and a male one at that," she said with a grin. "He will not have the first idea how to raise a human baby."

"But hell-spawned demons would?"

"Some would, yes," she replied, her smile disappearing. "The Nether does not simply imprison the spirits of the damned. There are plenty of pure demons that live there. Some of them are quite adept at human behavior and more than willing to serve Kraegor simply for the opportunity to be freed from their current confines."

"So he will have brought along some of his new friends?"

"I am almost certain of it," she answered. "Kraegor was always a very capable sorcerer. Gating in servants from the Nether would be well within his abilities, particularly with his new connection to it."

"I suppose it is what it is," he sighed, looking deep into her ice blue eyes. "But for now, let's keep warm and get some sleep. We'll need all our energy tomorrow, I'm guessing."

She smiled again and nodded, then worked her body in very close to his. They wrapped their arms around each other and nestled their faces into the warmth of each other's necks. Neither, however, was able to sleep.

"Notyet," Zarandrae said softly after some time, her lips brushing his throat as she spoke.

"Hmmm?" he tried to remain calm, conscious of the electricity that was tickling his neck and running through his body.

"Can I ask you something you might consider personal?" she said, pulling her head out of her warm cocoon, so she should look him in the eyes again.

"I don't see why not," he replied, breathing a little easier. "We've shared quite a lot over our time together."

"It has been an enjoyable time at that," Zarandrae admitted. Her eyes took on a thoughtful gaze and she went on. "When Draven was lost to me, I thought I would remain alone for the remainder of my days. It was something I dreaded. Loneliness is difficult for any living being, but dragons are particularly hurt by it. We are weakened, sometimes severely, but the worst is simply living an existence devoid of contact with another."

"And now?" he asked, more than curious at her response.

"Now, I'm stuck wrapped in a tent with a human," she said lightly, but he knew she was joking. He could hear it in her voice.

"Ironic, isn't it," he chuckled and then asked, "Do you regret it?"

"I regret many things," she answered softly. "But not this."

He felt a quiet thrill run through him and felt her shiver in his arms. Whether it was from the cold or not, he wasn't certain. "So what happens next?" he finally asked.

"I would be lying if I said I have not wondered at what might happen in the future," she answered, closing her eyes as a hint of silvery blush traced across her pale cheeks.

"Aye, the same would go for me," he said thoughtfully, holding her close and realizing how nice it felt to hold her. He was very aware of the curves of her body pressed up against him and he found himself wanting it to last. He let the silence hang for several minutes before he finally asked, "So, what is it that you wanted to ask me anyway?"

She raised her head again, as if she had completely forgotten it in the moment. "Oh, I was just wondering about your name," she said. "It's quite unique."

"You mean odd," he smiled.

"Unique," she repeated. "May I ask how you came by it?"

"You really want to know?"

"Absolutely," she said, lifting her head up and looking in his eyes.

"Well," he replied with a sigh, "if you insist." He grinned as he spoke. "So, I have nine older brothers. I was the tenth and last child born to my mother. I am also the biggest of my family and was the biggest baby by far. According to my father, my mother had a very difficult delivery with me."

"Did she survive your birth?"

"Oh, sure," he replied. "My mom was a farmer, very tough. But she was also very tired after I came into the world."

"I can imagine."

"Anyway, to hear my father tell the story, he asked her a few times what she had decided to name me and she finally got tired of him bothering her while she was trying to sleep. So she finally said 'Not yet, damn it!' My dad went and told everyone that was my name."

Zarandrae buried her head against Notyet's shoulder, her body suddenly shuddering with suppressed laughter. "I have never heard such a thing," she said between giggles. "You swear you are telling me the truth?"

"Without a doubt."

"It's a good thing your father didn't add the second name," she laughed.

"What makes you think he didn't?"

She paused and looked at him, then burst into laughter again, a sound he thought was the most wonderful sound in the world.

"Yes, my full name is Notyet Damit," he deadpanned. "For obvious reasons, I never use my second name."

Notyet held Zarandrae as she laughed into his shoulder. Finally, she pulled her head back up, working hard to get herself under control. Wiping away silvery tears of laughter, she finally said, "That has to be one of the most refreshing and enjoyable tales I have ever heard," she said warmly. "Thank you."

"For what?"

"For reminding me what it is to be human."

Without another word, she snuggled back into him, burying her face against his neck. She fell asleep quickly this time, and Notyet laid there for a while longer, marveling at the wonder of fate, before he, too, fell fast asleep.

They reached the summit far later in the day than Zarandrae had thought they would. The rest of the climb had been the worst part of the journey, with many rock slides and boulders to work around or over, and deeper and deeper snow to trudge through. Now, as the sun began to draw near the horizon, they were tucked in behind a large boulder, a small gated entrance just a few short yards beyond them down the path. They were finally prepared to breach Frosthold.

"It doesn't appear to be guarded," Notyet whispered, his eyes scanning the snowy rocks all around, "but then again, what would he need to guard against?"

"Kraegor knows we are coming, so I have no doubt we will encounter beings that he has summoned to protect the keep," she answered.

"Can you still sense him?"

She closed her eyes for a moment and was silent, before shaking her head. "No, he must be away, perhaps searching for us."

"That gives us the advantage. Should we wait until night falls before going in?"

"It would not matter," she replied. "Anything he has summoned from the Nether is not going to be hampered by darkness. The light actually favors us, because we will be able to see them. Many demons do not need the light to see us."

"Sounds reasonable," Notyet said as he shifted his position to face his companion. "So before we do this, can I ask you a question?"

"Certainly."

"This may very well come down to fighting a dragon," he said solemnly. "That's obviously not something I am going to be particularly successful at."

She smiled, but did not comment.

"What are our chances?" he asked.

"Kraegor is a dragon," she shrugged, "but so am I. If I am able to face him in my true form, I will have the advantage. I should be able to defeat him, as he will not be able to use his magic."

"And if we face him in his human form?"

"He is a sorcerer, as dangerous as any other alive, and will likely keep the fight inside so he does not have to face me in my true form," she answered. "Fighting a wizard will take brains, not brute strength, and this kind of fight will be to his advantage."

"What about his time in the Nether?" Notyet asked.

"That is the unknown," she admitted. "Until we actually face him, there is no way to know what new powers, if any, he possesses. But he will be formidable regardless and his magic will be steeped in darkness and destruction."

Notyet nodded and took a deep breath. "Well, I suppose that in the end, none of that really matters. We're here, so we're committed." He paused and looked at her. "If we don't survive this, I just want you to know that I have enjoyed our travels together. You've become a true friend to me."

"We will survive, Notyet," she said softly, leaning forward and embracing him. "I, too, have enjoyed the friendship we have forged. And who knows, maybe it will lead to something more."

She gave him a wink and before he could reply, she was moving down along the rocks, working her way closer to the gate. Shaking his head, but smiling nevertheless, he followed. It was truly a strange feeling, going toward what was probably the most dangerous challenge of his life and knowing he may very well not survive it, but happier than he had been in years. His feelings for Zarandrae had grown and it seemed as if hers had grown for him, too. The possibilities were a source of deep satisfaction to him and he realized that he had a good reason to survive whatever was coming.

As they got closer to the gate, they could see that the entrance was indeed guarded. A large, hulking figure was lurking in the darkness of the archway, completely still and watching. It was a demon of some sort, with a large muscled frame and piercing red eyes over a long snout filled with jagged teeth.

Notyet placed a hand on Zarandrae's shoulder to get her attention. *What is it?* he signed, reverting to his old way of communication and knowing that Zarandrae understood it.

Zarandrae shook her head, uncertain.

I will work my way around to the other side of the gate and get its attention. You get it from behind.

Be careful.

It turned out that he didn't have to do anything to get the demon's attention. He had not moved far when it suddenly lifted its head, large nostrils sniffing the air. Notyet had only a moment to curse his luck when it lumbered out of the darkness, red glowing eyes fastened on his position.

"No sense in putting it off," he grumbled aloud, stepping out from behind the rocks and drawing his sword.

The creature shifted its gaze directly to him now and then came on, long dagger-like claws flexing in anticipation. For its size and ferocious-looking image, it wasn't that intelligent. Its thinking was very one-dimensional and Notyet turned to the right, stepping quickly and drawing it toward him. He slowed his retreat, timing the creature's advance with Zarandrae's quick approach from behind.

As it closed with him, it opened its jaws wide, black teeth dripping with thick rancid-smelling ichor. Its head snapped forward and Notyet sidestepped the attack, slashing his sword across the monster's torso, opening up a deep, bubbling wound. A guttural roar erupted from it and it slashed its maw in his direction. Notyet was comfortably out of range, but the creature's movement slung long strings of thick fluid from its jaws. Several strands and droplets found their mark on

Notyet's chainmail and skin and immediately began to sizzle.

With a howl of pain, he dropped his weapon, desperately trying to scrape a thick blotch of burning poison from his hand and suddenly appreciating the fact that the monster wasn't so dumb after all.

Knowing its prey was now defenseless, the creature attacked again, lurching forward, long claws raking the air. That's when Zarandrae struck from behind, her great sword cleaving through the demon's skull with a dull thunk of breaking bone. The creature stiffened, mouth hanging open, eyes seeming to shiver in their sockets. Then it pitched forward in death, a low final rumble bubbling from its throat.

Notyet was still concerned with the creature's vile secretions, and he was quickly removing his armor as the acid-like poison continued to eat through the hardened steel links of chain. Zarandrae left her sword in the creature's skull and rushed to help him pull off his ruined armor, eventually leaving him standing in his leather jerkin.

"Well, this certainly hasn't started out very well," he grumbled, grabbing his hand and looking at the wound. Fortunately, he had managed to scrape the fluid off before it had eaten through his entire hand, but as it was, the skin near his thumb was black and bubbled.

Zarandrae gently took his hand and pulled a water skin from her belt. She poured some water on it, washing away any residue and bringing a bit of relief to the sting of the burn. "These are demons," she said. "They will have many different ways to kill us."

"Obviously," he agreed as Zarandrae wrapped a strip of cloth around his burned hand.

Looking down, Notyet toed his discarded chain mail. The acid continued to slowly eat away at the steel links, leaving a black tar-like substance in its place that hardened into fragile globs that broke underfoot. "Acid spit," he sighed glumly, kicking one of the cooled clumps aside. "If we run up against a bunch of these things, I'm going to be fighting Kraegor in my skivvies."

"Skivvies?" Zarandrae looked at him questioningly.

"Underwear," he explained. "Picked up the term hanging around Rick Branson, the outworlder. They have some colorful words for things on his world."

"Well, we will have to be more careful," Zarandrae said with a smile. "Come, we should get inside. Chances are, our enemies know we have arrived."

Notyet grunted his agreement and they retrieved their weapons, which were thankfully not affected by the creature's blood. They approached the gate, finding it protected by heavy iron bars. The gate itself moved on large hinges protected by steel plates and a thick chain, and a lock secured it to a locking bar embedded deeply in the stone. Zarandrae used the last of the freezing potion that Link had given them, destroying the chain and allowing them to pull the gate open. It squeaked loudly on rusty hinges, but opened the way for them, revealing a long hall that led deep into darkness.

Notyet retrieved a torch from his pack and, leaving the rest of their supplies hidden in the rocks, they proceeded into the keep and toward a foe so dangerous, it chilled his very blood. He knew what they had to do, but even with Zarandrae at his side, he was nearly overwhelmed with the hopeless feeling that they simply could not win against a being as evil as Kraegor.

Sensing his distress, Zarandrae reached out and grabbed his free hand, twining her fingers with his as she looked into his eyes. She didn't need to say anything; he understood perfectly that she was telling him they would face the dragon together. Unfortunately, it still did nothing to lessen the thought that they were hopelessly overmatched against a terror so great, it rivaled anything the world had ever seen.

He could not know how true those thoughts would be.

Mirror

They moved through the long tunnel, passing numerous closed doors on either side, most of them exhibiting signs of disrepair and long disuse. They encountered no other demons or creatures and searched for some time before they found what they were seeking. It was a set of stone stairs that circled upward into the castle, hugging the wall and disappearing into the gloom above.

With silent nods to each other, they began to climb, Notyet leading the way with his torch and Zarandrae following close behind, her senses on the alert. Some fifty feet up, the stairs ended on a wide landing inside a square-shaped chamber, a closed wooden door in each of the four walls. Unlike those in the halls below, these looked to be in good repair.

Notyet paused, looking around the room and trying to make sense of what might lie beyond any of the doors. "I guess one is as good as another," he finally whispered, moving toward the nearest one.

Zarandrae grabbed his arm, causing him to stop. She then went to each door, her eyes closed as she listened and felt with senses that Notyet did not possess. Several silent minutes passed before Zarandrae opened her eyes and looked back at him.

"I still cannot sense him," she said worriedly.

"That would be exceptional," Notyet replied, his hopes rising slightly. "If we can find the baby while he's away, we might actually get out of this alive."

"We have already killed one of his guardians," she pointed out. "He will know soon that we are here, if he doesn't already. I find it difficult to believe we have made it this far without facing any more opposition that a single demon."

"All the more reason to make this quick."

"There is another possibility," she warned, her voice thoughtful and concerned. "He may have found a way to mask his presence from me."

"Now that's a cheerful thought," Notyet replied darkly.

"We must proceed carefully," she went on. "There is no telling what he could be planning."

"Can you get a sense of anything beyond Kraegor?"

"Not much. I can sense the negative planar energy of creatures from the Nether. Unfortunately, that is all around us."

"So we know he has help," Notyet reasoned. "Any chance of pinpointing the baby?"

"No," she shook her head. "Conceivably, if Rayne is indeed the child of Kraegor, I should be able to sense her dragon blood. But she would be only a tiny life force and, at the moment, the negative energy of the Nether blots everything else out."

"Okay, then let's pick a door and see what we find. Any preference?"

"Your guess is as good as mine," she replied.

Notyet took a deep breath and then turned to the door he was closest to. He paused, placing his ear to it and hearing nothing, took hold of the latch and quietly released it. The door swung open on rusty hinges, but he held it steady and slow so the sound was only a small squeak. It opened into another hall, this one lit by torches running the length of it. There were other doors spaced at even intervals down the hall, some of them closed and others opened. The hall was well maintained and lounging against a wall near the far end of the hall were a couple of humans. One looked remarkably like one of the Zent warriors from Iszenmar. The other was a smaller human with darker skin and wrapped in robes of black. They were conversing and, although too far away to hear what they were saying, Notyet could tell by their body language that they were relaxed and seemingly at home in the keep. What alarmed him the most, though, was the presence of a monstrous reaver that stood motionless at the end of the hall, not more than a dozen yards from the two mortals.

Thankfully, the reaver was facing away from him and the two men were too engrossed in their conversation to notice the opened door. Slowly, he pushed it closed again and latched it, then leaned against it and blew out a long sigh.

"Humans," he finally whispered. "He has humans working for him, as well as demons and monsters."

"That he has both living and undead servants in his midst attests to his mastery over both," Zarandrae said. "He has grown in power."

"There was a reaver at the end of the hall and those two certainly didn't appear to be worried about it," Notyet agreed.

"Shayene kept her minions separated," Zarandrae pointed out. "Apparently, Kraegor does not segregate them and the mortals are not threatened. If he is able to control his minions to such an extent, he is much stronger than we believed."

"So the Nether affected him more than we thought."

"Agreed."

"What now?" Notyet asked. "This place is probably crawling with troops and undead. Sneaking in and finding the baby is going to be practically impossible."

"The only thing we have going for us is that he doesn't know exactly where we are right now," she pointed out. "If he did, we would already be dead or captured."

"You know we're probably not going to get out of this alive."

"That is a distinct possibility," she said sadly. "But if it is our fate to die in this keep, we will face it together." She held out her hand to him.

Notyet took it, staring into her eyes and then suddenly, she was in his arms. He kissed her passionately, pouring his soul into the act and, to his happy surprise, she was hungrily kissing him back. They remained that way only for seconds, but for Notyet, it held a lifetime of good feelings. As their mouths parted, he started to say something, but she placed a slender finger against his lips.

"Shh," she whispered with a smile and a single silver tear rolling down her cheek. "Let us finish this."

With that, she slipped out of his arms and went to a different door. Giving him a nod, she slowly opened it. Notyet, his heart swelling with love, stepped past her and into a hallway, his sword drawn.

He met the first charging demon head on.

Chapter 13

Notyet leaned against the door and let his body sag to the floor as exhaustion threatened to overwhelm him. They had been fighting almost non-stop for an hour, their enemies alternating between savage demons, blood-thirsty undead, and cunning mortals, and sometimes a mixture of all three. They came at them from every direction, forcing them deeper into the keep and seemingly always into more enemies.

Notyet had taken a beating. His sword had broken some time ago and his left arm was now useless, his bone shattered just above his elbow by an iron mace. That same iron mace, dripping with the blood of his enemies, was now held in his right hand as its former owner would no longer need it. He had stripped off his ruined leather jerkin, and his heavily muscled torso was crisscrossed with bloody gashes and cuts and splotched with blossoming bruises.

Zarandrae knelt across from him, tying a strip of cloth around her own bicep to staunch the flow of silvery blood from where a crossbow bolt had torn a hole in it. She was still wearing her armor, but it had been dented and rent in a number of places and her body, too, had suffered numerous wounds.

The upside—if it could be called one—was that the two of them had killed many enemies, including the deadly reaver, and had gained a small reprieve from the fighting. For the moment, others still hunted for them through the maze of halls that wound throughout the keep, but there was silence in the corridor they were now in. It was a brief lull at best and Notyet knew better than to find hope where there was actually none. Their enemies would discover them soon enough and they would be forced to fight again, weary and injured. What was worse was that they were no closer to finding the infant. He knew that even if they did find the baby, they would likely find Kraegor, too, and they were both well short of the ability to face him now.

"You have...to change," he panted, reaching up and wiping a trickle of blood that was running down his cheek. He wasn't sure if it was his or from one of those he had killed—not that it mattered now. He was bleeding bad enough from plenty of other wounds. "It's the only way...you're going to escape."

"There is not the room to do that," she replied, equally winded. Her face was also streaked with blood—a mixture of red, black, and her own silvery-blue. "If I do, my transformation would bring the castle down around me. If that doesn't kill me, it would certainly kill you."

"It doesn't matter," he said with some finality, leaning his head back against the door and closing his eyes. His strength was nearly spent and he marveled that he was even still on his feet. "I'm not getting out of here, Zarandrae. We both know that."

"Listen," she said softly, reaching out and gently touching his face with long slender fingers. He opened his eyes at her touch. "I swore an oath to you when you asked me to join you. It was because of you that I was freed from a prison that would surely have meant my eventual death. I will not abandon you now, not for any reason."

"There are too many of them," he tried to argue. "We simply cannot defeat them all and we're no closer to finding the child."

"I agree that Kraegor is too well prepared," the human-form dragon agreed. "Perhaps we were never meant to survive this at all. Regardless, though, there can be no turning back."

"But..." he started to protest, but she waved him off.

"Even if we were to escape the castle, Notyet, you know he would find us eventually and the outcome would be the same." Zarandrae smiled and leaned forward, giving him a quick kiss on the forehead. "No, we will see this through to the end and we will do so together."

He sighed and shook his head wearily. "No talking you out of this?"

"No," she replied, a sad smile on her face. Both of them knew they were going to die. She just wanted to die by his side.

"You know, this is not how I envisioned things working out between us," he said, struggling to climb to his feet. It took great effort and he grimaced in pain as he did so. "But if you're not going to leave me here to die, then I suppose you're right. Let's finish this."

"Together," she smiled.

They embraced each other for what would be the last time and Notyet turned and opened the door. The hall beyond was clear. They stepped out and began moving cautiously forward, deeper into the center of the keep. Ahead lay a closed oaken door, arcane symbols carefully engraved in the wood. Two alcoves flanked the door and Notyet motioned ahead to them. Zarandrae understood his cue. The two warriors flattened themselves against opposite walls and moved silently forward toward the recesses. Without hesitating, they both stepped out in front of niches and thrust in their weapons. Notyet's alcove was empty and his mace clanged off the stone, but Zarandrae put her sword directly through the heart of a man clad in black leather. His eyes momentarily grew wide in shock before she pulled her blade free. He slumped to the floor, dead.

"Too bad this whole outing hasn't gone that smoothly," Notyet remarked drily, looking down at the body of the assassin. "He's a Dom," he added. "That's the first of my people that I've seen in here."

"It would seem that Kraegor has gone far and wide to recruit his soldiers," Zarandrae said. "He is up to something."

"But what? And what would he need the child for?"

"I don't know," she answered. "The child is important to him or he would have killed everyone in the cave when he escaped from the

Nether. But he didn't, and that troubles me. What's more is the presence of so many mortals and demons in his service. This is particularly alarming."

"Why would that be any different than Shayene gating in creatures from the Nether?"

"Because dragons do not take on followers," she answered. "It's not in our nature."

"But it is in his now?" he questioned.

"It has to be the Nether," she nodded. "Something about his time in hell changed him."

"All the more reason for you to leave me and get back to Nykiva to warn everybody," he said with some difficulty. He felt like he was dying inside and certainly did not want to die alone. But he also knew that Zarandrae could and should escape, even if it was only to warn the outside world that an even greater evil was stirring.

"A noble request, but pointless," she smiled. "I've already told you that I'm not leaving you."

"Not buying it, eh?"

"No."

"Well, I had to try," he sighed, moving to the door. The wood was polished and in good repair. He hadn't the foggiest idea what the runes meant and at the moment, he didn't care. He placed his ear against the wood and listened, his brow furrowing

"Anything?" she asked.

He looked at her, his expression strange. "It's…singing," he whispered. "But it's nothing like I've heard before."

Zarandrae put her own ear to the door, conscious of the fact that their battered faces were only inches apart. Pushing down her own feelings and thoughts about the kiss they shared earlier, she concentrated on the voice she heard from within. It was soft and feminine and singing in an ancient language that she quickly recognized. The innocence of the voice immediately vanished and Zarandrae knew they were at the end of their quest. She closed her eyes, concentrating harder, feeling into the room with her dragon senses. For a moment, she felt only the terrible blackness of the singer's presence. And then, ever so slightly, there it was—a tiny life force radiating the blood of a dragon. They had found Kraegor's daughter. However, any faint hope she might have had of rescuing the child, was now gone. The singer would see to their end.

"It is ancient speak," she whispered, opening her eyes, her face grave. "The words are from a lullaby from before our age."

"A lullaby?" Notyet asked in puzzlement, before a victorious grin suddenly crossed his face. "Like you would sing to a baby!"

"Yes, but the voice is not human," she cautioned. "It is a demon; a succubus."

"I suppose that it's powerful," Notyet sighed, shaking his head.

"Very much so," she answered. "It presents the gravest of danger to us. But it would also make the perfect nursemaid for a mortal baby."

"So that would mean Kraegor has decided to raise Rayne as his own," Notyet reasoned.

"Yes," she answered. "Bear in mind that a succubus is fiercely independent and free-spirited and would not willingly serve anyone, even a dragon, unless it stood to gain much. If this one is truly acting as a nursemaid for Rayne, it is an extremely ancient and powerful being and will not be subservient to Kraegor in the least."

"So, his consort maybe?"

"Most likely his queen," she corrected.

"That's just bloody perfect," he grumbled. "An all-powerful evil dragon with a demon queen. Can we defeat it?"

"I don't know," Zarandrae answered helplessly. "At the moment, she is singing. That means she will have the baby close to her."

"Isn't that a good thing?"

Zarandrae shook her head. "It will give her a much bigger advantage than she already has. I doubt she would be as interested in protecting the baby as we would be."

"So she would fight dirty then."

"She's a demon," was the simple answer.

"This is not going to end well, is it," he added.

"No," she replied. "Her magic is powerful and, in a truly ancient demon, it will be nearly unmatched. But her strategy will be simple. As I am a woman, she will want to kill me outright. She has destructive magic that she will use to that end. However, it is you she will use her most potent magic on."

"Me?"

"Yes, you," Zarandrae answered. "She will sing to you and, in her singing, she will control you. Your thoughts and actions will be devoted solely to her and nothing else. Such is the nature of a succubus."

"Not if I have anything to say about it," he said grimly, laying his weapon on the ground. He unwound one of the bloody strips of cloth he had used to bind a wound on his arm and tore off two small pieces. Wadding them up, he shoved one in each ear and then rewrapped the cloth around his arm. Picking up his weapon, he nodded at Zarandrae, who gave him a grim smile.

Nothing more needed to be said. They knew what they had to do.

Zarandrae opened the door.

Chapter 14

They stepped onto the floor of a large circular chamber, obviously the main living quarters for the master of the keep. At one time, many years ago, it would have been Shayene spending much of her time here in study, blissfully unaware of what the future held for her. Today, it was a different master.

The room itself was well-appointed with a variety of fine furnishings—comfortable couches, overstuffed chairs, and exceptionally carved tables and pedestals—and large bookcases filled with countless books placed up against the walls. Around the room were numerous standing candelabras, all with colorful candles alight and brightening the room. Against the far wall, an iron staircase ran up to a second level that was open to the ground floor and looked more like a wide circular walkway where one could gaze down at the floor. All around the walkway were openings, likely leading into other rooms and more living spaces. Some were dark; others were lit from within.

Finally, the domed ceiling above was a masterpiece, an intricate mosaic of stained glass and painted stone; something any king would be proud to own, to gaze upon its myriad of colors and patterns at their whim.

"Wow," Notyet breathed in wonder. "Kraegor is living in style."

"It is not by his hand, but by mine," a melodic female voice said and they both turned to face her. A woman was leisurely descending the far stairs and, at first glance, she was strikingly beautiful—pale skin and soft features, with long, raven-colored hair that seemed to shimmer in the flickering candlelight. However, she also had a pair of curved horns sweeping back from her forehead and a set of large, black, leathery wings protruding from her shoulder blades.

The demon—for a demon she was—wore loose satin harem pants

in a deep shade of midnight blue, with a flowing silken sash of gold tied at her hip. Beyond that, she was barefoot and naked from the waist up. And there, nestled in the crook of one arm and nursing at her right breast, was a baby.

They had found Rayne.

"Seems you were right about the demon," Notyet said, already feeling the allure of the demon's appearance and finding he had to fight against her invisible pull.

"M'Zabareth," the succubus said silkily.

"Say again?" Notyet deadpanned, pointing at his ears. "I don't hear too well. Mostly deaf since birth."

"I am known by many names, but on your world, I was once known as M'Zabareth," she repeated, her voice not changing at all. But to Notyet, it sounded like she had spoken to him directly in his mind. That changed things considerably.

With a sigh, he reached up and pulled the cloth out of his ears. "Guess I won't be needing these anymore," he stated sheepishly, tossing the scraps of cloth to the floor.

"I know you," Zarandrae said quietly, stepping forward. She had not bothered to draw her weapon, knowing now that it would be a pointless gesture. While Notyet had no clue as to how powerful this demon was, the dragon did know. M'Zabareth's name was well known to the Arcai and their companions. Zarandrae also knew that by the mere presence of M'Zabareth on their world, they were all in more trouble than they could have possibly imagined, and saving the life of this child would ultimately be meaningless.

"And I know you, dragon," the demon replied sweetly, gently rocking the child as she fed her.

"Your presence here is not possible," Zarandrae stated flatly.

"Why would you ever say that?" M'Zabareth teased, a mischievous smile on her face. "I am here, therefore it must be possible, wouldn't you say?"

"I don't know how powerful Kraegor has become, but he could never possess the strength needed to summon one such as you," the dragon went on. "The power needed for you to cross over to our world is beyond any of this world."

"Perhaps the convergence is closer than you think," the demon said with a sly wink.

"The convergence does not pertain to the barriers to the Nether," Zarandrae countered acidly. "Do not mistake me for a fool."

"I'm a little lost," Notyet spoke up, feeling very tired and struggling to get the words out. "What are we talking about?"

"M'Zabareth should not be here," Zarandrae answered, ignoring the demon's smile. "She is not only a succubus; she is *the* succubus. She is their matron mother and is among the highest caste of demons in all of the Nether."

"So why can't she be here?" he asked, his words seeming to slur.

"Because I am one of the thirteen," M'Zabareth answered brightly, turning sultry eyes on the battered warrior.

"The thirteen?" he mumbled.

"M'Zabareth, the Temptress, is one of the thirteen demon lords that rule the Nether," Zarandrae picked up the explanation. "They are not spoken of in any texts of this age. Only the Arcai and their godly parents are aware of their existence and we do not speak of them. Ever."

"Why?"

"Because she was one of the architects of the fall of the First Born," Zarandrae answered. "It was the thirteen that orchestrated the falling away that led to the gods cleansing the world with the Earth Storm and starting anew."

"So how does that keep her from coming here?" Notyet shook his head, aware of a buzzing sound seeming to sweep through his brain. His thoughts were muddled, but he pressed on through the confusion.

"Only a god has the power to allow a demon lord to cross into the world of the living as a physical being," Zarandrae said, eying the succubus carefully. "It is the safeguard to keep them from occupying and destroying our world. Or any world, for that matter."

"All true," M'Zabareth said, still smiling.

"Wait a second," Notyet said, trying to pull his thoughts together. Whether it was a loss of blood or the demon's presence, he was finding his thoughts more and more jumbled. "You're saying only a god can gate her into our world?"

"That is precisely what she is saying," the demon replied, her voice almost a purr. She continued to smile, as if she and only she was privy to a grand joke and she was just waiting for the others to figure it out.

"So how…" he began, but faltered. She was in his head and he knew it, yet he was powerless to do anything about it. The buzzing sound turned into a musical hum and it began to fill his mind. His vision swayed and he felt his weapon sliding out of his hand to clatter uselessly to the floor.

"Enough!" Zarandrae commanded angrily.

"Or you'll do what, my dear sister?" a new voice spoke out and, as it did, a mist began to form before her. It coalesced into the shape of a man and Kraegor suddenly stepped out of the void. He looked as he always did—tall and angular, dressed in black and silver robes. But a dark power seemed to emanate from him, swirling about his feet and giving off wispy tendrils of icy shadow.

"Give up the child, Kraegor," Zarandrae commanded, her own voice like ice. "You have no claim to her."

"Oh, but I do," the black dragon replied. "She is my daughter, taken by right and given over freely to my queen to raise as her own."

"Demons cannot create life," Zarandrae challenged. "She will never be the child's mother."

"But some can sustain it and nourish it in their own way," M'Zabareth grinned, her eyes going to the baby still feeding at her breast. "The child is mine, dragon," she continued as her eyes narrowed and rose again, this time her voice finding a steely edge. "You have no right to claim it from me."

Noting Zarandrae's fingers tightening on her sword, Kraegor raised his hands. "You must control yourself, sister," he said easily. "Your weapons are meaningless here. You cannot defeat her. She is a lord of the Nether."

"A dragon has never battled a demon lord," Zarandrae replied dangerously, her eyes never leaving M'Zabareth. "Perhaps we should test the truth of your statement."

"Don't be ridiculous," Kraegor scoffed. "She is one of the thirteen and you are not even a dragon anymore. You are human. You are wounded. Better to rest and regain your strength and perhaps see things with a brighter countenance in the morning."

Zarandrae suddenly stumbled, feeling her strength leech away and she locked surprised eyes on Kraegor. The dragon had not moved, yet she keenly felt power surging from him, seeping into her body and robbing her of her strength.

"Yes, I think that would be best," Kraegor went on, stepping forward. Reaching out, he placed his hand on Zarandrae's shoulder.

Unbearable pain flared through her body, causing her to cry out in despair and she fell to her knees in front of her brother. Silver tears welled up in her eyes as she looked up into his face. It was peaceful and serene, yet she saw the dark malevolence lurking behind his eyes.

"You have been confused, my dear Zarandrae," he said soothingly, sending more debilitating magic into her body. "Draven has been taken from you and your heart has been broken. To compensate, you have allied yourself with this pitiful human," he spit, giving the motionless Notyet a disdainful glance. "The loss of your companion has clouded your thoughts and your judgment," he finished, turning back to her.

Agony roared through her and she found herself on her hands and knees, fighting with everything she had to remain upright. Kraegor maintained his grip on her shoulder and somewhere, deep in her core, she felt something begin to fade. It was her essence, the spark of life that made her unique; that made her a dragon. In a moment of clarity, she realized that Kraegor was stealing it from her.

Frantically, her eyes scanned the room. She saw the demon still cradling Rayne, but smiling coldly as she watched what was transpiring before her. Notyet stood motionless beside her, his features slack, completely in the thrall of the succubus queen. Zarandrae did not need an imagination to know how her mortal friend would die. And then there was Kraegor, slowly leeching away her soul.

It was over.

They had lost.

As she began to sink into nothingness, one final desperate thought took hold. With a rising scream that turned into the deafening roar of her true self, she used the last of her failing strength to fling herself away from Kraegor's grasp. Crawling on the floor, she gathered her fading essence together, channeling it into a final frantic attempt to keep her identity. The transformation was among the most painful she had ever endured, the task of gathering her scattered spirit almost too great to bear. But she fought through it and felt her strength begin to return. Her essence flared anew and alive inside her. Then, her body began to change.

Kraegor took a startled step backward. "No!" he shouted, his calm countenance vanishing, replaced by sudden shock as he realized what was happening.

But Zarandrae did not hear him. She was lost in the ecstasy of her true self and lightning began to encircle her body as it changed. She knew she would not likely survive the change, but neither would Kraegor or the demon, she hoped. She would destroy the keep around them, burying them all in the rubble. Rayne would die and so, too, would Notyet. But it was a far better fate than living and serving the unholy alliance of the dragon and the demon.

And then suddenly, she heard it. It was the sound of a crying baby.

Rayne was awake in the arms of the succubus, her cries becoming desperate as the lightning-charged dragon transformation took place near her. Energy suddenly began to form around her tiny body, sending off streaks of its own lightning that merged with those surrounding Zarandrae. The energy snapped and popped and then suddenly folded around the changing dragon.

Zarandrae had never felt anything like it in her long life. It was as if her whole body was being turned inside out and ripped apart. She roared in agony as her essence began to fade once more, the dragon part of her winking out. As her vision faded, she sensed, rather than saw, the vortex begin to form around her and, with a last desperate realization, she reached out, her fingers latching on to Notyet's limp hand. A moment later, the energy exploded around them and, amidst the final combined scream of a dragon and a human, it ended.

They were gone.

As the air popped and crackled with dissipating energy, Kraegor stepped forward, his features dark, but thoughtful. M'Zabareth stood beside him, comforting and rocking the baby as she stared at the spot that Zarandrae and Notyet had last been. As Rayne's cries quieted to whimpers, the demon shifted her in her arms to begin feeding her again. Rayne quickly fell into contented silence as there was a final loud pop of electricity in the air and a faint wisp of burning ozone.

"Where did they go?" the dragon asked, his voice deep and contemplative.

"They are no longer of this world," M'Zabareth answered plainly, as if the answer should be obvious.

"A gateway?" he reasoned. "But how?"

The demon looked down at the nursing child and smiled. "It was the baby," she said in dawning understanding. "She was the catalyst. It was she who brought the gateway into existence."

"Yes," Kraegor said, thoughtfully stroking his chin. "Yes, that would explain my escape from the Nether. I have long considered that possibility and this proves it. The child is a gatekeeper."

The demon nodded, still gazing at the sleeping baby.

"But where did they go?" Kraegor asked, looking back to where the two had been moments before.

"It is a big universe, dragon," M'Zabareth said with a shrug.

"Quite," he smirked knowingly. "But not for long."

"Just remember our bargain," she reminded him as she turned away and walked back toward the staircase.

"Gods do not break their promises," he snarled.

"You are not a god yet," she warned him, "and you have debts to pay to those that are." Ignoring the angry look that flashed across his face, she swept up the stairs, talking and cooing softly to her baby.

Kraegor watched her go, but his irritation at her claim faded. He wasn't concerned about debts to any god. Once he found the Nexus, none of them would even matter anymore. Nothing would.

Only him.

Interlude III

As the bronze dragon winged her way overhead, the old hermit looked up and shook his spear at her in impotent rage. He was still boiling mad and had nearly forgotten why he was seeking her in the first place. The last time he and the bronze dragon had met, they had been in a terrible fight, both in dragon form and then finally as humans, when they were too exhausted to continue their battle in the air. Both bore scars inflicted by the other and they had carried a mutual anger, even a hatred, for each other ever since.

He knew the anger was justified on both their parts and he would never claim otherwise. Siranschae had believed he had betrayed their kind in his desire to annihilate the Vi'Raaji people in retaliation for the death of his companion. He had simply believed she had no business interfering in what he believed was righteous vengeance for Jayra's murder. They had gone to war over it and it had eventually taken the gods themselves to intervene and stop the fight. Otherwise, he was fairly certain they might still be fighting to this day.

But while the past decade and sudden mortality had mellowed Diaman—for that was his true name—Siranschae had apparently not found the same peace he had and was now seeking a final resolution. Diaman's problem was that, since the gods had taken his dragon abilities from him, he was merely human now and Siranschae could just swallow him up and be done with him, should she so desire.

Still muttering angrily, he watched her circle and descend, disappearing over the tree line some distance to the west of him. Gripping his weapon tightly, he began marching forward into the woods, fully intending end their decade long feud one way or another.

Five minutes later, he stepped out of the trees and found her. He was surprised to see that she was not alone. Siranschae had transformed into her human form, and her bronzed skin gleamed in the sun. Her sword hung in its customary place in a chain loop at her belt.

Next to her was a young woman clad in white, who he did not know. Long dark hair contrasted with pale skin and she stood close to the human-form dragon, both of them talking quietly together. Diaman looked closer and could swear she looked like a Tae. Before he could consider why the young woman would be accompanying a dragon, their conversation ended and Siranschae drew her weapon. As the dragon began walking forward, a look of singular purpose on her face, Diaman was suddenly struck by how much he missed his friend over the years, despite their long feud.

With a sigh of regret, he lowered his spear into combat readiness and braced his feet. He took small solace in the notion that at least she wasn't going to eat him outright. Still, he knew how formidable a warrior she was in human form and he hadn't fought or practiced with his spear in years. This wasn't going to end well for him at all.

Siranschae stalked in and then did something that completely shocked him. In stride, she threw her weapon down, the sword point sticking into the ground. Then, without breaking her pace, she simply swatted his spear aside with her hand and then threw her arms around his neck, hugging him close.

Diaman did not know whether to try and run her through or pass out from surprise. He stood in astonishment as his former friend-turned-enemy-turned-friend-again embraced him fiercely, before finally holding him at arm's length and looking deeply into his eyes.

"You know, you truly are a bastard," Siranschae said, but there was a genuine smile on her pretty face. Not a trace of anger remained.

"You'll pardon me if I say I have no idea how to respond," he stammered haltingly in true confusion. "The last time we were together, you were trying to kill me."

"I was trying to prevent the genocide of an entire race," Siranschae corrected him, narrowing her eyes. But the anger never returned.

"They killed my companion," he argued, his voice suddenly pained again. "They deserved their fate."

"Do you still believe that?" she asked, her face sympathetic and understanding. "Do you honestly believe destroying the Vi'Raaji people would be what Jayra had wanted?"

Diaman paused, searching her features. Truthfully, he supposed that he did not believe that any more. But that didn't mean it was easy to admit. Instead, he said, "The years living alone have allowed me to search my feelings. I do not know if I will ever be able to accept Jayra's death or even forgive them for it. But I grew tired of hating them for it a long time ago."

"I remind you that a single Vi'Raaji assassin was responsible for Jayra's death, not the entire race," Siranschae pointed out.

"Not an easy thing to explain to someone as distraught as I was."

"No, but you'll remember that I tried."

"I remember that you tried to kill me," he said ruefully.

"You and I remember our fight in far different terms," she corrected. "But that is long in the past and no longer matters. I am simply glad to see you, my old friend." She hugged him again.

Diaman did not have a reply to that, so he merely nodded and shrugged and then looked past Siranschae to the young woman, who had been waiting silently nearby. "Who's your friend?" he asked.

Siranschae turned and smiled at the girl, motioning her forward. "This is Arianna, my dearest companion," she said warmly.

"Indeed?" he questioned, one eyebrow arching and looking back and forth between the two women. "And where is Donaran?"

Siranschae's face momentarily darkened and Diaman did not miss the sudden sadness that crossed her features. "You have missed much in the last decade, particularly the past year," she responded as Arianna joined her, slipping her arms around Siranschae's waist and resting her chin on her bronzed shoulder, her sparkling eyes on Diaman. Just her presence seemed to lighten the human-form dragon's mood, and Siranschae was smiling again in no time. "But that is a discussion for later," she added. "You sought me out, Diaman. Tell me, what could be so important to force you from your self-imposed exile?"

He cleared his throat and looked around, as if he thought someone might be eavesdropping on their conversation. "Well," he began with a tired sigh, figuring it was best to get to the truth of the matter right away. "What would you say if I told you that I think someone from another world has crossed over into ours?"

"I would say you were right," Siranschae said without missing a beat.

"Really?" he asked, genuinely surprised.

"As I said, you have missed much. Where is this outworlder?"

"He's hurt, but still alive. Or at least, he was before I came looking for you," he answered. "I left him on my island."

"Come, you will take me to him," Siranschae said, turning away and quickly effecting her transformation into her true form, a sight that left pangs of regret coursing through Diaman. Arianna climbed upon her back and then reached down and helped the old hermit up to sit beside her. Then, they were airborne.

For the first time in over a decade, Diaman was soaring through the sky again. It didn't matter that it was on the back of another; it just mattered that he was flying. He closed his eyes and felt the air stream past his face and, not for the last time, offered up a silent wish to the gods that they would restore his birthright to him.

It was time to fully let go of the past.

Part 3

Fyre

Mirror

Chapter 15

Terion stepped out of his world and into another, Rick Branson right next to him. Behind them the gate remained in existence for only a few moments, long enough for him to turn around and view the worried expression of Loken and the strained concentration of Eric. He raised a finger to his forehead in silent salute and then the gate winked out of existence. They were on their own.

Terion knew that he would likely never see his own world again and it filled him with a moment of panic. But he pushed it down into the same pit he placed all his fear when he went into battle and calmly considered their task. Avenrael was in this world, somewhere close most likely, as was her daughter. Both would need help. Terion hoped Notyet would succeed in finding Rayne and he wondered briefly if he would ever know.

One step at a time, he told himself and then considered their surroundings. They were in a room, a small one with a single window. He stepped softly to it and looked out. It was a clear night and he could see stars; stars that he recognized. He didn't suppose he would be able to get used to that whole concept of worlds upon worlds, all existing in the same place. But that was the least of his concerns.

Turning back to the room, he saw that it was neat and orderly, with only a few furnishings—a wooden chest of drawers, an odd-looking table, and what looked like a wooden cage without a top. When he peered into the cage, he recognized it for what it was. It was a bed that a small child would sleep in.

Fyre.

"Looks like we're on the right track," Branson whispered next to him, looking down into the empty crib. "But she's not here and the sheets are stripped."

"Does that mean anything to you?" Terion asked.

"Means she's probably not coming back," the marine said grimly. "Let's see if we can find out why." He turned and padded silently across the room. Approaching the closed door, the soldier paused and listened.

As Terion watched, he realized that he had not considered what their plan would be beyond finding Avenrael and the baby, but he didn't assume it would matter in the end. Whatever happened, they were not going back to their world. If Terion and Branson were able to find and rescue the woman and child, they would have to create new lives here on this world. For the marine, that probably wouldn't be much of a problem since this was his original home. For Terion and Avenrael, it would be more of a challenge, although the baby would have no such issues growing up in the world, as it would be all she would ever know. Still, all that could be considered later. They needed to find Avenrael and the child first.

Branson turned the knob and slowly cracked the door. It opened silently, the hinges well-maintained. The hall beyond was dark and the soldier paused, listening carefully. Terion joined him and heard nothing. After nearly a minute, Branson finally stepped out into the hall, Terion right behind him. It was dark, but he could see the outline of a stairwell at the end and several more doors along the hallway, all of them closed. He considered trying them, but there was a soft glow from the stairwell that beckoned them forward.

Turning to Terion, Branson brought a finger to his lips and then pointed to the stairs. Terion nodded and slipped into the hall and against the wall across from Branson. Together, they moved silently down the hall, freezing at the top of the stairs as a floorboard creaked loudly underfoot. They waited, barely breathing. But again, all they heard was silence.

The glow was coming from somewhere on the lower floor, and Terion looked at Branson to see if the man knew what it might be. Judging by the marine's look, he did, but the man wasn't about to take the time to explain it to him. After waiting several minutes for something to move or make a sound, Branson began to descend, keeping his feet on the edge of the stairs near the wall, where he would have less chance of hitting a squeaky board. Terion mimicked his actions and together, the two men moved silently down to the landing.

At the bottom, Branson held them up again, making sure they were alone. After several long moments of silence, he stepped off the stairs and followed the glow around a corner and into another room. Terion followed and they entered into a room that was a little bigger than the bedroom they had arrived in. The glow was coming from a rectangular mirror of some sort. There were several pictures in the mirror, one of them seemingly alive as people moved in and out of the door to a building. The other was a still picture of a woman, someone Terion recognized immediately. His heart soared.

It was Avenrael.

"We know we're definitely on the right track," Branson said, pointing to the picture of the woman.

"What is it?" Terion asked, looking all around the picture frame. It was unlike anything he had ever seen before. "How is it that people are moving?" he asked, pointing to the picture opposite Avenrael's portrait.

"Security feed on a computer screen," Branson answered and then, seeing Terion's questioning look, added, "It would take too long to explain right now."

Terion moved closer, his eyes going back to Avenrael's picture, a portrait with a string of numbers and letters across the bottom. Her face was haggard and her hair damp and limp. Her crystal blue eyes appeared dead and dull and she was looking away, as if searching for something that she could never see. Terion didn't think he had ever seen a look so hopeless and full of despair and he felt the anger flare up within him at what she had gone through.

"That's a booking photo," Branson went on, pointing to her picture again. "It means she's been arrested."

That was a term Terion did understand and he wondered what had happened. Before he could say something, he heard an audible click as he became aware of the presence of another person. Instinctively, he spun his body, one hand sweeping out toward the presence, his other hand pulling the long knife from his belt. There was a grunt and then a counter blow struck him in the shoulder and knocked him off balance. He rolled through it, bringing himself around full circle to face the direction of his assailant, his blade out before him.

By the glow of the computer screen, Terion saw their attacker. The man was older, with dark eyes and short-cropped gray hair. He was pointing a strange object at him.

"Whoa! Whoa!" Branson said in alarm, raising his hands in the air as he faced the man. "This isn't what it looks like, sir. Don't shoot!"

Seeing Branson's reaction, Terion understood the meaning and straightened, letting the tension leave his body. With a deft flick of his wrist, he flipped his dagger in the air and caught it by the blade. He held it out, presenting it hilt-first to the old man. "I have no wish to fight you," he said, keeping his voice neutral. "Here is my weapon."

"That's a good thing, son," the man said, his own weapon firmly trained on Terion's chest, "because I reckon it would be a really short fight." He inclined his head toward the desk. "Put your knife down. And your sword, too," he finished, pointing to the blade at Terion's waist. "What are you doing running around with swords on you, anyway?"

"I'm no threat," Terion said, following the man's directions. "But I have two more blades wrapped in the bundle over my shoulder."

"Do you intend to use them?" the man asked, his eyes narrowed in suspicion.

"No, they are bound," Terion answered, reaching back and patting the cloth-wrapped bundle. Inside were Avenrael's dragon-forged daggers. He wasn't certain what they could do in this world, but he felt it was wise to mention to the man that he had them. "As I said, I am not a threat."

"That remains to be seen," the man replied guardedly. "How about you?" he asked, looking sharply at Branson. "You armed, too?"

"Just a knife in my boot."

"No guns?" he said skeptically, but then motioned toward the table. "Put it there with your buddy's."

Branson nodded and slowly placed it with Terion's.

When the man felt they were suitably disarmed, his face pinched up in anger and he raised his weapon to point it at Terion again. "Now, who the hell are you and what are you doing in my house? And don't lie to me, because I don't like liars and I'm liable to shoot you if I think you're tellin' me a story."

Terion wasn't certain if the man meant it or not, but he saw no reason not to be completely honest. "I'm looking for her," he said, pointing to the picture on the screen. "Her and her baby."

For the longest time, the man was silent, staring at Terion closely, his eyes taking in everything. Finally, he lowered his weapon and slipped it into the shoulder holster he was wearing. He stepped over to the wall and flipped a switch, bathing the room in a soft glow. "Have a seat," he said, pointing to a chair and making it obvious that it was not a request. "Both of you."

Terion obliged, lowering himself into the seat next to the desk, his eyes straying again to the picture of Avenrael. Branson pulled over a nearby stool and sat down next to him.

"How do you know her?" the man questioned, taking a seat in his desk chair across from them. He folded his hands across his chest and looked at them expectantly.

"She's a friend of mine," Terion replied.

"A friend," the man repeated, his face carefully neutral. "You got a name?"

"Terion."

"That seems about right," he said cryptically.

"Why's that?"

"Only word she's spoken since she was found," he replied, pointing to the photo of Avenrael on his computer screen.

"What about the baby?" Terion pressed. "Is she here?"

The man raised an eyebrow. "You the father?"

"No," Terion replied darkly, considering the real answer to that question. "As I said, I'm just her friend."

"What about you?" he asked, turning to Branson and peering closely at his face.

"No," Branson shook his head, raising his hands. "Not me."

"I believe you. But judging by those scars you're carryin', I'd say you have a helluva story to tell yourself."

"You probably wouldn't believe me if I told you, sir," Branson replied. "But the name is Rick Branson. I am...I was a United States marine. I'm just a friend of Terion's, that's all."

"Once a marine, always a marine, isn't that how the saying goes?"

"This is a little different," Branson said and sighed deeply, seeing that the man was expecting some sort of explanation. "We had an op up north. Nachvak Fjord. Turned out to be a spectacular failure."

"What happened?"

"It's a really long story, sir, but let's just say we had an out-of-this-world experience."

"Hmph," the man grunted and then wheeled his chair back in front of the desk. Pulling his handgun and laying it next to the keyboard, he began typing. "Don't get any ideas," he warned without looking up. "If I have to go for my gun for any reason, I'll just save time and shoot the both of you."

"Understood, sir," Branson replied. He didn't think for a moment that the man wouldn't follow through with his threat. But Branson felt they could trust him and would at least listen to their story.

The man typed for a minute and then brought up a screen, turning the monitor so that they could see it. It was a picture of Branson in his marine dress uniform. "Major Rick Branson. United States Marine Corps. Missing in action and presumed killed," the old man said. "Doesn't say much about why you guys were in Canada, but does mention it concerned the Russians."

"Actually, the Russians weren't on site when we arrived," Branson said. "The French were and when the shit hit the fan, more than a hundred of us ended up on another world."

"You've missed a lot in the last year then."

"That so?"

"Yep," the man replied tiredly, leaning back in his chair. "The Russians control Europe and NATO has been dissolved," he said matter-of-factly. "We're not that far from an all-out nuclear war. I'm guessing it's only a matter of time before all hell breaks loose."

"Doesn't surprise me, I guess," Branson agreed somberly. "Never were any happy feelings with the Russians before we...er, before we got called away."

"So what happened when you took your little trip? Where's the rest of your men?"

"Most of them are dead," Branson answered grimly. "With all due respect, sir, it's definitely a story for another time. I'd be happy to share it with you, but right now, we're a little pressed."

"I suppose you're right about that," the old man agreed, "but at least I know you ain't lyin'."

"So what can you tell me about the girl?" Terion prompted, reaching over and tapping Avenrael's picture on the screen.

The man folded his arms and regarded Terion closely. For the longest time, he just looked at him, as if struggling to come to a conclusion. When he finally did, he stood up and said, "Let's go for a ride, boys."

"Will you take us to Avenrael?" Terion asked.

"That her name?" he asked, sliding his gun back into the shoulder holster and picking up a set of keys from the desk.

Terion nodded.

"Pretty name," the man said. "I'll tell you everything on the way."

"Where are we going?"

"To get your friend," he said and this time, he smiled.

It took Terion some time to get used to riding in a car, but the discomfort barely registered. He was too interested in listening to what police sergeant Carson Dorsey was telling him about what had happened to Avenrael and the baby. They were in a city called Minneapolis, in a state called Minnesota, something Branson had mentioned earlier.

They were found in Huset Park, near the pond off Mill Street," Dorsey explained. "We got a couple calls about a wild homeless lady and a baby, so we came out to check it out. I was along on the initial call."

"So it was her then?" Terion asked.

"Yeah, it was her," he answered. "She was pretty disoriented and damn strong. We tried calming her down, but she was really upset. Kept going on and on about losing her baby, even though the baby was with her."

"There was…another," Terion explained. "Twin girls."

"Oh," Dorsey said as if a piece of the puzzle suddenly fell into place for him. He paused as if remembering something distasteful and then went on. "Anyway, we had a rookie on the scene who thought he needed to taze her."

"What does that mean?" Terion asked, keeping his concern masked.

"Boy, you really aren't from around her, are you?" Dorsey said.

"He's not," Branson added with a humorless smile and then answered the question himself. "It's a device that is supposed to take the fight out of someone. Uses an electrical shock. Unfortunately, in some people all it does is piss them off."

"Right," Dorsey agreed. "That's exactly what it did to your friend."

"What happened?"

"She went berserk," the officer answered. "Never seen anything like it in my life. Damn near a machine in how she reacted."

"Did she kill anyone?" Terion asked worriedly, knowing that with an assassin of Avenrael's skills, that was a very real possibility.

"No one killed," Dorsey replied, prompting a sigh of relief from Terion, "but she busted a few of the guys up pretty good. Would have been a lot worse if she wasn't in bad shape herself, so we were able to finally take her down and subdue her."

"Where is she now?"

"Booked her in for assault on a police officer and then had her confined to the psych ward at Ramsey. Baby went to Amplatz. They cleared her after a day and then she went into foster care."

"Foster care?"

"Fill-in parents," Dorsey explained. "It's complicated."

"Was that you?" Terion asked, remembering the baby bed back at the house.

Dorsey nodded. "Wife takes care of them mostly, but I have a soft spot for the little ones. Hate to see them go through hard times."

"Is she still with you?" Terion dared to ask, hoping that Branson was wrong in his earlier assessment that the child was gone.

"Unfortunately, no," Dorsey answered. "We're just kind of a stopover before they're permanently assigned. The baby got placed last week with the woman's sister in New York."

Terion was silent, trying to digest what he had just heard. That was impossible. Avenrael, if she had a sister, didn't have one on this world. He felt a pit open up in his stomach as he considered what that meant.

"I'm guessing this whole sister bit is probably a ruse, right?" Dorsey guessed, seeing Terion's reaction. "Wanna tell me your story now?"

"How much time we got?" Branson prompted.

"Enough."

Branson looked at him. Terion nodded, sighed, and told him.

Chapter 16

Terion related the story in its entirety of the birth of Avenrael's twins, leaving nothing out. Speaking of dragons and magic and portals to this man from another world seemed an extremely odd thing to do, but Dorsey took it all in, asking minor questions here and there, but generally letting Terion tell the story. Terion knew that having Branson with him was a great help, but he was pleased that Dorsey was still willing to believe him on his word alone.

When he had finished, the police officer was quiet for quite some time as he drove, considering everything Terion had told him. "You know," he finally said, "that's a pretty tall tale when all is said and done."

"I'm certain it seems like it," Terion agreed. "But I have no reason to lie to you. Everything I told you is the truth."

"Oh, I'm not saying I don't believe you," Dorsey said.

"Why not?" Branson pressed, interested to know why Dorsey—someone they'd just met by breaking into his house—would buy into a story as crazy as what Terion had related.

"I've been a cop for thirty-five years," Dorsey replied, his eyes distant as if he was remembering better times. "I've seen a lot of terrible things over the years. Some of it was pure human depravity. Some of it I'll never be able to explain." He paused again, thoughtful, before adding, "Been telling myself to retire for more than five years now, while I still have my health. But for some reason, I never did. Always figured there was something more I had to do." He shrugged and scratched his chin thoughtfully. "Who knows? Maybe this is it."

"We all have our journeys," Branson agreed. "Odd that ours deals with another world, eh?"

"Yeah," Dorsey chuckled humorlessly. "Ain't that a kick in the pants."

They drove in silence for a while longer, before Dorsey turned into a parking lot. He pulled into an empty space between a van and a pickup, and shut the car off. Turning to Terion, his face was serious. "All right, listen closely," he said, stabbing a finger at Terion. "Your buddy probably already knows this, but I'm going to lay it out for you as simple as I can. I don't know how things work in your world, but in mine, you can't just march into a psych ward and check someone out, especially at night. This girl of yours is going to be doped up and probably in restraints and definitely not allowed any visitors. So just be quiet and let me do the talking."

"I assume she'll be under guard?" Branson asked.

"She's considered dangerous, so she'll probably have one officer keeping an eye on her, providing she hasn't been a problem since they checked her in."

"Has she?" Terion asked.

"I have no idea," he shrugged, "but I guess we'll soon find out." He pointed through the windshield to the big building. "That's Ramsey County Mental Health. They'll keep her here until they figure out whether or not she's sane, before processing her through the system and getting her ready to stand trial for assault and anything else they can throw at her."

"Are there generally not a lot of people here at night?" Terion asked, looking toward the building.

"Not usually," Dorsey answered, cocking an eyebrow at him. "Why do you ask?"

The warrior nodded toward the building. "No lights."

Dorsey looked and realized Terion was right. "Wonder what the deal is with that?" he asked more to himself than the others, an edge of concern in his voice.

"This is not expected?" Terion questioned.

"No," Dorsey replied. "Night time means the patients are mostly asleep and individual room lights would be off. But there are still people on staff here, keeping things running."

"So there should be some lights on in the building," Terion reasoned.

"Right."

"Then why aren't there?" Branson asked grimly.

"That," Dorsey said, opening his door and stepping out onto the pavement, "is what we're about to find out."

Moments later, all three men were standing in front of his car, looking toward the mental health center. It was a boxy five-story building, with a longer two-story addition running off one side of it, giving it an L-shape. There were no lights burning in any window of either wing. Even the entry was dark. Dorsey pointed out to Terion that nearby buildings like the staffing center next door and the cab terminal with its rows of green and white vehicles, as well as the Goodwill warehouse across the street, all had power.

"I don't completely understand what you mean," Terion admitted, "but it doesn't sound right."

"It's not," Dorsey said, reaching back into his car and pulling out what he quickly explained was a radio that allowed him to communicate with other people he worked with. He clicked the transmit button. "Dispatch, this is Dorsey," he spoke into it. "Come back."

"Up late tonight, Carson?" a female voice came back over the radio after only a couple of seconds.

"Yeah, got a couple friends in town and out showing them around, Donna."

"At two thirty in the morning?" the woman asked skeptically.

"You guys drinking?"

"What are you, my mother?" Dorsey asked sharply, but there was no anger in it.

"Har har, Carson," she replied drily. "What's up?"

"Drove past Ramsey a little bit ago and they had no power," he said. "Rest of the area seems lit up just fine. You get any calls about it?"

"Nothing that I've taken," she replied and then was silent for a few moments, the sound of paper rifling in the background. "Nothing in the logs, either. Want me to send a unit?"

"Nah, hold tight," Dorsey answered. "It's probably nothing. I'm nearby, so I'll swing around and check it out and let you know if there's anything wrong."

"Ten-four, Carson," she replied and there was a click on the other end. Dorsey tossed the radio into the car and looked at the building again.

"You going in armed?" Branson asked.

"Yep," the cop replied, "and so are you." He walked around to the truck of his car and opened it. Reaching in, he pulled out a Mossberg 590 shotgun and handed it to the marine. "I take it you remember how to use one of these?"

"Like riding a bike," Branson grinned and accepted the weapon.

Turning to Terion, Dorsey looked him up and down and then promptly closed the trunk. "No time for a shooting lesson and I'm not up to getting an ass full of buckshot. Besides, I'm sure you'll do just fine with your blades if we run into any trouble in there."

"Agreed," Terion said, fingering the knife that was back at his belt. For a moment, he thought about taking out Avenrael's daggers, but then decided against it. Better to give them to their owner when they found her.

"Just stay close to me and let's figure out what the deal is," Dorsey finished. "Let's go."

They moved across the lot, Dorsey in the lead and Terion and Branson close behind. The officer and the marine had their weapons out, but Terion kept his blades sheathed, figuring that walking into a hospital with swords drawn in a world that didn't use them, might cause more than a few problems for everyone involved.

That thought immediately vanished as they entered the building and saw what was waiting for them. A pair of bodies were on the floor just inside the door, a man and woman lying face up in spreading pools of blood, their throats savagely torn out. Terion quickly drew his sword, while the other two men chambered rounds in their respective weapons.

"What the hell?!" Dorsey whispered in shock, kneeling beside the first body. There was no reason to check for a pulse. "What kind of animal would do this? And how did it get inside?"

Terion stepped past him, eyes scanning the darkness. He knew immediately what they were up against. The story Dorsey told of Avenrael's sister taking custody of the baby had sparked the first hint of doubt. Now, after seeing the bodies, he knew for certain. It was Shayene. There could be no other explanation. A year ago, he was there in the Wraithlands when they defeated the Arcai—his half-sister—and found out the horrible truth about what she had become. That was just before he watched her disappear through a gate into another world. This world. Shayene was here and somehow, she knew they were, too.

"Listen to me closely," he instructed, turning back to face the other two men.

"We need to get some help," Dorsey interrupted him, and Terion noted the underlying tone of apprehension in the man's voice. The man had seen a lot in his long life, but this had him unnerved.

"No," Terion countered, placing a reassuring hand on Dorsey's shoulder. "You will only get them killed. Trust me on this."

"Listen to him, sir," Branson said, also fairly certain he knew what had happened, having lived the same nightmare that Terion had a year before. "He knows what he's talking about."

"What do you mean?" Dorsey asked.

"This is not an animal attack. What did this is not from this world," Terion answered plainly. "It's from mine."

"Explain," Dorsey growled.

"This is the work of a creature born of dark magic. It takes the blood of its prey, moves only at night, and only in the dark. Light is harmful to it and sunlight will kill it."

"You're talking about vampires?" Dorsey asked incredulously, screwing up his face in disbelief.

"So, you know of them?" Terion asked with some surprise.

"Yeah," Dorsey replied, sounding insulted. "It's a damn fairy tale."

"Not in my world," Terion countered. "If you believe my story, then you believe I'm not from your world. In my world, this is as real as it gets."

"Are you kidding me? This was really done by a vampire?" Dorsey still was not convinced.

Terion nodded, his look grave and deadly serious.

"Well, I'll be double-dipped in hell and rolled in sprinkles," the grizzled cop said, shaking his head in disbelief. Then a thought occurred to him. "So, if this was really done by a vamp, are these people going to turn?" he asked, pointing at the bodies.

"No," Terion replied grimly. "These were just kills, likely done by thralls. True vampires are far more elegant in how they deal with their victims."

"Thralls?"

"Servants," Terion answered, "and facing one of them would be highly preferable to facing their master."

"So what do we do?" the old cop asked after a moment's hesitation. He'd already seen and heard enough to cause him to seriously question everything he thought he knew about his world in genera—and beyond.

"Use your weapon," Branson replied, casting a glance at Terion for confirmation that he was on the right track. "Aim for the head and be accurate. Anywhere else and you'll be dead before you can take a second shot."

"He's right," Terion nodded, "but even that isn't permanent unless you ultimately take the creature's head. Right now, your best hope is to simply incapacitate it. A head shot is the best way to do that."

"Roger that," Dorsey said, sounding stronger and a little more sure of himself. "Where to?"

"The creature has to be here for Avenrael," Terion ventured. "There is no other explanation for this to be happening right now."

"Yeah, I guess it would have to be a pretty hefty coincidence, otherwise," Dorsey said, climbing back to his feet and walking toward the front desk. He stepped around the back and stopped abruptly, looking down, his face crinkling in revulsion. "There's two more nurses back here," he said somberly.

"Dead?" Branson asked.

"Yeah," Dorsey nodded, his jaw tightening in anger as he picked up a clipboard from the desk. Several moments of flipping through the dog-eared pages and he had a room. "Your girl's on the third floor," he said and looked back up at Terion. "How many of these things are we going to have to deal with?"

"Should be just one," Terion answered and then followed it up with a fervent, "I hope."

"Well, you better be right," Dorsey said grimly. "Follow me."

The three men moved down a darkened hall, ignoring the occasional feeble call from behind a closed and locked door, a patient looking for a nurse who wasn't going to come. They all took that as a good sign that the intruder was indeed there for only one reason and wasn't bothering with any of the other patients. But the nurses and orderlies wouldn't be so lucky. They found the body of another hospital staffer at the end of the hall, killed the same way.

Weapons out and ready, Dorsey led them through the fire door and they hurried up the stairs. On the third floor, the detective held up a hand to stop them and then slowly opened the door. Another nurse lay dead at his feet, her terrified eyes glassing over as the last of her blood bubbled out of the torn flesh of her throat.

As Dorsey knelt beside her and witnessed her last shuddering breath, Terion stepped past him and into the hallway, looking at the rows of doors on either side. "Which one?" he asked, feeling the need to act quickly. "We have to stop this now."

"Three ten," the cop replied as he got back to his feet, an angry scowl on his face. Together, all three hurried down the hall and around a corner. They reached the room in seconds, but it was too late.

The door to room 310 was no longer there, having been ripped completely from its hinges and flung down the hall. The creature was in the room, a man in camouflage military fatigues. He was perched on the bed, straddling the still form of a woman, his face buried at her throat.

"No!" Terion shouted in desperation, charging into the room, his sword sweeping out.

The man's head jerked up and he rolled off the bed with frightening speed as Terion's blade slashed through the air where he had been only a split second before. Terion only had a moment more to see it: black fathomless eyes, oversized jaws dripping crimson, and the man's name—Bonheur—sewn onto his tattered fatigues. Then he was gone, flinging himself through the window and into the night.

"Sonuvabitch!" Branson snarled, rushing to the window. Below him, the creature hit the pavement and rolled to its feet, before disappearing into the night. The three-story drop had meant nothing to it. "That can't be!" Branson spit out, shaking his head. "It can't be!"

Terion hurried to the bed as Dorsey stood by the door, his gun drawn. At the bed, Terion leaned over the still form of Avenrael. Her wrists and feet were strapped down, as Dorsey had said she would be. She had been the perfect victim. Utterly helpless. Her throat was smeared with blood, but her eyes were open and terrified. Pressing his hand to her wounded neck, Terion leaned over her, allowing her eyes to focus on his.

"I'm here," he whispered, forcing a smile, but his heart nearly breaking. Her throat hadn't been torn out like the others. Instead, there were two neat punctures, blood still pouring from the holes. The vampire had not been here to kill the Vi'Raaji. It had attacked her for a wholly different reason. And that left Terion cold and horrified.

"How…" she gasped, her throat working under Terion's hand. He could feel her warm blood welling around his fingers and he pressed harder against the punctures, trying to seal the wound, but knowing it wouldn't really matter. In time, they would heal themselves.

"Never mind," he went on hurriedly. "I need to get you out of here."

"Terion," she began, tears filling her eyes. "You know…"

"Not now," he said, shaking his head and slipping his dagger under the restraint strap. "Stay with me," he finished, quickly cutting her free with one hand while keeping the pressure on her wounded throat with the other.

"I thought you said this thing was from your world," Dorsey said angrily from the doorway. "That looked an awful lot like a United States soldier, son!"

"French commando," Branson corrected him from the window, his eyes still locked on the shadows where he had seen the thing disappear. He was still haunted by the memory of his first encounter with the man. "He and I have met before," he added. "I thought I killed the bastard over a year ago."

"Fancy him showing up here tonight," Dorsey went on. "How's that possible? Part of your long story?"

"Yes, sir. He and his commandos came through the gate with us when we crossed over into his world the first time," he explained, nodding his head toward Terion. "We were put in a situation where we had to kill each other, and I was the one who survived."

"Seems that you missed," Dorsey pointed out drily.

"It's a little more complicated than that," Terion broke in, helping Avenrael into a sitting position. "The one that turned him into that thing is from my world. That commando is her thrall. One of them, anyway. Every bit as deadly, and completely under her control."

"You mean she has more of them?" Dorsey asked sharply.

"Undoubtedly, but probably no more that we have to worry about," Terion answered. "This one had a purpose. He meant to turn her."

"You know, she never did say what happened to him," Branson mused, moving away from the window as he considered what had happened between them. They had fought to the death at Shayene's command. They'd had little choice. In the end, he'd been ready to kill Bonheur, before Shayene had suddenly ended the contest. He thought she had killed the man for his failure. Apparently, she hadn't. "The bitch has had him working for her all this time."

"Then it's all true, isn't it," Dorsey sighed. "Damn, and here I was hoping this was just going to end up being a bad dream," he added and then nodded toward Avenrael, his look sympathetic. "And what about her? How is she?"

"The laws of vampires work the same in any world they are part of," Terion said softly, his face pained.

"So she'll turn," Dorsey stated.

Avenrael looked at Terion with eyes that were both fearful and sadly accepting. She knew exactly what had been done to her.

"We still have time," Terion added, pushing aside his panic of what it would be like to lose her all over again.

"Before what?" Dorsey snapped. "Before she turns into one of those things and tries to make us like her? That's what vampires do, right?"

Terion looked up, his voice measured. "We have to get the baby."

"Is there a cure?" Dorsey demanded.

"I need your help," Terion went on, ignoring the question.

"Is...there...a...cure?" Dorsey repeated slowly, enunciating every word.

Terion looked hard at him and then let his eyes slide to Avenrael's face. For the longest time, he looked into her pale crystalline eyes, wondering what might have been; wondering what would soon be. "No," he finally answered in resignation, his voice a whisper as he gripped her hand tightly with his free hand, his other still pressed to her neck. "If she feeds, she'll turn immediately, but even if she doesn't, the change cannot be stopped. If she is killed before she is fully under the control of her master, though, she will simply die."

"What happens when she turns?" Dorsey asked.

"Then we're facing a full-on vampire and you already know what they can do," Branson answered him. "Sorry, brother," he said sadly, turning to Terion. "I truly am."

"How long does she have?" Dorsey questioned.

Terion shook his head, bowing his head in shattered silence.

"I have a little time," Avenrael was the one who finally spoke, reaching up and gently pulling Terion's hand away from her throat. The wound had already begun to close and the bleeding had slowed to a thick, dark dribble. "I can fight it for a day, maybe two," she added. "Beyond that, I cannot say."

"Then I guess we better get this over with," Dorsey said gravely.

Terion looked up, expecting the worst, only to find the man sliding his weapon back into his holster. "What do you mean?" he asked hopefully, having fully expected the man to demand they end Avenrael's life.

"The baby is in New York City," Dorsey answered matter-of-factly. "It's a bit of a drive, but I can take you right to her."

Chapter 17

They retreated to the car and Dorsey radioed in the emergency, reporting multiple deaths and nothing more. A short time later, the parking lot was crawling with emergency vehicles, and sirens pierced the night.

Ordering the others to stay in the car and keep out of sight, Dorsey met with the watch commander and relayed most of what he knew without divulging what they had seen in the girl's room. He offered up both the theory that some wild animal had gotten loose inside or some psycho nutjob had gone completely off the reservation. Raving to them about vampires would be a one-way ticket to finding himself a patient in the very same building.

After his report and an empty promise to get an official account on paper in the morning, he rejoined the others in the vehicle.

"Time to get out of Dodge," he said, sliding into the driver's seat and starting the car.

"Are we heading to New York?" Branson asked.

"Yep. Going to make a quick stop by the house first, though. If we're going to storm a New York City penthouse and face a vampire, we're damn well going to be armed to the teeth."

"What about your wife?"

"She's down in San Antonio, visiting her sister," he answered. "She usually takes a little sabbatical any time we place an infant."

"So no uncomfortable questions when you leave."

"None."

"And I take it you have a personal stock of equipment back home?" Branson asked.

"Thirty-five years on the force is a long time to accumulate a small arsenal," Dorsey affirmed without smiling.

"Bad ass cop," Branson chuckled.

"I prefer the term 'prepared for any situation,'" Dorsey replied grimly.

"Where is New York?" Terion asked from the back seat. He was cradling Avenrael's head in his lap and gently stroking her hair. Her eyes were closed and her breathing shallow, as she fought the change that was going on inside her.

"About twelve hundred miles due east," Dorsey answered. "Should take us about a day to get there, depending on traffic."

"And you know exactly where she is?"

"I have copies of the adoption paperwork at the house, including the destination address of the baby," he confirmed. "Perks of being an officer of the law, as well as a foster parent. So yeah, I know exactly where she's at."

"And what happens when we get there?" Terion asked. "Shayene will undoubtedly be protected. She'll have guards and wards that you likely are not prepared for. We need a plan."

"We've got a lot of time on the road to plan the op," Branson cut in. "As long as Dorsey has a laptop, I can get something figured out during the drive. We won't go in blind, Terion. None of us wants to die."

"Laptop's back at the house," Dorsey said. "We'll grab it when we cowboy up. You should be able to find some sort of building plan online, at least."

"Then that's where we'll start," Branson agreed.

They drove the rest of the way in silence and, once back at Dorsey's place, the detective ordered Terion to stay in the car with Avenrael.

"Why?"

"Because I'll feel a lot safer if you keep an eye on her out here," the officer answered evenly. "Besides, Branson will understand the gear I have. No offense, but it'll be beyond you."

"Understood," Terion nodded and turned his gaze back to Avenrael. Her eyes were moving rapidly behind her eyelids and he silently wondered what nightmares she was experiencing.

Dorsey and Branson hurried into the house where the detective grabbed Branson by the arm. "Hold up a second," Dorsey said. "I need to know something."

"What?"

"How well do you know this guy?"

"Terion? I've known him most of my time on his world. Why?"

"Do you trust him?"

"Implicitly," Branson assured him. "Not many other people I'd want on my side than him."

"Let me rephrase my question, then," Dorsey went on slowly. "He's obviously got a thing for this girl, right?"

"I guess so."

"Do you trust him enough to do what's right if she turns on us?" Dorsey voiced his concern. "We're going to be in that car for a long time with one of those...*things* in the back seat."

"Look, I can't tell you I know exactly how this is going to play out, but Terion has a good head on his shoulders," Branson answered, giving the man a reassuring pat on the shoulder. "He won't let it get out of hand. If she turns, he'll do what he has to do."

"I hope you're right," Dorsey let out a long sigh. "This world is screwed up enough, without being responsible for turning one of those monsters loose on New York City."

"By my calculations, there's at least one there already," Branson pointed out.

"Yeah, there is, isn't there," Dorsey mused. "Damn, can you

imagine what would happen if you turned a whole city of vampires loose on the world?"

"I don't even want to think about it."

"You might have to," the cop said, heading into his living room and motioning the marine to follow. He went directly to a closet and, pushing aside a bunch of coats, uncovered a locked door in the back of the closet. It had a keypad where a doorknob would be and Dorsey entered a string of numbers. There was a series of clicks and the door swung open on silent hinges. Behind it was a large wall rack bearing numerous weapons of all types, as well as a variety of high-end tactical gear.

Branson whistled in admiration. "And I thought my pad was well stocked," he said. "You look like you're ready for World War III."

"That's not so far off if you listen to the news these days. It ain't a question of *if*, son, it's a question of *when*, and that doomsday clock is sitting right on the midnight hour."

"That close, huh?"

"Russia is gonna do something stupid and the good 'ol USA is going to go into lockdown mode. Personally, I'm shocked it hasn't happened already. You guys might have come back just in time for the fireworks show to end all shows."

"All the more reason to get this done and then disappear."

"So, you going to stick around here or go back to the other world?" Dorsey asked and then laughed. "Man, listen to me. I sound like a freakin' nutball."

"You would, if I hadn't spent the last year living in that other world," Branson said, absently running a finger down one of the raised white lines on his cheek. "Remind me to tell you how I got my scars one of these days."

"And you still want to go back there?"

"Truthfully, I'm not sure we even can," he answered. "But from what I've heard—and I've got no reason not to believe it—I'm not sure any place is gonna be safe in the end. Assuming we can't return, we'll be better off just heading to high ground somewhere remote once we get this done."

"Sounds like you know a lot more than you're letting on."

"Like I said, it's a long story, sir," Branson said again, nodding as he did. "A really long story."

"And it's going to be a long trip," Dorsey replied. "I'm sure you'll have the time, and I'm always up for a good story."

They continued talking as they pulled out the gear they thought they would need, both to get into a high-rise apartment and then to survive on the run afterward. Less than ten minutes later, they had it loaded into the car and then got in themselves.

"How's she doing?" Dorsey nodded at Terion as he got behind the wheel.

"No change," Terion replied. "She's out right now, but she's fighting it."

"You'll tell us if she's losing, right?" Dorsey prompted.

"She's already losing," Terion admitted sadly. "It's just a matter of how long she can fight it."

"Doesn't give me a lot of confidence, son."

"I'm just being honest with you," Terion replied. "Just get us there. She'll be with us as long as she can."

"And if she can't make it?"

Terion didn't answer, but the look on his face was enough to apparently satisfy Dorsey. When it came down to her turning completely—and she would turn eventually—Terion would end her suffering and kill her before she became one of them. He couldn't let that happen to her.

Dorsey started the car and had them on the road a minute later. Branson got right to work on the laptop and he and the detective began talking, strategizing together on what they were going to do once they got to New York.

Behind them, Terion continued to hold Avenrael, stroking her hair and her cheek, silently hoping for a miracle and that they would get there without incident.

They wouldn't.

The opening salvos of World War III began four hours later.

Chapter 18

It started with a small nuclear device detonating in the Iranian city of Tehran. Thousands were killed instantly. As accusations began to fly between world leaders, a second and larger bomb exploded, this time in Beijing. Within an hour, Russia and China were at war, trading rocket and artillery attacks, while threatening worse. The United States and other countries began nervously mobilizing their own forces, and across the world, panic, terror, and despair began to take hold.

As the world unraveled, the three men listened to the radio in shocked silence for more than an hour. The internet had gone completely offline shortly after the first reports of air-to-air combat came out of Russian and Chinese air space. News reports attributed it to hackers, and countries were locking down their borders, both the real ones and those in cyberspace.

As the morning sun rose higher and the interstate began to get thick with traffic, Dorsey decided to pull them off the main highway and look for alternate ways to keep going east. He began talking grimly about checkpoints that were sure to start popping up as conditions around the world got dicier. Terion didn't understand most of what was happening, but knew the situation was dire and only going to get worse.

"I think we need to reexamine our goals here," Dorsey said as he pulled the car off onto a gravel road. He drove for a bit, before coming to a stop under a large oak tree overhanging the road. There were no other vehicles anywhere near them. "I'm not sure it's smart to keep heading east," he went on, directing his comment toward Branson. "Whether or not we're involved in a global war by the time we get to New York City, it's still going to be tricky getting around. People are going to be panicking and National Guard troops are going to be all over the place trying to keep order."

"I agree. But right now, it sounds like we're just dealing with heightened security in the States," Branson said, recalling the radio reports. Panic and tension was certainly in the air, but major cities around the country were still relatively peaceful. "Corporate America is still working and Russia and China are going to be too wrapped up fighting each other to worry about us. As long as they don't look our way and we stay out of their fight, we should have plenty of time to get in and out of New York and be long gone before everything falls apart."

"If we get pulled over, we're going to be detained," the detective argued. "Even if America doesn't get involved in the conflict right away, I'm guessing we're going to be seeing checkpoints popping up along the main routes. We'll have to stick to the back roads if we want to avoid them. But there ain't no back roads getting into the city, and running around with a tactical arsenal in the trunk of my car is going to get us shot on sight."

"What do you suggest?" Branson asked.

"I think we need to find a place to lay low," the detective went on. "Big cities are going to be a bad place to be right now, especially ones like New York. When it gets out of hand and riots start popping up everywhere, we're likely to see martial law enacted."

"What about the baby?" Terion asked, checking his frustration.

"Man, I feel for you," Dorsey said helplessly. "I really do. But I don't know how we're going to be able to pull this off now."

"Look, I understand your world is in a lot of trouble, but I'm going to go after the child," Terion stated plainly.

"How do you propose to do that?"

"On foot and alone, if I have to."

"With her?" Dorsey questioned dubiously, pointing to the

shivering form of Avenrael.

"Hang on a sec," Branson broke in before it could turn into an argument. He looked at Dorsey. "We're in completely uncharted territory here and I do understand your concerns, sir. But I say we soldier on and try to do what we set out to do. The longer we wait things out, the worse it's going to get."

"You're sure you want to do this?" Dorsey prompted.

"If we're gonna go out in a blaze of glory, we might as well do it in style, right?"

"Safer finding a bunker to hole up in," Dorsey grumbled.

"That just prolongs the inevitable," the marine said. "Last thing in the world I want to do right now is bunker down and wait for everything to go to shit. If I can make a difference—any difference— I'd rather take the shot."

"Well, it's your call," Dorsey sighed deeply. "Personally, I think we're gonna get our heads blown off, but hey, I'm not sure living through a nuclear winter is on my bucket list anyway."

"Thanks," Terion said, offering a tired smile from the back seat.

"Eh, don't mention it," Dorsey said and started off again. "You need to plot me a course," he said to Branson as he pointed to the glove compartment. "I doubt we'll see free internet again, so we'll need to do things the old-fashioned way. There are maps in the glove compartment. Get to it."

For the rest of the day, and well into the night, they drove carefully on, avoiding potential checkpoints and most other people. They kept the radio on, listening to a constant stream of news. It wasn't good. Fighting was raging on the ground now and had spilled over into the Middle East as the two super powers tried to take control of the oil fields. Many countries condemned the fighting, but no one moved to intervene, unwilling to risk the conflict escalating into a nuclear conflagration. So the United States, at least, remained mostly quiet and behaved, with only sporadic flare-ups in some of the bigger cities.

Their journey east was mostly uneventful, beyond experiencing the greed of some unscrupulous business peoples. They still needed gas and many service stations and other stores were predictably closed until further notice. Those that were open were already posting gas prices beyond the ten dollar mark. Cash was low, but thankfully those locations hadn't thought about what the future might be like and were still accepting credit cards using hand written receipts, since electronic communications were currently at a standstill. As long as he kept his tank full, along with the half dozen ten-gallon containers he'd purchased the first chance he got, Dorsey didn't much care what they charged. He doubted he would ever have to pay another credit card bill again.

They eventually stopped at a small convenience store in a tiny town in Ohio, run by a very old couple who were mostly oblivious to what was going on in the world. Prices were normal and panic hadn't hit the town yet, so the store was stocked. Branson filled whatever room was left in the car with food, water, and supplies, while Dorsey topped off the tank. Then they drove off into the night.

None of them spoke much beyond the fevered mumblings of Avenrael as she fought the change going on inside her. Most of it was pained snippets revolving around her missing children, and the heartbreak in her voice told Dorsey and Branson they were doing the right thing by pressing forward.

They had made it to Montclair, New Jersey, when the front windshield shattered as a hail of bullets stitched themselves across it.

"Heads down!" Branson yelled as Dorsey wrenched the wheel to the left and sent them careening down a side street.

"Damn, I'm hit," Dorsey mumbled, twisting the wheel again and dodging several cars as he accelerated, trying to put distance between them and the shooters.

"How bad?"

"Enough to piss me off," the cop went on angrily, wiping blood from his scalp where the bullet had creased it.

More gunfire erupted behind them and they heard tearing metal and breaking glass as several more bullets found their mark. Swearing again, Dorsey dodged down another street and killed the lights. A moment later, he put the car up against a curb and cut the engine. "Terion, you stay put," he hissed in the darkness, turning to face him. "This ain't your world."

Terion nodded and Dorsey turned to the former marine. "You remember how to shoot?"

"Already on it," Branson replied, grabbing the Mossberg from the floor. He opened the door and slipped out into the night.

"I don't know what we're dealing with here, but I imagine there's going to be a lot of this crap going on as we get deeper into the city," Dorsey said, looking back to Terion. He nodded toward Avenrael's form huddled on the seat. "How's she doing?"

"She is still fighting it," Terion answered quietly.

"Well, let's hope she keeps at it," the cop said, then reached up and brushed his hand across the side of his head again. It came away wet with blood. Muttering angrily to himself, he got out of the car, leaving Terion alone with Avenrael.

Dorsey met Branson across the street between two parked cars. Around them, lights were on in some homes, but window shades and curtains were drawn tight. No one was about to stick their necks out and help them, not that it surprised either of them. Both men were well-aware of humanity's overriding desire to remain uninvolved when bad things happened around them. They heard voices approaching from down the street.

"Amateurs," Dorsey whispered, looking in that direction. "Probably just some idiot looters."

"Agreed," Branson replied. "You cover the corner. I'm going to cut through the back yards and see if I can come in behind them."

"You want to take prisoners?"

"Are you kidding? As far as I'm concerned, they signed their death warrants the second they pulled the triggers," the marine said coldly.

"Ah, the joys of a society in decay." Dorsey sighed. "Alright, Cochise. Get going. I'll cover from here."

Branson took off between the two houses nearest them as Dorsey settled in behind the car. The detective had a very good view of the street corner as it was bathed in the glow of a street light. Another indication that they were dealing with everyday thugs was when three figures hurried into view a couple minutes later, all of them looking down the street he had turned down. All three men carried what looked like automatic rifles and were talking among themselves, making no attempt at silence or even at hiding their weapons.

Because of their hardware, Dorsey immediately pegged them for local drug dealers, probably looking to settle some scores or just sow terror. So, he thought nothing of putting a bullet into the head of the middle one, and did just that. As his gunshot rang out and the thug flopped to the pavement, there were two quick blasts from the Mossberg as Branson took out the other two from behind. They had never known what hit them.

Dorsey came out from behind the car and began to advance, weapon still drawn, eyes scanning the street in all directions. He saw

Branson moving up the sidewalk toward him, pushing another man forward with the barrel of the Mossberg. Dorsey could tell that Branson's prisoner wasn't much more than a teenager. He was wearing a hoodie with the hood pulled up and a bandana, which had been ripped away from his face. Blood seeped from a cut over one eye that was rapidly swelling shut.

"I thought you weren't taking prisoners," he grumbled.

Branson shrugged and shoved the young man hard, causing him to stumble to his knees. Dorsey centered his gun between the teenager's eyes. "Give me one reason why I shouldn't pull the trigger," he snarled and took some satisfaction when the kid begged to be spared, tears streaming down his cheeks.

Behind him, Branson shook his head. "Just a group of stupid punks," he said in disgust. "End of the world brings out the would-be bad-asses that don't know any better."

"Just gettin' some while we had a chance," the thug whined, head still lowered. "That's all we was doin'. Please don't kill me!"

"Screw it," Branson said, stepping up behind him and smashing the butt of his shotgun into the base of the kid's skull. The punk dropped to the pavement, unconscious. "We don't have time for this."

"Agreed," Dorsey said and both men trotted back to the car.

Terion met them at the bumper, his face ashen. "We have to move fast," he said urgently. "She has little time left."

"Before she turns?" Dorsey asked with rising suspicion. "I'm not sure I like the idea of being in a car with her, if she's getting that close."

"I don't think that's going to be a problem anymore," Branson said dejectedly, pointing to a spreading puddle of gasoline underneath the vehicle. "Bastards got the fuel tank."

"Damn," Dorsey cursed and looked down the road. "I guess we'll have to hoof it."

"What about Avenrael?" Branson asked.

Before anyone could answer, the door opened and a figure stepped out. Dorsey cursed again and raised his weapon.

Avenrael had lost her fight.

Chapter 19

It was midnight the following evening when Terion looped his arm around the throat of an unsuspecting security guard and tightened his hold, keeping the pressure on until the man went limp. He carefully eased the body to the floor and looked up to catch Dorsey's eye.

"You didn't kill him, did you?" Dorsey warned, looking back from his post near the lobby entrance.

After the gun battle in the streets across the river in Jersey, they had holed up for the day in a house in the suburbs that had been recently abandoned. They needed the rest and also to bone up on the news. It was ominous. The war still raged across the ocean and the United States had deployed her fleets and air forces to protect her coastlines, all while ambassadors and diplomats burned the midnight oil trying to prevent the war from escalating and spilling over onto American soil. Although curfews had been enacted in most major cities and police departments were fully staffed and on high alert, ready for any developing civil unrest, things were still relatively peaceful, which Dorsey found to be a small miracle.

Avenrael had needed to stop, too, due to her new inability to survive in direct sunlight. She had emerged from the car a totally different person from the one he had seen strapped to the hospital bed back in Minneapolis. Of the wound at her throat, not a trace remained. Her cocoa-colored skin was smooth and perfect, her white hair shiny and lustrous. Dorsey thought she could easily pass for a supermodel, were it not for her eyes. Coal black and glittering with something more than ambient light, they were thoroughly unsettling to him. He had almost killed her at first—or tried to anyway—but she had moved too quickly and disarmed him before he could pull the trigger. Branson had fared no better, but instead of killing them, she had handed their weapons back to them and then begged them to help her.

"I will not harm you," she had said almost pleadingly. "You have to believe me. I only ask you to help me reach my daughter." Had it not been for Terion's added convincing, both he and Branson would have tried to kill her first chance they got. She moved like a predator, and that scared him. Something about her brought to mind the image of a sleek and powerful panther, with absolutely nothing above it on the food chain. He would be lying if he said he wasn't terrified about what would happen if her control ran out. One look at those razor-sharp canines told him it would not be a pleasant end for any of them. It was obvious that she was under some sort of internal pressure and occasionally struggled against the hunger inside of her, but she had stayed true to her word. She was a vampire, yes. But she had not fed yet. And that was something.

"No, I didn't kill him," Terion replied as he bound the unconscious guard's hands with a length of zip cuff. "He'll sleep for a while, long enough to keep him out of danger."

"She's here," Avenrael interrupted softly, slipping out of the shadows of a nearby hall, her eyes straying upward as if she was able to see through the forty-plus floors that separated them from their target.

"The baby?"

"Shayene," she corrected darkly. "I can sense her and hear her call. That means Fyre will undoubtedly be with her."

"Then we best get to rescuin' her, so we can get the hell out of here," Branson added, stepping out of the hall behind her. He was armed to the teeth and Avenrael's presence no longer unnerved him. "If things go south with Russia, we don't want to be anywhere near a big city when the nukes start flying. Especially this one."

"Avenrael," Terion cautioned, taking her by the hand, trying not to wince at the icy coldness of her skin. "Have you considered the outcome of this?"

She paused, her eyes locking with his. There was a hardness in them, something Terion had seen in the past when they were enemies. But there was sadness, too, and it could not quite be masked by their fathomless black depths. "I am not strong enough to destroy an Arcai," she said softly. "But I am enough of a threat to give you a chance to rescue my daughter." She paused and leaned closer, her face inches from his. "You must promise me, Terion, that you will do whatever you can to rescue her. You must promise that you will do whatever it takes to free her from the life Shayene plans for her. Save my baby. Take her home."

"And you?" he said with feeling, hoping against something he knew could never be.

"You see what I have become, Terion," she said with a sad smile. "This is not a battle I will win. Eventually, I will not be strong enough to resist Shayene's power over me and I will have to feed. When I do, she will control me completely."

He started to respond, but she leaned forward and brushed his lips with hers. It was brief and agonizing in what it told him—what he hoped for and what he wanted could never come to pass. Shayene had taken it all from him.

Avenrael pulled away, her features tightening. Closing her eyes, she steadied her breathing and when she opened them again, the softness was gone. The predator was all that remained. "Let us finish this."

They moved quickly, securing the area and then took the elevator upwards. They got off three floors below their target.

"Remember what I told you," Terion warned them as they moved toward the stairwell door. "This is a fight well beyond any of us. We are to get the baby and flee."

"Let me deal with Shayene alone," Avenrael added. "If you try to interfere, she will kill you."

Without another word, they entered the stairwell. They climbed silently, arriving at the door to the penthouse lobby. Dorsey took a deep breath, adjusted the battered ball cap on his head, and tightened the tool belt about his waist, items he had taken from a maintenance room off the main lobby. He hoped the ruse would work.

Steeling his resolve, he stepped out into the hall, suddenly huffing and puffing with faked exertion. His intuition had been right. A single man stood in front of a large set of double doors at the end of the hall. He was dressed in combat fatigues, much like the French marine they had encountered in Minneapolis.

"Elevator's on the fritz again," Dorsey gasped, placing his hands on his knees like he was out of breath. "Gimme a second."

The man's body tensed, dark eyes narrowing. The marine was some twenty feet away, but Dorsey could see the hunger in those eyes. It was the same hunger he saw in Avenrael's eyes. The man wasn't human.

"Look pal," he said, straightening and stepping into the hall while reaching into his tool bag. "I got a work order to…"

He never finished the statement. The soldier leapt at him, covering the twenty feet in just a couple of huge bounds, fanged jaws unhinging and opening wide.

Avenrael saved Dorsey's life. She shot from the doorway in a blur of motion, catching the soldier around the waist and slamming him into the wall. Terion was behind her, leading with his blades. As the thrall rolled back to its feet, she rushed past him, going for the double doors and leaving the soldier for Terion, who ended the creature's existence with one quick sweep of his sword.

"Save some for me," Branson said, following him through. He held a Glock 17 in each hand, his eyes scanning for targets. Several of them emerged from the doors on either side of the main entrance to the penthouse.

Avenrael closed with a pair on the right, while Branson opened up on three more coming out of the left-hand door. All of them moved like alpha predators.

Branson fired purposefully, aiming for the heads of the vampires. His old movie monster lore reminded him that vampires were not particularly affected by mere bullets. But he was shooting Radically Invasive Projectile ammunition and headshots didn't leave much left above the shoulders. It was easily as effective as a sword, though messier, and he took down all three of his targets.

He swiveled to help Avenrael, but she had made quick work of the two she faced, leaving both writhing on the ground with broken necks. Terion then separated their heads from their bodies.

Dorsey was shocked as he watched it all unfold, as much at the speed as at the brutality of the fight. The plan had been to try and quietly gain entrance to the apartment. He had even expected a guard to be in place at the door. But he had not been prepared for the carnage and incredible pace of the battle.

As her enemies fell, Avenrael hit the door like a thunderclap, blasting through it like it was made of paper and sending shards of metal and wood into the apartment beyond as she breached it.

Another soldier met her almost immediately, launching his body into hers, taking them both back into the hall in a tangle of limbs. They were up in a moment, circling each other like wolves, snarling in fury through razor-sharp canines. The man was Bonheur, the same man who had attacked Avenrael in Minneapolis and was responsible for what she had become. He was a combat-trained French marine, but Avenrael was a Vi'Raaji witch from another world, born and raised to be a killer. She was also a mother, desperate to make her last act that of saving her infant daughter. Bonheur leapt forward again, hands outstretched as he sought to grasp her throat, but she met his attack by stepping into his charge and catching the thrall underneath his armpits. A strong fighter under normal circumstance, Avenrael's strength was now augmented and she flung him upward, where he slammed into the ceiling, sending plaster and wood raining down.

Bonheur crashed back to the floor and quickly leapt to his feet. But Avenrael had already turned away from him, stalking into the apartment, her mind consumed only with facing Shayene. The French marine might have taken her then, but a blade suddenly appeared from his chest, thrust through him from behind. Terion circled his arm around Bonheur's throat, pinning him tight as he turned the blade in the man's heart. With an inhuman roar, the former French marine spun around, launching Terion into the wall. Growling, he looked down at the blade, as if contemplating how to remove it.

That was when Branson stepped next to him and placed the muzzle of his gun against the man's temple. "Remember me?" he asked and then pulled the trigger.

Bonheur's body flopped on the floor as thick black blood drained out of what remained of his head. Branson stepped over him and reached down to help Terion back to his feet.

Dorsey, however, stared down at Bonheur's body in shock. These weren't men they were killing. They were monsters and in his world, monsters like this did not exist.

"Bravo," a smoky voice sounded from the apartment and all three men suddenly looked up. A woman was walking toward the shattered doorway, her hands folded at her waist. She was dressed in a simple silk robe of black, streaked with crimson blood. Dorsey shuddered to think who it could belong to and if they were going to find more victims in her apartment.

Avenrael crouched ten feet from her, her body tense. She looked at Shayene with a cold fury.

"I see you are fighting it, witch," the woman said slyly, smiling at the assassin. "You must know that it is hopeless, though. You will shortly be mine and, when you are, I will make you kill your friends," she added, casting a glance down the ruined hall at the three men. "Fitting that they should be your first."

"My daughter," Avenrael hissed. "I want her back."

"Or you'll do what?" Shayene taunted, then threw back her head and laughed. "Do you honestly think you can harm me in any way?" she continued, her cold eyes scanning all of them and then dismissing them as if they were nothing.

Branson tried anyway, pulling the trigger, hoping to end it before it even got started. But the bullet impacted against something invisible before reaching her head and a sudden wave of very-visible bluish energy blasted back at them. Avenrael missed the brunt of it just by being low to the floor, but the blast wave struck all three men fully, throwing them backward and slamming them against the closed elevator doors hard enough that they bowed the metal inward.

It was the perfect distraction for Avenrael and she attacked, launching herself from her crouch. She hit Shayene solidly, sending both women flying back into the apartment. In moments, they were locked in a titanic struggle, doing everything in their power to kill the other.

"Holy…" Branson mumbled, picking himself up off the floor. He had never been hit that hard in all his life and he knew he was lucky that nothing had been broken. "You okay?" he asked, reaching down and helping Dorsey climb shakily to his feet.

"What the hell was what?" the cop asked.

"Kinetic blast," Terion said through clenched teeth, leaning against the wall and holding his arm close to his body. He hadn't been so lucky, as it appeared to be broken. "It's a very effective spell that wizards can employ against physical attacks."

"You mean she's got a force field?" Dorsey asked incredulously.

"Not anymore," Terion said grimly, looking down the hall at the fight that was raging inside the apartment.

"And it looks like your girl is all over her," Branson pointed out.

"Now's our chance," Terion said, pushing away from the wall and hurrying forward. "Check all the rooms! Get the baby!"

They hurried into the apartment. Two halls, both seemingly made of stone, led off the main living room where Avenrael and Shayene were locked in ferocious combat. Avenrael had taken the fight in close right away, hoping to keep the formidable sorceress from employing her magic. She was striking as quickly as she could, keeping Shayene off balance. They all knew it would be a losing effort, but while she was busy, they still had a chance.

While Branson pushed Terion toward the left side hall, trying to keep him focused on the task and not the danger Avenrael was in, Dorsey hurried off down the other. The penthouse was enormous for a New York City apartment, with several closed doors along both sides of the halls. Dorsey pushed open the first one and was immediately met by a horrible shriek of rage, as a small, scaly creature lunged out of the darkness at him. He barely got his arm up in time to keep the thing from tearing his face off, but sharp claws and teeth bit into the flesh of his arm, all while the creature screamed curses at him. Dorsey wasn't sure what was more unsettling—the fact that such a creature existed or that it was swearing at him with words so vile it would make a drunken sailor blush.

Dorsey screamed in terror and revulsion as he tore the little demon away from his bleeding arm and flung it against the far wall. He pulled his service pistol as the little monster climbed back to its feet. "What the hell are you?" he asked breathlessly, not expecting an answer.

"I am Grum," it growled, taking a menacing step forward, narrow eyes glinting wickedly, "and I will eat you! She promised me!"

It leapt at him again, but this time the detective was ready and he shot it through the head. For a few almost comical moments, Grum staggered backward and then forward as if drunk, a thick black ichor bubbling from the hole between its beady eyes. "But…she promised," it gurgled, before finally pitching forward at Dorsey's feet. Grum twitched once and then was still.

Whatever fear Dorsey had felt, suddenly vanished. It didn't matter what was happening in the other room where Avenrael and Shayene battled or what Terion and Branson would be facing. What mattered at that moment was his own small victory. He had overcome his own personal demon, literally, and lived to tell the tale.

As Grum's body dissolved into a steaming black puddle of tar, Dorsey took a quick look around the room and, seeing nothing of the child, stepped back into the hall. There were several more doors on each side, but the one at the end of the hall caught his attention. The door frame was arched and the door itself apparently cut from stone. It was the entrance to an important room and, holding his weapon at the ready, he hurried down the hall. The door wasn't locked and he pushed it open. Taking a deep breath, he stepped into a room lit by sconced candles, surrounding what appeared to be a stone table, the only other furnishing in the room. On the table was not the baby that he had expected to find, but a young man.

Dorsey cocked his head, taking in the unexpected situation. The man was dressed in tattered gray robes and appeared to be sleeping peacefully, oblivious to the sounds of fighting beyond the door. His hands were folded across his chest and Dorsey could see they were covered with intricate tattoos that ran up his hands, disappearing about half way up his forearms.

"Hey," he called out cautiously. "Hey buddy, you okay?"

There was no reaction.

He stepped forward, eyes scanning the room for hidden danger, until he was standing over the sleeping man. There didn't appear to be anything odd about him; he looked to simply be sleeping. His eyes were closed and his features, while somewhat gaunt, seemed peaceful. Reaching out, he touched the man's shoulder. Just like that, it was as if a light switch was turned on. The young man's eyes snapped open and his hands shot forward, reaching for Dorsey.

Both of them screamed.

On the other side of the penthouse suite, Terion and Branson were rushing down the hallway, opening doors and checking rooms as they went. They found nothing important until they reached the one just before an arched stone door at the end of the hall.

As Terion opened it, an apparition rose up before him. It was a man, or might have been at one time. Now, it was emaciated and gaunt, its skin drawn tightly over protruding bones. Empty eye sockets sought Terion out, but the blackened holes didn't seem to stop the creature from sensing him. With a guttural snarl, the thing lunged forward, sharp clawed hands tearing at the flesh of Terion's good arm. With a shout, he threw himself backward, the creature coming down on top of him. Jagged and rotted teeth snapped toward his face and the stench of fetid death was so strong, Terion thought he might pass out.

Before the monster's teeth could descend, the heel of Branson's heavy combat boot connected with the side of its head, sending it sprawling. A length of heavy chain was fastened to a manacle around its ankle and Branson scooped it up. Before the creature could recover, he looped it around the monster's throat and pulled it tight, wrestling it back to the floor. As it thrashed, Branson placed his knee against the back of the creature's neck and then, with a single mighty pull on the coiled metal links, he snapped the thing's neck. It bucked several times and then went limp, sliding back to the floor.

"Why do there always have to be surprises," Branson griped, climbing to his feet and helping Terion stand. Together, they looked down at the body, ignoring the faint twitching in one of its legs. "What's with the chain?" the marine asked, looking at Terion.

They followed the chain into the room and found that the other end was attached to a heavy steel hook drilled into the wall next to the door. The chain was to keep the creature imprisoned, with enough room for it to get into the hallway, but not enough for it to reach the far end of the room. The reason for that was obvious.

"Pretty effective guard dog," Branson said as the two men cautiously approached the baby crib set against the far wall. Looking in, they saw her. She lay quietly sleeping, her thumb in her mouth, oblivious to the chaotic world around her.

They had found Fyre.

Avenrael and Shayene continued to fight, screaming and cursing at each other as they clashed. The battle had carried them through the glass patio door and onto the balcony. Both women were wounded, but every time Avenrael would inflict a cut or a gash on her opponent, Shayene would open three more on the Vi'Raaji. Avenrael was weakening, her wounds mounting, her supernatural strength ebbing. Shayene, on the other hand, seemed to heal her wounds as fast as

Avenrael could inflict them, and there seemed to be no end to her strength.

The end finally came when the assassin struck and missed, overbalancing and stumbling forward. Shayene caught her and spun her around, driving her long razor-sharp claws deep into the flesh of the witch's lower back. She slipped her other arm around Avenrael's throat, pulling the woman close to her and then tightening her hold, pushing her claws in deeper. Avenrael felt her flesh tearing and knew the wound was terrible, perhaps even mortal. But she was helpless in Shayene's grasp. She was spent. Her strength was all but gone. She only had one thing left to do now. She only hoped she could.

With Branson supporting him, Terion stepped out of the hall, holding the precious baby in the crook of his good arm. His weapons were sheathed, which didn't matter anymore. They would have been useless to him anyway with his other arm broken as badly as it was.

He looked toward the balcony, watching the end of the fight unfold. It was no shock to Terion how it ended, with Avenrael dying at Shayene's hands. The Arcai had always been beyond their powers to defeat and they had known that from the beginning. But holding Fyre closely to his chest, he also knew he would have made no other decision. Even if Avenrael had not committed him to finding and rescuing Fyre, he would have taken it upon himself to do so anyway.

On the balcony, Shayene sneered at him as she ripped her bloody claws from Avenrael's torn body. A shudder ran through the Vi'Raaji's form as Avenrael gazed at Terion with a look of finality. Her eyes had cleared, fading from blackened orbs to crystalline blue and he could see the tears welling at the corners as she saw her child nestled in his arm. The curse had lifted as death had come. She smiled at him then, a faint upturn of her mouth. Terion felt all the loss rise up within him and, in that one searing moment, he realized he truly did love her.

Avenrael must have seen it in his face and mirrored it. Then, with a final burst of strength, she spun in Shayene's arms, turning to face her killer. Terion glimpsed the horrible wound in her lower back, the torn flesh and pouring blood, red now, not black. Avenrael locked her arms around Shayene, drawing her close. And then they were gone, Avenrael flinging them over the railing and into the night.

It was a forty-six story fall.

Terion went numb. It was the second time he had watched Avenrael sacrifice herself to save others. A year ago, she took Kraegor into the Nether through the collapsing portal, saving them all from the dragon's wrath. Now, she took Shayene over the edge of the balcony, saving those with her once again.

A small sound caused him to look down, his eyes straying to the little baby's face. Fyre's skin was dusky, like her mother's, and her dark eyes were open now, looking at Terion's face closely. For just a moment, Terion's heartache faded. The emotional and physical toil was gone and it was simply he and Fyre. He smiled then, thinking he must look rather frightful to the curious baby, who reached up with chubby fingers and lightly touched his cheek. It was a moment that Terion would have been happy to live in forever.

Then reality came crashing back with the sound of Shayene's voice cutting through the sudden quiet of the destroyed apartment.

"You pathetic fools," she snarled, vaulting herself back over the railing to stand on the balcony again, the fingers of one hand curled tightly into Avenrael's long blood-streaked hair. The assassin lay motionless on the floor, held up only by Shayene's grasp, and the Arcai shook the woman's head like a ragdoll. "Did you really think it would be so easy?" She stepped back into the living room, dragging Avenrael and then contemptuously flinging her blood-soaked body at Terion's feet.

Terion looked down in shock. Avenrael's eyes were closed, her form unmoving. Her features were slack, her face seemingly at peace. The heartache flared up inside him and he fought back his own tears as he slowly looked up, his eyes settling on Shayene; on his sister; on Avenrael's killer. How the Arcai had survived, he had no idea. But here she stood, gloating in her victory and, despite her torn robes and blood-spattered body, she appeared relatively unscathed. The last of her wounds, deep gashes across her face, were closing even as Terion looked at her. He took a halting step back and then turned away from her, a hopeless attempt at protecting the baby he held.

"You have caused me much in the way of trouble," Shayene said, her voice dangerous, almost feral. "You have invaded my home and destroyed my servants. And now you attempt to kidnap what is rightfully mine!"

"No, Shayene," Terion said, daring to look back at her. "The baby is not yours and never has been. You will not have her."

"You dare oppose me?"

"I opposed you even after I found out you were my sister," he said quietly. "Nothing has changed between us. And nothing ever will."

"Oh, but things have changed," she said, her voice dripping with venom. "You believe you saved our world, but in doing so, you doomed it while letting me escape to this one. And make no mistake, this world is mine. It has always been mine. And you helped bring that about, my dear brother."

"You should get out more, lady," Branson said drily. "Not going to be much of a world left once the missiles start flying."

"I care nothing for the petty wars fought by mortals," she spat derisively. "It will end soon enough. It only waits for me to awaken my soldiers and send them forth to begin building my army."

"What are you talking about?" Terion asked, fear rising that something more was at play here. Something much more.

"You think you understand what is happening, but you truly don't," she responded with a laugh, her eyes hard. "You believe you know what my plans have been, but in truth, you never have."

"You tried to rule our world," he responded shakily. "I thought that was pretty obvious when you unleashed your armies on everyone that opposed you."

"What happened on our world was but a means to an end," she scoffed. "It was never about our world, and I'm surprised you still haven't realized that."

At this, Terion narrowed his eyes.

Seeing his look, she smiled and said, "It was all carefully planned to allow me to rule *this* world first, my dear brother. Here is where my true armies will rise. Here is where they will gather in preparation for the final blow."

"For what?"

"Why, to return home," she replied, her smile widening. "And it will be a grand homecoming indeed."

"You keep settin' them up and we'll keep mowin' them down," Branson put in. "Just like we did tonight."

"You killed my personal servants, fool. Hardly irreplaceable."

"But dead, just the same."

"True," she agreed. "But, I'm certain you will both become adequate replacements for those you killed." She smirked and touched her lips with one long finger, seeming to appraise them both. "Adequate indeed, I think. I will make you mine and then you will watch me raise the child as my own, until such time as I decide to make her my servant as well." She stepped forward, hands flexing. "Only then, will I kill you and, I promise you, it will be an exquisitely slow execution."

"She will never be yours," Terion whispered in desperation, clutching the baby tighter, understanding what he was going to have to do; what Shayene was forcing upon him. If he was going to die, he would have to make sure the baby died with him. It broke his heart, but it was the only way. He could not allow Shayene to raise her. He had promised Avenrael that.

"Well, this ain't what I was hoping to see," another voice sounded, stopping Shayene in her tracks and causing all of them to look toward it. Dorsey limped into the living room, his battle with the little demon evident in the bites and cuts all over his arms. The scratches down his face still oozed blood, but it wasn't his wounds that were surprising. A young man clad in tattered robes of gray cloth was leaning heavily on his shoulder, a dazed look on his face. "I don't suppose it would make any difference to say you're under arrest for kidnapping, will it?" Dorsey went on, casting a weary look at Shayene.

"You dared to awaken my prisoner," Shayene growled, her eyes narrowing. "His was a special task and he was not to be awakened until the final hour."

"Yeah, well now his task will be to get to the hospital and get checked out," Dorsey answered, clearly unafraid. "You gonna stand down? Or are we gonna do this the hard way?"

"Clearly, you do not comprehend the situation you are in," she said, before turning back to Terion. "I see you brought an outworlder into your fight, dear brother. So much the pity for him. How much does he know?"

"Enough."

"Then he will be your first victim," she snarled angrily, before launching herself at the wounded warrior.

The Arcai, Shayene , was more powerful than any other being on the planet. Her strength was unmatched and her power beyond compare. But in that moment, the young gray-robed man's eyes cleared and his head snapped up. He uttered a single word, "No!" and flung his free hand toward Terion. Shimmering power in ribbons of blue and purple energy flashed into existence, surrounding Terion and Fyre, Branson and Avenrael, before snapping back and enveloping Dorsey and the young man.

Energy crackled and popped even as Shayene suddenly comprehended what was happening and screamed in defiance. But her realization came too late. A moment later, the world gate collapsed back in on itself and they were gone.

Shayene stood alone.

Mirror

Chapter 20

The moon was high the next evening when Shayene again stepped out onto her now-ruined balcony. The fight with Avenrael had been vicious and she was still somewhat surprised at how hard the woman had pushed her. But it did nothing to mar her current anticipatory mood. Killing the witch had been pleasant revenge for what the Vi'Raaji had done to Kraegor last year. But it had been by no means necessary. Losing the child, though, was a greater loss and one she still had to reconcile. She knew of Fyre's lineage; had sensed it in the baby when she had first arrived on this world along with her mother. Shayene could still feel the child faintly, but reclaiming her would have to wait. She had far more important things to deal with now. The fighting across the ocean had grown fierce in the past twenty-four hours and she knew she must act now.

She thought about the people of this world, an odd world of machinery and non-belief. She had found it strange at first—men and women, even children, most with little or no belief in higher powers. Their beliefs were in their worldly heroes and in their money and in themselves. Always in themselves.

On one hand, that had made it more difficult to exert her mastery over them as a demigod. On the other hand, it made it much easier to find a different method of control, one that turned out to ultimately be better suited for what she had intended all along.

She simply remade them.

She closed her eyes and reached out to them, feeling those already under her power, nearly a thousand strong in New York City alone. Others existed in other cities across the world—she had not been idle during the past year. They were the forgotten of this world; homeless and discarded, the refuse of humanity living on the streets or in boxes or beneath bridges. They were ignored for the most part and, when they weren't ignored, they were reviled. She had taken them sometimes four or five a night, giving them hope and purpose, telling them that, while the world hated them, she cared for them. She would watch over them. She would protect them. And when the time was right, she would give them the power they needed over those that would harm them. All they had to do was give themselves to her, flesh and soul.

And so they did. A moment of pain, a flash of horror, and then it was over. They were sworn to her, and her instructions were always the same. *Go and sleep now, my child. Find the darkest hole and hide yourself away from the world, but only for a short while. Sleep and hunger and listen for my clarion call.* They obeyed, one and all, hiding themselves in the deepest parts of the cities, down in dark sewers and holes and basements, slumbering and hungering. Waiting.

On this, the night after the fight with Avenrael, she stood on the balcony, her unmarred body naked in the moonlight, stretching forth her power and feeling their presence beneath her. They were hers and they were ready. With the world on the verge of its own war, the time had come. Terion had escaped with the baby and, worse, with her captive gatekeeper, largely because of that very gatekeeper. Bonheur was dead, freed from his service to her. Grum was gone, as well, her last contact with her former world. But no matter. They could all be replaced. She would do so after remaking this world.

She closed her eyes and sent her thoughts into the night.

Awake.

Ground zero for the outbreak that would ultimately destroy the world was not only in New York City, but in a dozen other cities around the world. In every one, it was the same. It began with panicked phone calls to police departments and then hospitals; then anyone that would listen. The calls were always the same—frantic descriptions of brutal murders followed by screams of terror and silence. In the first couple hours in every city that it happened in, the police departments and other emergency services were utterly overwhelmed.

By the end of the first horrifying night, thousands had been killed and the attackers had melted back into the darkness. As the sun rose, the affected cities began to pick up the pieces and understand the nightmare that had just occurred. Most news organizations called it spontaneous riots of unprecedented proportions attributed to the expanding war in Russia, China, and the Middle East. People called it a supernatural event of terrifying implications. Some said it was the beginning of the end of days and flocked to their respective churches to pray. Whatever the cause, the whole world was talking about it. Many were packing up to flee the affected cities, while politicians the world over bickered and fought over blame and aid, and hospitals and morgues were inundated with bodies. But, it wasn't over.

When the sun went down the following evening, the original attackers returned. They were joined by many of the victims they took during the first horrible night. The bloodshed escalated exponentially and, by the time the sun rose that second morning, many countries were in various states of emergency and scrambling to contain the outbreak. But by then, it was too late. Even limited nuclear attacks were unable to quell the spread of violence. The balance had tipped. The world had been undone.

It would take nearly two months for the United States and most other major countries to fall completely under military rules as the murderous plague spread unchecked within their borders; less than six more before most countries and nationalities ceased to exist altogether.

In less than two years, the world that had been, was gone. There were no nations, no standing armies, no patriotic fervor to spur on the survivors. There was only the day, when the survivors could sleep, and the night, when they would try to survive until dawn.

More than half of every attack resulted in death. Those who died outright, torn to pieces by ravenous monsters that were once their neighbors, their families, and their friends, were the lucky ones. Those who were taken instead and turned were imprisoned within Shayene's soul, hungering as she did. They worshipped her and loved her, even as they hated her.

Shayene cared nothing for them. They were hers and would always be. They would worship her, trapped within their new existence forever. Their gods were silent and had been for many years as the people's faith had dwindled into unbelief. Their Arcai were dead, each of them by her hand, one after another until none remained. Her dominance over the world was complete and she ruled it without challenge. She still felt the small glimmer of their souls, crying out for deliverance during the days when they slumbered. But no gods answered them. Only she would, filling them with her hunger and, when the sun set the next day, they would venture out to hunt once more.

They would continue feeding on the world, whittling away at the survivors as pure predators, taking the sick and the weak when they could separate them from the strong, and taking the strong when the strong made mistakes. In time, there would be none left. It was inevitable. Her numbers were simply too great. Eventually, the last settlement would be abandoned; the last survivor would be taken. And then the world would be empty and only her soldiers would remain.

When that happened, she would lead them back to her own world to complete what she had started. She would have her vengeance.

The coming convergence would take her there.

Interlude IV

Siranschae knelt beside the mangled man and gently placed her hand on his forehead. Upon returning to Diaman's little island, they had found Rook behind the hut, where he had been attempting to reach the water basin. They were uncertain why, for there was still plenty of water on hand in the shack. "Fever has taken him," she said softly, looking at her companion.

Arianna knelt on the other side of Rook and began touching his face—what was still flesh and not machine—and closed her eyes. "He is in pain," she said immediately, her features growing tight as she began to experience what he was feeling. "Great pain."

"He seemed better before I left," Diaman offered, watching the young woman work, his face lined with concern.

"His body views the metal and wire as an infection," Arianna continued softly. "He fights it, trying to dislodge it."

Diaman looked quizzically at Siranschae, who returned his gaze with a smile. Standing up, she took her friend by the arm, turned him away, and started walking back toward the hut, leaving Arianna with Rook. "You have many questions," she said, briefly looking back at the young Tae, who was now fully at work trying to heal the outworlder.

"Who is she?" he asked suspiciously. "She is not like other mortals. This, at least, is clear."

"She is a Tae healer," Siranschae answered. "More specifically, she is an empath."

"An empath?" he scoffed. "They are nothing more than legend!"

"Arianna proves that they are much more than simple legend," Siranschae explained. "She learned of her birthright at a very young age, but, because of what it meant for her, she purposefully kept it hidden from her people."

"Why?"

"She did not want to be shut away in a temple the rest of her life, forced to be a symbol to be worshipped. So when she was old enough to travel, she left Taer Blys and fell in with a group of adventurers who became her surrogate family."

"I see," he mused thoughtfully. "Quite a tale, I imagine?"

"Yes," she answered, her voice distant. "In your absence, much has happened, particularly with our kind and our Arcai companions."

"You understand that my exile means I have not had the ability to know or even sense what has been happening in the outside world."

"It hasn't been good, my old friend. If you were to ask me, I would say that our age is in its twilight."

"So I'm beginning to believe," he lamented. "First an outworlder shows up who seems more metal than human, and now I find that empaths are not quite the legend that I always thought them to be."

They continued walking past his hut and toward the shoreline, before Diaman asked the question that had been on his mind for some time, ever since Siranschae had introduced Arianna to him. "What happened to Donaran? And to you, for that matter?"

Siranschae was silent before answering and, when she did, her voice was distant and sad. "About a year ago, he was killed on the battlefield by Draven. During their fight, I was engaged with Zarandrae. When Donaran died and the weakness claimed me, Zarandrae landed a killing blow against me. I should have died, too, and would have if not for..." she trailed off, looking back from where they had come.

"Arianna," he finished.

"She came to me as I lay dying," Siranschae explained. "She healed me, where there should have been no hope of healing."

"How was she able to heal a dragon, I wonder? I thought the

legends stated that an empath can only heal their own kind."

"I though the same, until she healed me," Siranschae answered. "When I realized what she was doing, I fought her because of what I thought it might to do her. I did not want to be responsible for her death. But in my wounded state, I could not stop her. She saved my life and paid a terrible price to do so."

"What kind of price?" he asked.

"Saving me nearly cost her life," she answered. "It was only the intervention of Jayadra and Volsaun that brought her back in the end."

"Jayadra and Volsaun?" he asked, eyes widening is surprise. "How many more of our brothers and sisters are involved in the happenings of mortals today?"

"As I said, there is much that you do not know, Diaman."

"Like how Arianna is your companion now?" he asked, eyeing her expectantly.

"She saved my life when I should have died," Siranschae repeated her earlier statement. "She is my soul sister, as close to me as Donaran ever was."

"Do you miss him?"

"Always," she said softly, looking out across the ocean waves as the gulls called overhead. "In his final days, Donaran was a drunk and rarely sober enough to even have a conversation. But he was always a good man and, in the end, he died with honor."

"Well, he will be reborn one day," Diaman consoled her. "In time, he will return to you."

"Perhaps, if the gods see fit to do so," she said. "But I'm not certain they will, though. Not anymore."

"Surely the gods would not keep him from you, any more than they would keep Jayra from me."

"I do not believe the gods hear us anymore," she said somberly.

"And even if they do, perhaps they are simply content with letting our kind depart this world."

"You really believe that?"

"I don't know," she shrugged.

"What about Arianna?" he pressed the subject. "She is mortal, Siranschae. She will die. If you are bonded with her in the absence of Donaran, the next severing could kill you."

"We all die, Diaman," she replied. "But in truth, I do not know how long Arianna has in this world." Siranschae paused, contemplating something more. Then she added, "She is more than a mere mortal anymore."

"What do you mean?"

"When she saved me, she nearly died. Jayadra restored her health with a healing potion brewed from the blood of Volsaun."

"That's…rather unpredictable," Diaman said, shocked at the revelation. "Jayadra gave her dragon's blood? By the gods, what happened?"

"She was healed, but because of the potion, she possesses the blood of a dragon within her now," Siranschae answered simply.

"And it didn't kill her?"

"It did not. But it did lead to unforeseen changes within her."

"What kind of changes?"

Before should could reply, from behind the hut came the roar of a great beast. Diaman turned, his eyes going wide in shock, but Siranschae merely smiled

"Those kinds of changes."

Part 4

Wasteland

Mirror

Chapter 21

Rick Branson trudged through the gray-tinged snow, glad to be getting back to the cabin before night fell. It had been a long trek down and back up the mountainside, but the outcome had been what he'd expected. The small group of survivors that had taken shelter in the cave at the base of the mountain had indeed been hit the night before. Branson had found several mangled bodies in the cave, but no survivors. Whether anyone had escaped, he didn't know. But he doubted it. More than likely, anyone left alive had been taken. And that meant they would have been turned.

That was what life was all about anymore. You ran and ran until you couldn't run anymore. Sometimes you got lucky and could hunker down for a spell in one place. Other times, the vampires found you quickly and the outcome of that confrontation was foreordained. The humans who survived in the wastelands that covered the Earth were the ones who remained on the move and stayed ahead of the packs. Those that didn't usually paid with their lives or ended up as part of those packs the next time the sun went down.

He crested a rocky ridge and looked up the slope. He could barely make out the shape of the small cabin nestled into the side of the mountain. It looked cold and lifeless, exactly how they wanted it to. As homes went, they had been able to stay in this one for nearly three months, almost a record for the sixteen years they had been on the run. But he knew their time here would be coming to an end. The attack on the survivors at the foot of the mountain told him that the undead were getting closer and would eventually sniff them out again.

The question was, should they push north into what used to be Canada or try their luck back to the south? North meant even colder temperatures, but far less night activity by the creatures. South meant warmer weather—if only by a few degrees—and less snow. It also meant fresh fish, if they could find a boat and get it out far enough from the contaminated zones where the cold ocean water still supported an abundance of sea life. But the monsters were more active in the south, especially near the coastlines. The last time they had been south, tragedy had nearly cost all of them their lives. He didn't think Terion would agree to going there again.

He trudged toward the cabin, keeping his eyes on the trees around him, alert for any movement. The creatures rarely climbed. Hell, most of them couldn't even see anymore. Sixteen years and a dwindling food supply had reduced the bodies of the vampires to dried husks, even though they were no less lethal. Their eyes were gone, but they didn't need eyes to track their prey. All they needed was to sense the pumping of blood through veins to draw them and, in some cases, that sense was extraordinary.

That said, there were other things besides vampires that surviving humans had to contend with. Over the course of sixteen years, people had been forced to evolve as humanity desperately tried to avoid extinction. Billions had died at the hands of the vampires, but millions more still survived, and some of those did so by mimicking the creatures and feeding on other humans.

Branson shuddered at the memory of one of those encounters a couple years prior, where they had come upon what appeared at first to be little more than a hole in the ground. They had started exploring, wondering if it might turn into a potential safe hold for them. Instead, they found that the elaborate maze of tunnels was home to a particularly nasty group of cannibalistic survivors. After killing several just to escape, he and Terion had made the decision to leave the area and never return. Every map they possessed now had that area, in what used to be Montana, marked to avoid at all costs.

Despite the danger inherent in being outside at any time, the rest of his trek back to the cabin was without incident and he breathed a sigh of relief as he pushed open the front door and slipped inside. Several pairs of eyes looked up at him.

"Shut the damn door," Dorsey growled from his place next to the fire. "Didn't your momma ever teach you any manners?"

Branson chuckled at the old man's cantankerous attitude, but couldn't blame him for it. Carson Dorsey was in his 70s now and showing his years. His hair was white and stuck out in every direction, and it framed his wrinkled face almost comically. The last five years had been hard on him as arthritis took hold and began to gnarl his fingers and bow his back. While he was always barking at them that he was as fit as anyone else, he had slowed considerably, enough that Terion had finally put an end to him making any scouting or supply runs. So he stayed in "HQ," as Dorsey like to call it, making plans, looking at maps, and making or repairing weapons when his arthritis wasn't flaring up. It was valuable work to their little group, but Branson quietly worried that his old friend would not survive should they be forced to run again. And after his scouting expedition down the mountain, that situation looked to be looming in the very near future.

"Where's Terion?" Branson asked a much younger man sitting next to Dorsey, knowing the old man would never hear him anyway, his hearing going along with the rest of his aging body.

They knew the younger man only as Uncle, the poor lost gatekeeper they had rescued from Shayene's penthouse apartment in New York City. It had been an accident, really, that Dorsey had stumbled upon him after killing the little demon, but it had been the best possible luck. Uncle had saved them all by opening a gateway and transporting them several floors below Shayene's apartment. It had then been a true Houdini escape from the building, with Uncle getting them through walls and floors with his still-very-weak magic, all the way to the ground floor and always ahead of Shayene's pursuing goons. They found shelter in an abandoned apartment several blocks away, patched up their wounds as best they could, and then left New York City when the sun came up. The undead apocalypse began the next night. Uncle never did recall his real name and no one had assigned him one until Fyre started calling him Uncle when she was two. It had stuck with him ever since.

"Oh, you know how it is with those two," Uncle said drily, moving his hand in the air and manipulating a small sphere of magical portal energy above their fire, the shimmering circle no bigger around than a tin can. "They won't roll in until the last rays of sunshine go away."

Branson chuckled and watched the gatekeeper play with the magic. It never ceased to amaze him, watching Uncle's smoke trick. For the longest time after they had gone on the run to escape the spread of Shayene's vampires, they had hidden at night, never using a fire or anything that would attract attention to them. As countries fell and cloud cover grew from last-gasp nuclear options around the world, temperatures began to plummet. Mid-summer was now usually a balmy 40 degrees at best, and winters were deathly cold. One night, as they contemplated freezing to death, Dorsey had made a suggestion. "Why not have the boy portal the smoke somewhere?"

After a lot of discussion on what effect, if any, that would have on the barrier, Uncle had finally tried it. At first, there had been mixed success, but he eventually perfected it over several months. Now, they could build a fire in any structure and Uncle could portal the smoke to a place they had already visited. It was so amazing that Branson had to see for himself one day, trekking back to their previous location where he watched a lazy stream of smoke wafting up from nothing. Even upon closer inspection, he could not find any trace of the portal. He figured it would make a hell of a puzzle for anyone who stumbled across it, and it made them all feel a little bit safer.

"Probably making out or something," Uncle added with a grin, shooting a glance across the room at a teenage girl who was lounging in a battered thread-bare chair, her eyes glued to a book.

"Oh, that's just so gross," Fyre mumbled off-handedly, her eyes never leaving her battered copy of Harry Potter and The Deathly Hallows. The teenager was obsessed with reading, and books were the one thing they still found in abundance during their travels.

Branson pulled off his parka, clumped across the room, and began to remove his gear.

"How's it look out there?" Fyre asked, setting her book aside and looking at him with concern. She was an extremely bright young girl, with untapped power of her own, and she was always well-aware of their precarious situation, since her parents had decided early on that the truth was always best.

"Not good," Branson replied evenly. "A pack hit the lower caves last night."

"Any survivors?" she asked, running her fingers through her mane of silver hair, one of her defining characteristics. It had been dark brown as a baby and a toddler, but as she grew older and it became apparent that she possessed some kind of magic about her, it began to change, until it closely resembled her mother's.

"None that I could find," Branson answered glumly.

"Are we going to have to move again?"

"Depends on what your dad finds, but I'd have to say it's probable," he finished, casting a worried glance back at Dorsey, who now appeared to be sleeping in his chair, hands folded over his chest.

As if in answer, the door opened again and a pair of figures slipped into the lodge. Both were dressed in dark clothes, from coats to boots, with fur hats and scarves pulled tight across their faces, showing only their eyes.

"What did the south slope look like?" Terion asked Branson immediately, pulling his scarf from his face. He was older and wiser looking, but the 16 years had not affected him too much. Even in his fifties, his piercing eyes still held their fierce glint of life.

"Got hit last night," Branson replied somberly, shaking his head. "They're close."

"We found the same thing," Terion said, looking at his companion, who was busy removing her own gear.

If the years had been kind to Terion, they hadn't even touched his wife. Avenrael had not changed at all in their decade and a half on the run. Her youthfulness had been a discussion point numerous times in the past and the best any of them could understand was that her short time as a vampire had imbued her with certain characteristics. When Shayene had killed her in their fight, the curse had been lifted because she had not yet fed. However, some of the benefits had remained when she had been brought back to life. And to be sure, she had indeed died at Shayene's hands. But when Uncle had delivered them all from certain death, Dorsey had used CPR—a completely foreign concept to Terion at the time—and restarted her heart. The detective worked frantically on her, packing and wrapping her wounds as they fled, and always ready to pound on her chest when her heart stopped.

The Vi'Raaji's survival that night was as close to a miracle as anyone could have hoped for. Between the woman's indomitable will to live and Dorsey's stubborn refusal to let her die, they had gotten past that first 24 hours until she had finally stabilized. Some of that survival could be attributed to Dorsey's understanding of medicine and his insistence that they all take a turn giving her some of their precious life-giving blood. The rest was on Avenrael and her accelerated ability to heal the horrendous wound that Shayene had inflicted to her lower back. Today, all that remained of the ordeal was a large, star-shaped scar just to the right of her spine. It was a reminder of how close she had come to leaving them forever.

Avenrael went directly to Fyre, smiling as she knelt next to the teen and ran her long fingers lovingly through the girl's hair. "How's your book?" she asked, her crystalline eyes glittering in the firelight.

"It's good, Mom," Fyre answered, leaning forward and kissing her on the cheek. She looked very much like her mother—dark skin, silver hair, and beautiful exotic facial features. But where her mother's eyes were ice blue, Fyre had her biological father's eyes. They were dark, extremely so, and if one looked closely, one could see glittering flecks of green within their depths. They were the eyes of Kraegor. The eyes of a dragon. "Are we going to have to leave?" she asked.

"I believe so," Avenrael answered truthfully and then joined the others around the fire.

"The caves are occupied," Terion stated flatly, referring to a cluster of caves that existed on the other side of the mountain that he and Avenrael had been scouting. Three months ago, he and Branson had found them to be empty. But the cabin provided a better shelter for them at the time, so they had opted to settle in the lodge instead.

"Bloodsuckers?" Branson asked.

"Looks like it," Terion nodded. "We found signs of fresh remains at the main cave entrance."

"No chance of waiting it out and hoping they move on, I guess," the former marine sighed.

"No. This is a big pack."

"We also have another problem," Avenrael added, warming her hands by the fire. "We found additional tracks. Humans."

"More survivors?" Branson asked guardedly.

"Trackers," was the woman's terse, one-word response.

This caused Dorsey to open his eyes, and the undertone of sudden concern in the room was palpable. Vampires and cannibals were bad enough, but trackers were human collaborators protected by and working directly for Shayene. Their job was a simple one. They acted the part of survivors, finding and infiltrating groups and reporting their location to Shayene, allowing the Arcai to send her vampire packs to eliminate them. Trackers were the biggest reason that large groups of survivors didn't band together anymore. Once you were with a group and knew them, you didn't want to take chances adding an unknown person who might be a tracker.

That was what had happened to them in Louisiana several years ago. Tired of going it alone for so long, they had finally joined with a larger group of survivors that had established a stronghold on the coast and were turning it into an actual town with fortified homes and even a fishing trawler to provide food. The township was accepting new additions all the time, welcoming weary survivors in and preaching strength in numbers. They had walls, weapons, and plenty of capable fighters. Unfortunately, one such addition turned out to be a tracker, and the swarm of undead that attacked shortly after had decimated the town. Hundreds had been killed and more had been taken as slaves. Very few had escaped. It had only been Terion's insistence that they have an escape plan in place, that had allowed them to get away. They had avoided the clusters of survivors ever since, occasionally meeting some to trade, but never more than that. Such was the case with the group that had perished on the south slope the night before.

"How do you know they're trackers?" Branson asked.

"Ski tracks on the higher slopes," Terion explained. "I make two or three of them at least, but they're taking precautions to mask their presence, skiing and moving about single file for the most part."

"Definitely not regular survivors then," the soldier agreed. "Sucks for us."

"Is it possible they know we're here?" Dorsey spoke up, his craggy voice sounding utterly exhausted. He knew that if trackers had found them, they were going to be hard pressed. The vampire packs were driven by hunger and need for blood; they didn't think and didn't plan. If they came across survivors, they simply attacked en masse in their desperate need to feed. That made them easier to avoid. Trackers, on the other hand, were human. They planned and schemed. If trackers were on their trail, they were in a world of danger.

"I don't think so," Terion replied. "But they're looking for someone or something. The tracks are all over the mountain side."

"So we bug out," Branson said with finality. "What's the plan?"

"We move out in the morning, about an hour before dawn breaks," Terion answered. "The packs should be back in their lairs by then. That way, if trackers are about, we have a better chance of getting out before they see us, especially if they are zeroing in on this place."

"Which they will, sooner or later," Branson agreed. "We going north or south?"

"We head deeper into the forest."

"That means north then," Branson said, somewhat dejected. He was getting tired of the bitter cold and he would absolutely kill for some fresh fish. But he knew Terion wasn't about to risk their lives and head down into more active territory again. Still, he wondered if the day would come when they could move south. Better yet, maybe the day would eventually come when they could stop running all together. He voiced the only point of contention the two men had ever had by saying, "One of these days, Terion, we need to think about settling in somewhere. We're getting too old to keep running."

"Come on, Rick, you know that's not possible," Avenrael spoke up. "Any time we find something, the packs eventually close in."

"Hey, I'm just sayin'," he added, holding up his hands, clearly not wanting to fight. "I just want to make sure we're always thinking about it."

"If we can find a suitable cabin still standing or some other shelter, we can probably bed down for the winter," Terion said, feeling the same frustration as Branson. "We're far enough north that we'll avoid most of the packs now as winter sets in, and it'll get too cold for trackers to be chasing around. Who knows, maybe we can turn it into something more permanent."

"If we don't freeze to death first," Dorsey added with a growl.

"Alright people, let's start packing," Branson said, ignoring the old man and personally okay with where he left things with Terion. Once they found new shelter, the two of them could revisit possible destinations and think of something more permanent that would give them protection. Right now, though, with trackers and vampires about, that was the least of their concerns.

As one, the little group got to work, packing their gear and supplies and preparing to flee. It would be a long night for all of them.

Chapter 22

They departed well before sunrise and Avenrael ranged out ahead to scout as she always did while Terion led the rest of them. Fyre and Uncle did their best to help Dorsey along, who quickly began showing signs that the journey might be more than his old body could handle this time. Branson brought up the rear, hanging back to watch for any type of pursuit, while nursing dark thoughts about what would happen to Dorsey if they found themselves in a fight-or-flight situation. He didn't like to think about their options. There were precious few, and none of them were any good.

All of them were seasoned outdoorsmen and women and, despite Dorsey's difficulties, they moved quietly through the forest, grateful for the trees' natural windbreaks and the lack of snow drifts hampering their way. Out on the open slopes, the snow was powdery and, in a lot of places, extremely deep. If they stayed inside the tree lines near the base of the mountain range, they could move along fairly easily, unimpeded by the deeper snow. That was the plan, anyway.

They traveled for nearly two hours before Avenrael returned and Terion brought them all to a halt for a quick rest. "How are you holding up?" he immediately asked Dorsey, helping the old man settle back against the trunk of a wide oak. Dorsey's face was white and a thin sheen of sweat shone on his forehead, despite the cold. He was in obvious pain, but wouldn't even consider complaining. That concerned Terion most of all.

"I'll live," Dorsey answered through gritted teeth. "But I'd give anything for a cup of coffee right now."

"Want me to run by an old Starbucks for you and get you something floofy?" Branson chided him as he walked up and patted the old man affectionately on the shoulder. None of them had had coffee in over a decade, but Dorsey had never outgrown his desire for it, even though it was a pleasure that no longer existed in the world. "As if you'd rather have some yuppy Frappuccino instead of my own home-brewed tea," he chuckled, referring to a leafy mixture he made out of plants and tree bark. The others all thought it tasted horrible, but he liked it.

"I'd rather die," Dorsey grumbled.

"Yeah, but at least you'd be warm," Branson countered. "You know my brew will bake your bones, once you get past the taste."

"Like I said, I'd rather die," Dorsey repeated sourly.

"How's it look up ahead?" Terion asked, turning his attention to his wife while Branson and Dorsey continued to talk quietly together.

Even wrapped up tightly against the cold so that only her pale blue eyes were visible, Avenrael was still the most beautiful woman he had ever laid eyes on, inside and out. When Dorsey had saved her life all those years ago, Terion had abandoned any lingering second thoughts he had about a relationship with his former enemy. He'd boldly stated his love for her, lest he lose her again and, with that, any chance to tell her how he truly felt.

He would no longer concern himself with what others thought and he figured that even Cavanah, one of his oldest friends before he had been killed, would have been happy for him in the end. When Avenrael was known as Vendetta, she was a Vi'Raaji assassin who had been his deadliest enemy and she done some truly terrible things, including murdering Cavanah. But when the dragon, Kraegor, had assaulted her in Nykiva, something within her had broken during the rape and everything had changed. When Terion found and rescued her, she threw her lot in with him and his companions and was ultimately willing to sacrifice her life to help them defeat Shayene and her dragon. Nothing beyond divine providence had saved her from the worst possible fate anyone could imagine, and he had been drawn to her ever since.

Now, looking into her eyes as she unwound her scarf, he found her warm and compassionate, a wonderful mother and loving companion. She completed him, like no one else could. She was his soul mate and he, hers.

Seeing the look in his eyes, she smiled and leaned forward, kissing him warmly on the mouth.

"Eww, Mom! Dad!" Fyre complained, ever the teenager. Even growing up in a savage world where death lurked around every corner, she remained, first and foremost, a teenager easily embarrassed by her parents, particularly when they were amorous.

"Get a room, you two," Branson added with a grin, reaching up and bumping knuckles with the girl, who grinned back at him.

Avenrael hugged her husband close, pausing only to playfully stick her tongue out at her daughter, who promptly returned the gesture and rolled her eyes. Then pulling back, Avenrael was serious once more. "The way is clear for some distance," she reported. "I see no tracks from the creatures, nor any from trackers."

"Any signs of shelter?" Terion asked.

"Nothing that would offer us any kind of defense against an attack," she replied worriedly. "If we don't find something by nightfall, we will be in very real trouble."

"Hey, Terion," Branson spoke up suddenly. "Remember when we went out for a couple days a few months back, right after we found the cabin?"

"The building on the mountaintop," Terion immediately guessed what his friend was suggesting. Shortly after they had claimed the lodge as their home, he and Branson had ventured north, traveling for two days to scout out any other potential safe holds, should the lodge not prove safe enough. Before they turned back, they had spied, on a distant peak, a building with several metal structures next to it—microwave or radio towers, Branson had explained to him. The building was on a mountaintop and a good many miles away, not to mention it would be a torturous climb if they could not find an old road or path. It was not much, but it was something, even if it might take them days to get there.

"Wouldn't be a bad idea to think about heading in that direction," Branson suggested.

"Maybe," Terion nodded thoughtfully, casting a glance at Dorsey. He knew the old man wouldn't be able to make the climb, let alone the long journey to get to the right mountain. They would have to carry him, and Terion already knew how much of a fit the man would pitch when he suggested it.

"Do you think the building will be occupied?" Avenrael asked.

"It's doubtful," Branson was the one to reply. "Before the world went to hell, those buildings were only used for maintenance and sometimes research. They were never any place to hole up for any length of time. Too far out of the way, and the vamps definitely wouldn't use it as a lair that far up the mountainside."

"What about other survivors?"

"It's possible, but I doubt it," Branson shrugged. "It's on a peak and well above the tree line and any decent hunting areas. It would be a bitch to haul a 200-pound deer up that mountainside."

"That's what we have you for," the woman smiled, before turning back to Terion. "We can stay on this track for a time and then we should move to higher ground. There's a ridge beyond this mountain that we can reach and it goes on for some distance. It would afford us a clear view of anything below."

"Agreed," Terion said, tightening the straps of his pack. Then, to everyone he said, "Let's get moving."

They traveled on, the gray sky growing only marginally brighter as they pushed on through the snow. They spoke little, conserving their energy for the journey. Around noon, nearest they could tell, Terion again called a halt so they could rest and eat. They ate in silence, all of them chewing on strips of dried deer jerky and thinking about what might lay before them. They all knew that traveling—even during the day—was dangerous, and the looming aspect of night falling while they were still in the open was not a pleasant one.

After about fifteen minutes, Terion had them back on the path ascending to the ridgeline that Avenrael had mentioned. It was a long strip of rock, a few feet wide at its narrowest and nearly a hundred feet at the widest. It ran for several miles and gave them the vantage point needed to see below and behind them and whether they were being followed. Better yet, the wind had swept it clear of snow, so it was easier to traverse, which was especially important for Dorsey. Trudging through waist-deep snow would have been the end of him.

They continued, taking turns helping Dorsey along. Even with the clear path, it was an effort for him to put one foot down in front of another. Worried, Terion brought them to a halt again and knelt beside Dorsey, who had sunk to his knees, his breathing rapid.

"You can't keep this up," Terion said quietly, his hand resting on the man's hunched shoulder. "You need to let us carry you."

"Over my…dead…body," Dorsey wheezed.

"That's going to be happening if you don't stop being a stubborn ass," Branson said, taking a seat next to their old friend. "We're out in the open and going to have to hoof it if we want to find shelter before nightfall."

"Hey guys, look," Fyre suddenly said, turning everyone's attention to her. She was standing on the edge of the ridge, looking back the way they had come. There, in the distance, a plume of black smoke was rising into the air.

"It's the lodge," Branson guessed, climbing to his feet with an angry scowl on his face. "Trackers must have found it and are burning it down."

"Scorched...earth," Dorsey said, his discomfort temporarily forgotten. "They're making sure...no other survivors...can use it."

"It also means they're on our trail," Terion pointed out. "It won't be hard for them to find us out here."

"Time to make time," Branson said hurriedly, leaning down and helping Dorsey back to his feet. The old man tried to smack his hands away, but Branson dipped his shoulder and scooped the old man up into a fireman's carry, ignoring his curses and threats of sticking a knife in his hind quarters.

"Let's move," Terion said. "Avenrael, you fall back and see if anyone is following us."

The woman nodded and hurried back the way they came. She moved with the grace of a hunting cat and, in moments, had vanished behind several boulders.

"We've got a head start on them," Branson said as she disappeared, "but if those trackers are on skis like you said, they're going to be moving fast. And they'll lead the vamps right to us as soon as the sun goes down."

"Agreed," Terion said. "We need to find shelter; some place that is defensible."

They hurried on, staying close together. Terion kept his adopted daughter near his side and noted with some satisfaction that the hilts of her daggers were within easy reach at her waist. The blades were once her mother's, dragon-forged weapons that Vendetta had used to ply her trade, secretly forged by Kraegor himself. Avenrael had forsaken them and Fyre had adopted them as soon as she was old enough to understand their use and their magic. She was quite proficient with them, too, as Terion and Avenrael had been teaching her how to fight ever since she could walk. Now, as they jogged along the ridge, she was as prepared as the rest of them, should they have to stand and fight. It wouldn't be the first time she had been put in that situation.

The sky was growing dimmer when Avenrael rejoined them, hurrying up to Terion. He started to pull them up, but the Vi'Raaji motioned them to keep going. "Don't stop," she said hurriedly, "They are coming."

"Trackers? They made us already?" Branson huffed, struggling mightily under the load of carrying Dorsey.

"No," she replied softly. "It's the pack."

"The pack?" Terion repeated in surprise. "How's that possible? It's still light!"

"They are staying inside the tree line," she replied. "The forest is mostly pines and it protects them enough that they can travel during daylight hours. That they are following us, though, is what truly disturbs me."

"How many?"

Avenrael didn't answer. She only shook her head sadly. That was all any of them needed to know.

"We have about an hour of daylight left," Terion said firmly, refusing to let fear get its talons into him. "We stay on the ridge and keep going. Look for some place we can defend."

"It's a long night, my friend," Branson pointed out, a resolute look on his face. He was prepared for the worst. "Unless there's a bank vault nearby, we're looking at Custer's last stand."

"Wait!" Dorsey suddenly called out, his voice shaking as he bounced up and down on Branson's shoulder. "Put me down!"

"What?"

"Put me down, you sonuvabitch!" the old man snapped with more energy than he had shown in some time.

Branson pulled up and slowly lowered the old man to the ground, his shoulders sighing in delight as the load was lifted.

"My pack," Dorsey said, looking around frantically. "I need my pack! Where is it?"

Fyre had been carrying it and she handed it to him.

Dorsey dove in, digging through it until he pulled out a bundle of papers. They all knew what they were. Dorsey's maps. He had built up quite the collection over the years and they were his pride and joy. Terion and Branson were usually the ones who decided where they would be going during their travels, but it was Dorsey who planned the routes. He knew each one extremely well and as they had been fleeing along the ridgeline, he had been silently going over every map he knew of the area. And that's when he remembered it.

Breaking into a fevered grin, he pulled one of the aged maps from the stack and carefully unfolded it, careful not to tear or rip it. It was faded and worn, but still legible. Dorsey spread it out on the frozen ground and looked around to get his bearings. Finally satisfied that he knew exactly where he was, he bent over the map and began running his finger lightly over its surface, mumbling to himself as he did. A moment later, he pressed a finger to the map and exclaimed, "Here!"

"What?" Branson asked.

"We are right here," Dorsey explained, tapping the paper impatiently.

"Great, but how does that help us?"

"This ridge was once a work road!" Dorsey went on, tracing his finger along the map before coming to a stop at a point just beyond where he had started. "Right here is where we want to get to."

They all looked closer, seeing only a small marking on the map, meaningless to them, but obviously not to Dorsey.

"It's a work tunnel entrance of some kind," the old man said excitedly. "If we can get in, we can defend it."

"If it's still there, where does it lead?"

"No idea," the old man answered. "But it's there for a reason, either to drain water or move cable. It's marked on the map, so it should be deep and will keep us from being surrounded."

"Not much of a hope," Branson said doubtfully. "We might be trapped with no way out."

"Perhaps, but it's the only chance we have," Terion said. "Gather your things and let's get moving." He motioned toward Avenrael, who silently nodded her head in understanding. She quickly disappeared into the deepening gloom.

"We have company," Uncle said softly, turning their attention to him. He had been silent while Dorsey had explained what might be their only hope, his eyes scanning the trees below the ridge while they talked. At first, he had seen nothing. Then slowly, a figure emerged out of the shadows of the tree line, standing safely in the dark beneath heavy pine boughs. Then there were two. Then five.

They watched the creatures appear along the base of the ridge, all of them facing them, eyeless faces tilted upward. There were now dozens of them.

"Well, that sucks," Branson sighed, his own eyes going to the sky. It was deepening to dusk far too quickly.

"It will if we don't get our asses in gear," Dorsey muttered.

"Run!" Terion urged, shooing everyone forward. "Go! Now!"

Without another word, they gathered their packs and hurried on, occasionally looking down the slope. Branson tried to hoist Dorsey back over his shoulders, but the old man threatened to shoot Branson if he tried picking him up again. Summoning what had to be a supreme amount of effort, Dorsey jogged alongside them, keeping pace and still rummaging in his pack as they went.

Below them, the vampires continued to shadow them, darting in and out of the trees, and keeping pace themselves. Once or twice, one of the vampires would slip too far out of the protective darkness of the tree line and the fading daylight would send it scurrying back into the shadows with an unholy scream of pain. But that would only last for a little while longer.

Fifteen minutes later, Avenrael reappeared in front of them and fell into step. "I found it," she said, but her voice was anything but hopeful.

"You don't sound excited," Branson was quick to point out. "That can't be a good thing."

"It is protected by a metal grate," she informed them. "We can't get in."

"It's…hinged, though, right?" Dorsey puffed, his face white with exertion. But still he hurried on, his legs pumping hard.

"Yes," she replied. "Chained and padlocked. How did you know?"

"Hmph," Dorsey said, turning his eyes forward and soldiering on as if it didn't matter.

"We have no choice," Terion said. "It's our only chance. How far?"

"Half a mile at the most," Avenrael replied.

"We'll never make it in time," Branson whispered, looking at the sky. Pure dusk was only minutes away and, when that happened, the vampires would no longer be harmed by the light. If they caught them out in the open like this, it would be a massacre.

"We'll…make it," Dorsey snapped back angrily, tossing his pack to Branson, forcing the marine to snatch it out of the air and continue running with it. "I didn't come…this far to…end up a meal…for those blasted…demons!" With that, the old man bowed his head and ran harder, pushing his body well beyond its arthritic limits. The others matched his stride, marveling at his sudden resurgence and hoping against hope that it wouldn't be in vain.

A short time later, Avenrael pointed to a depression in the rocks. "There!" she said, hurrying forward and leading them to the tunnel entrance. It wasn't big, maybe eight foot by eight foot, with a six inch trench down the middle. The trickle of water that had once come through the tiny canal now hung as dirty icicles, reaching down into a small frozen pool just beneath the entrance. As Avenrael had said, the opening was grated, hinged at one side and padlocked on the other.

"Move aside," Dorsey wheezed as he shouldered past Avenrael and dropped to his knees onto the cracked concrete in front of the bars. He immediately pulled out a small leather bag that had been tucked into his coat and yanked open the drawstring. Reaching in, he pulled out a handful of metal picks all attached to a small steel ring and then went to work on the rusty padlock.

"I'll be damned," Branson exclaimed. "Old coot's been holding out on us. You never told me you knew how to pick locks."

"I can…hotwire…a car, too," Dorsey hissed, his breathing ragged as he focused on his task. "Don't see…many of them…around anymore, though. Now shut up…and let me work."

As Dorsey worked feverishly on the old lock while Branson, Uncle, and Fyre looked on, Terion and Avenrael stepped back to the edge of the ridge. Looking down, they saw that their time was up.

"They're coming!" Terion shouted, seeing the first vampire rush out of the trees. It was an old one, with dry, desiccated flesh and empty eye sockets. But its oversized mouth was wide open and they could see its fangs clearly from where they stood. As it emerged from the gloom, it paused briefly and let out a strange cry of what seemed like pain. But it was only for a moment before it straightened and rushed forward, scrabbling up the gravely slope toward them. The fading daylight was no longer enough to stop them.

More of them began boiling out of the tree line. They came on as one and Terion sucked in his breath. There were more than dozens. A lot more.

There were hundreds.

Chapter 23

Dorsey picked the padlock in less than a minute, snapping it open as the first of creature topped the rise. Terion sent it flying back down the steep slope by planting a heavy boot in its chest. It went careening down, out of control, bowling over and slowing several others on the way down. But more were coming. There was no way they were going to survive the onslaught if they didn't get inside.

"Let's go, people!" Branson shouted from the tunnel entrance as he wrenched the door open, the rusty hinges squealing loudly. He pushed Fyre inside and reached for Dorsey, who had slumped down against the opened gate, his eyes closed tightly and his breathing harsh and ragged.

"You okay, old man?" Branson asked.

Dorsey didn't answer.

As the monsters began nearing the ridge line in numbers they could not hope to defend against, Avenrael and Terion turned and sprinted back to the opening. They slipped past Branson and into the tunnel as the marine reached down to help Dorsey to his feet.

"Come on!" Branson shouted.

"Leave me…alone," Dorsey wheezed through clenched teeth.

"Ain't got time for this," Branson said urgently, reaching for him again, only to have Dorsey feebly slap his hands away. The old man began fumbling for the pouch he had used to carry his lock picks.

"Listen," Dorsey said in a painful whisper. "Heart…attack. Ticker's goin'…down. I'm…done."

"Damn it, old man," Branson replied angrily, not wanting to leave his friend. This was not how it was supposed to end. They were all supposed to survive or die together. "Don't do this to me!"

"Never…gonna…make it," Dorsey said, pulling a couple metal

devices out of the pouch. They were grenades and his intention was obvious. "Need…to close…gate."

"Carson, you can't…" Branson began, his eyes opening in surprise, but Dorsey cut him off.

"Get…the hell…out of here," he gasped, pulling the pin on one and then the other, before hugging them close to his chest. "Take…the bag," he finished, indicating the small sack that lay on his lap. "Take it…and go."

"No…" Branson began, but the old man cut him off.

"GO!" Dorsey nearly roared this time.

With tears starting to sting his eyes, Branson looked up. The first vampires had come over the rise and were hurrying toward them. Time was up. Looking down, he placed a hand on his friend's head one last time. "See you on the other side, brother," he whispered back and then grabbed the bag. He hurried into the tunnel, pushing the others ahead of him as fast as they could run.

Despite the agony washing over him, Dorsey managed a small smile as his friends escaped further into the tunnel. He didn't know what they would find at the other end, but he knew they wouldn't be followed. He would make sure of that. He looked back to the ridge and watched the monsters come on, empty eye sockets facing him, oversized jaws with vein-piercing fangs snapping hungrily. They drew closer as his heart slowed.

Twenty yards. *Thump…thump…*

Ten yards. *Thump…*

Then they were on him, the closest vampire lunging forward, burying its fangs into his throat.

The old man never felt the pain of the bite as his failing heart beat its last and his blood ceased to flow in his veins. As the vampire began to tear at his throat in rage and frustration, the grenades rolled out of his hands.

Carson Dorsey's last heroic act saved his friends.

The other five were lucky. A short way down the tunnel, it bent at a forty-five-degree angle and began climbing. They had passed that point when the grenades went off. The blast was deafening, the concussion throwing the remaining survivors forward, sending them sprawling on the cold concrete, scraping skin and bruising flesh and bone. Had they been in a direct line from the blast, they would have been severely hurt or even killed. As it was, the change in direction had saved their lives. They were dazed and bruised, but they were alive.

And they were in pitch darkness.

"Holy…" Branson began as he shakily climbed to his feet, reaching out to find the nearby wall and steady himself. "I think it worked. Hang on a second, let me get some light." He fumbled at his pouches in the darkness, digging into one until he found the device he needed. Popping the handle out, he began to wind it, generating the small bit of electricity it would need to power the LED bulb inside. The old hand-crank flashlight glowed to life, illuminating the tunnel and the battered survivors. "Everyone okay?" he asked, sweeping the tunnel with the light. Acrid smoke and choking dust hung in the air.

Terion helped Fyre to a sitting position. The teenager was already sporting a goose egg on her forehead where the blast had thrown her into the wall. "I think so," he replied, looking worriedly into his adopted daughter's eyes. "You okay, hon?"

She nodded and gingerly probed the bump on her head. "Just banged my head, Dad," she replied quietly. "I'll be fine."

Avenrael knelt beside her, all mother as she examined the young girl, oblivious to her own bloody scrapes and bruises.

Uncle was already up, looking around. He seemed to be the least banged up of them all. "We should make sure the entrance is sealed," he said, looking back into the dust-filled blackness behind them.

"No doubt," Branson agreed. "Don't need any bloodsuckers sneaking up on us." He reached into his bag and pulled out a second hand-crank flashlight and tossed it to Terion. "That one doesn't hold a charge, but it will stay lit as long as you keep winding it. Scout up ahead and see if you can see anything."

Terion nodded and Branson turned to the younger man. "You're with me, Uncle," he said grimly. "Let's see what happened back there." As Terion moved up the tunnel, Branson and Uncle walked back, carefully scanning ahead. Around the bend, the passageway was noticeably more filled with dust and debris. Ahead, they saw no movement. The sound of trickling sand had Branson sweeping the light over the ceiling. Large cracks showed in the concrete above him and it looked like it could come crashing down at any moment. For the moment, though, it was holding.

"Looks like he did it," Branson said quietly, hoping his old friend had gone quickly and hadn't suffered. He missed the old buzzard already and it would be a long time before he would be able to get over what Dorsey had done for them. Clearing his throat, he pushed his emotions down and concentrated on the task at hand.

"Point the light up there," Uncle said softly, pointing ahead.

Branson followed his lead and swept the light to where he was pointing. What he saw sent a shiver down his spine. Dorsey's grenades had done a number on the tunnel entrance, collapsing it almost completely and burying him and who knows how many of the creatures. But toward the top of the rubble pile, there was a small opening and in that opening an arm had been thrust through and was waving around, jagged claws grasping. As they watched, it clutched at a rock, managing to dislodge it and send it tumbling down the pile.

The hole was a little bit bigger.

"Let's move," Branson whispered, turning away and hurrying up the tunnel with Uncle close behind. They caught up to the others quickly.

"What did you find?" Terion asked.

"They're coming through," Branson said urgently. "Might take them a bit, but they know we're in here and they're digging."

"How can they know we're in here?"

"You want me to go back and ask them?" Branson asked sarcastically.

"This is not normal behavior for them," Terion added grimly. "We need to know what's drawing these things—otherwise, they'll keep coming no matter what we do."

"You ain't wrong, but now's not the time for a committee meeting," Branson said, motioning them forward. "Dorsey gave his life and bought us a little time. Let's make the best of it and get moving."

Terion nodded and took the good flashlight from Branson. Then, leading the way, he began trotting up the tunnel, light sweeping ahead. The others fell in behind.

Deep in the mountain, lit only by the old LED bulbs in the flashlights, they quickly lost track of time. They kept going, following the tunnel as it continued deeper into the mountain and kept its upward slope. They saw no secondary tunnels branching off, so were forced to run on. Several times, they paused, listening carefully for pursuit. Once or twice, Branson thought he could hear bare feet slapping against concrete, but every time he cranked up and swept his light behind him, it was swallowed up by the darkness. He'd by lying if he said it didn't scare the hell out of him.

"There's something up ahead," Terion finally called out from his position some distance up the tunnel.

The rest hurried to join him. He had come to a stop and the reason was clear. The tunnel dead-ended. There were several nubs of metal imbedded in the wall they now faced and, as Terion shone the flashlight upward, they could see that the metal remnants used to be ladder rungs that ran up through a square hole in the ceiling and disappeared into darkness above. The hole was the width of the tunnel, eight feet across on both sides and allowing for plenty of room to climb. But unfortunately, the first viable rung was nearly twenty feet up. Below that one, the rest had been sawed away and it was clear the damage had been done relatively recently. Their cut ends shone in the light, bereft of rust.

"Now who the hell does something like that?" Branson asked, trying to mask his rising anger.

"It doesn't matter," Avenrael said quietly. "We need to climb."

"But how?"

"Shh!" Terion hushed them, sweeping his flashlight back the way they had come. "Listen!"

Everyone froze, staring down the tunnel. They saw nothing in the darkness beyond, but they heard it clearly now. It was the unmistakable sound of feet shuffling along the concrete. They were coming.

Avenrael muttered something in her own language—likely a curse—and pulled her pack off her back. A moment later, she had fished out a coil of nylon cord, picked up years ago during a supply raid on an abandoned and somehow forgotten hardware store. Throwing the coil over her shoulder, she jogged back down the tunnel, before stopping about twenty feet from the dead-end wall.

"What are you..." Branson began, but Avenrael raised her hand to quiet him.

"Move to the side," she commanded. "I need running room.

Terion, keep your light on the wall. Branson, start yours back up and point it up the hole so I can see what I'm doing."

In seconds, the lights were placed where she requested, Branson rapidly cranking his to keep as much light as he could pointing upward. A moment later, Avenrael burst forward, sprinting toward the wall. She leapt gracefully, the toe of her boot catching the lowest nub of metal and she propelled herself upward with incredible speed. Spinning in the air, she hit the back side of the hole and pushed off again with both feet and hands, hoping she had enough momentum to reach her target. She did, again spinning halfway around in the air, this time high enough that she could snag the first undamaged rung with one hand. Reaching up with her other hand, she secured her hold and pulled herself up until she was comfortably on the ladder. Working quickly, she uncoiled the rope and knotted one end around one of the rungs, before dropping it down to the floor below.

"Hurry," she hissed into the darkness "Climb!"

Below her, Branson dropped his flashlight to the floor, where it immediately faded out, the dead battery unable to maintain the charge. He settled himself into a combat stance, reached over his shoulder, and drew his favorite weapon out of a battered and stained scabbard that was fastened to his back. It was a Japanese katana, still brilliantly sharp and gleaming in the artificial light that remained from Terion's flashlight. Branson had had the sword for years, finding it in a burned-out pawn shop as the world was being overrun. It had seen a lot of use over the years and he smiled dourly, knowing that this was probably going to be the last time he got to use it. From the darkness, the pursuit was louder now and seemed to be quickening. The vampires must have sensed they were getting close to their prey.

"Hurry!" Avenrael urged them again from above.

Below, Terion directed Fyre to climb first and the young teen wasted no time scrambling up the rope. Above her, Avenrael moved to the side on the ladder, allowing her daughter to catch hold of the rung and pull herself up past her.

Uncle went next. He was not nearly as quick or as agile as Fyre, but he managed, grunting his way up the rope until Avenrael could grasp his hand and pull him up the rest of the way.

Terion looked down the tunnel and saw they were out of time. He set his light on the ground up against the wall, to lessen the chances that it would get kicked in the inevitable fight. Down the tunnel, the creatures were moving into the edge of the light's glow, two and three abreast. Resigning himself to what was about to happen, he looked upward and yelled, "Go!"

"Terion!" Avenrael cried from above. "You still have time. Climb!"

"They're too close!" he shouted. "Go!"

The first line of vampires surged forward, hissing in anticipation of the meal they were about to feast upon. Branson met them with his katana, taking the heads from the first two with short, rapid strokes, before going low and taking out the legs of the next one. He had hoped for a glorious battle to end everything, but he realized that his long blade in the confined tunnel was going to make that difficult. The tunnel restricted his movements too much and there were simply too many of them. They rushed forward, pushing him back.

Terion was right behind him, his own sword ready, but there was nothing he could do but wait. Both men fighting side-by-side with blades in a tunnel barely eight feet wide would get them killed before the vampires ever got a chance to end their lives. He winced as one of them got its teeth into his friend's arm. With a howl of anger and pain, Branson slammed the thing's head into the wall, crushing its skull even as several others overwhelmed him and bore him to the ground.

As Branson fell, cursing as he fought, several more vampires leapt over him and went directly at Terion, who had the same luck his friend did. He took down the first two with his sword before the next three slammed him to the ground, burying him under their horrid bodies. Above them, Avenrael screamed in desperation as she saw her husband fall and she yanked a long dagger from her boot.

But before she could drop to the tunnel floor, the air was shattered by a terrifying roar. A huge bulk plummeted past her through the hole, clawed feet slamming into the concrete floor on either side of Terion's head with enough force to leave cracks in the stone. A moment later, the vampires that had taken him down were suddenly gone, crushed into the walls on with such force that their bodies exploded.

Stunned, Terion rolled over and watched the beast pull vampires from the bloodied body of Rick Branson, sending them to the same fate. The surge of monsters seemed to falter and the beast paused only for a moment to glance at Terion.

In that moment, Terion was struck by the familiarity of what faced him. Their savior—for there was no other way to describe it—was humanoid in appearance, but with distinctly dragon-like features. He or it was dressed in loose-fitting clothing of animal skins sewn together— but where it wasn't covered, blue scales gleamed in the light instead of human skin. The most telling thing about the monster was its eyes. Framing a long snout and a mouthful of tearing teeth, the eyes were…human. Terion was reminded of a friend from long ago, a companion who had been given dragon-blood to save her life after she had given hers to save a dragon. In the final battle with Shayene, Arianna had suddenly transformed into a human-like dragon and single-handedly killed a deadly Reaver, saving his friend Notyet's life and enabling them to win the day. But Arianna was white.

This one was blue.

And a whole lot bigger.

With another deafening roar, the creature turned back to the flood of bloodsuckers and charged. The monsters never had a chance. The dragon-thing tore them to pieces or smashed them into the walls and floors in a terrifying frenzy. It drove forward, tearing through their ranks, obliterating the tide and leaving nothing but shattered bodies and body parts in its wake.

Terion crawled over to his friend. Branson's eyes were open, but it was apparent that they would not be for long. His throat was torn and blood ran freely from his wounds. Terion pressed his hands against Branson's throat, hoping to stem the flow. But he knew it was too late. He was already infected. If Branson survived his wounds, he would become that which they had fled from for sixteen years.

"I'm not...I'm...not..." Branson gasped, trying to find the words.

"Shh...," Terion shushed him. "It's going to be alright."

"Don't...lie," Branson whispered as he reached up and gripped Terion's wrist with a bloodied hand. There was already the hint of strength in it that told Terion the change was beginning. "Remember...our... promise," the dying man gasped. "Don't...let..." His eyes closed, his breath coming his shallow gasps.

Terion cried openly as he pulled the dagger from his belt sheath. There was no saving his friend's life. But he could save him from what was to come, a hellish damnation no one should have to face.

He placed the point of the blade against his friend's chest.

Branson's eyes snapped open, black orbs shining with hunger, mouth opening with a hiss and revealing two sharp fangs that seemed to grow longer as he watched.

Terion prepared to shove the blade through his friend's heart, but the voice of a boy stopped him. "Don't," it said gently. "He's not lost yet."

Raising his head, Terion saw a figure step out of the darkness. It was, but it wasn't, the beast that had saved them. The animal skin clothes were the same, but the blue scales were gone, replaced by pale human skin, where it wasn't covered with gore from its rampage through the vampires. He had the look of a young teenager, but had to be nearly seven feet tall. And beneath a tousled mop of hair the color of liquid silver, two eyes stared back at him. They were eyes Terion recognized.

Beneath his blade, Branson suddenly threw his head back and screamed, an inhuman howl that reverberated through the confines of the tunnel. As Branson rose and his claws reached for Terion, the boy roughly shouldered Terion aside and slapped a hand on Branson's chest. Lightning exploded from the boy's hand, slamming Branson's body back to the floor. The blackness in his eyes faded and a moment later, they were the eyes of the man again. Then they slipped closed and a moment later, Rick Branson was dead.

Terion lost track of time, stricken with grief. It was an odd friendship he and Branson had shared, two men from different worlds, thrown together in worlds gone mad. Other than his wife, Branson had become Terion's closest friend when Notyet was lost to him, trapped back on their world in his own quest to find Fyre's sister, Rayne. In Notyet's absence, Branson had become that same kind of friend and they had saved each other's lives several times over in the sixteen years they had been on the run. And now he was gone, as was Dorsey—two old friends dead in the space of an hour.

He suddenly became aware of the boy grabbing his wrists. "Pay attention," the boy was saying, shaking him roughly. "If I bring him back like this, he's going to bleed out and die again. Can you climb the rope?"

"Who…are you?"

"Can you climb the rope?" the boy insisted again and there was a hard edge to his voice. When Terion nodded numbly, the lad stood up and effortlessly hoisted Branson's body up, throwing it over his shoulder. "Meet me up top." With that, he leapt straight up, reaching out and grabbing the lowest available rung, before climbing rapidly up the ladder.

Terion looked up, expecting to see his wife and daughter and Uncle looking down at him. Instead, he saw only a distant light, some fifty feet up. The boy quickly reached it and climbed out of the hole at the top, disappearing from sight. Dazed, and with a sudden realization of where he had seen those eyes before, Terion wasted no time climbing up the rope and then the ladder. When he reached the top, strong hands grasped his wrists and hauled him out of the hole and into a room.

There, Terion stood looking in amazement into the scarred, but grinning, face of his long-lost friend.

Notyet.

Chapter 24

Terion threw his arms around his old friend and hugged him fiercely, unable to believe what was happening. Notyet hugged him back and then tapped him on the head. "I see your hair has gone gray, old man," he teased, indicating Terion's salt and pepper hair, although it was mostly salt these days.

"At least I still have mine," Terion replied through tears of joy, looking at his huge friend's bald pate, before growing somber. "Where's Branson?"

"Zak took him upstairs," Notyet answered, reaching down and swinging closed a thick metal lid that covered the hole. It clanged shut and he spun the huge wheel on top, locking it in place. "No sense in taking any chances," he added, making sure it was tightly sealed. Then he pointed up the stairs. "Come on, let's see if she can save him."

Before Terion could ask who *she* was, Notyet hurried up a set of metal stairs. Terion followed, stepping out into a brightly lit room, candles set all about and a fire burning in a fireplace. He saw a long metal table, and upon the table lay Branson's body. A woman, every bit as tall as Notyet, was leaning over him, her hands busy at the marine's damaged throat. Avenrael stood next to her, her shocked eyes alternating between Branson's body and the woman's face.

As comprehension began to dawn on Terion, Notyet reached out and patted the boy on the back. "Any problems, Zak?" Notyet asked easily.

"No, Pops," the young man replied, looking back with eyes that were exactly like his father's. "I ran them back to the end of the tunnel. Looks like your friends collapsed the opening, but the vamps had dug out a section at the top and were coming through there."

"Did you plug it?"

"Best I could, but if they're onto us, they'll eventually get back through. I can go back down and clear it again later, if you want."

"We'll keep the hole sealed for now," Notyet replied. "That will hold them back for a while, but if trackers are pushing them, they've got access to firepower that I'd just as soon not mess with. We better get ready to move out."

"Pops?" Terion muttered in surprise as he stepped toward the table to get a better view of the woman who was working on Branson. He saw that she was stitching the wound in his neck, her hands nearly a blur as she worked.

"Zak!" she said suddenly. "Get ready!"

The boy immediately placed his right hand on Branson's chest. It was obvious they had done this before.

"Now!" she commanded, raising her hands free from her patient.

Lightning flared from the boy's hand with a sizzling crack, slamming into Branson's chest and bouncing his body off the table. Branson twitched once and went still.

"Again!" the woman cried, hands still in the air, eyes still on Branson's form.

Zak obeyed, sending another jolt into Branson. This time, a cough and a low moan escaped Branson's blue-tinged lips and the woman's hands roamed over the man's stitched throat, pressing gently. Finding a weak pulse, she nodded satisfactorily and then went back to work on the man's other wounds, most of them on his shoulders and arms. She worked silently and slower now, stitching up what she could and bandaging the rest. Terion watched in awe, as much at what she had done for his friend as who she was. He could not believe it.

It was Zarandrae.

"I believe you've already met my wife," Notyet finally said with a toothy grin, looking at both Terion and Avenrael. Both continued to stare at Zarandrae in shock. "Fortunately, the years have mellowed her," he added, gently touching the woman's cheek, still grinning widely.

"Har har," Zarandrae smirked playfully.

"We've obviously got a lot to talk about," Notyet went on as he clapped his old friend on the back. Zarandrae looked up briefly and offered Terion a warm smile, before going back to work on her patient. Branson's eyes remained closed, but color was creeping back into his face and his chest now rose and fell with life. She had really done it. Zarandrae had brought him back.

"Come on, you two," Notyet urged, motioning them to follow him through a doorway and into another room. Dumbfounded, Terion and Avenrael finally tore their eyes away and followed. The living room, such as it was, was a collection of tables and chairs, most of them piled with camping gear, weapons, and other useful items needed to survive the harsh lands they all lived in now. Uncle and Fyre were already in the room, standing around a small corner table off to the side and excitedly thumbing through a pile of musty old books. Fyre was quite obviously in heaven.

"Welcome to our humble home, temporary as it might be," Notyet said warmly. With his mother no longer needing his help, Zak ambled out of the back room and joined Fyre and Uncle at the table.

"Zak?" Terion questioned, pointing to the big lad as he joined his daughter.

"That's our boy," the big man replied, tousling the lad's hair as he passed. "Go on, have a seat," he went on, grabbing a couple of rusty metal folding chairs and setting them out. "I already met Fyre. Glad you were able to find her and her mom. I know what that had to mean to you, Terion."

Terion nodded and smiled; words were unnecessary. He saw in

Notyet's eyes for his wife, Zarandrae, the same passion he held for his own.

"And he's called Uncle, is it?" Notyet asked, looking at the other middle-aged man.

Uncle held up a book and touched his forehead with it, indicating Notyet was correct.

"Uncle doesn't remember much of his past life," Terion explained. "We found him when we raided Shayene's apartment to rescue Fyre. That was sixteen years ago," he mused. "And all we really know about him is that he came from our world and that he's a gatekeeper."

"A gatekeeper?" Notyet asked, eyes widening in amazement. "Seriously? Why haven't you gone back, then?"

"No focus," Uncle spoke up, tapping his head again. "Whatever Shayene did to me, she took my memories. I have only the barest recollections of people and things, shadows mostly, but nothing to latch onto in order to anchor a gateway."

"Damn, that's too bad," Notyet groaned. "Almost had my hopes up there for a bit. And I sure wouldn't miss this place," he added, looking around, wrinkling his craggy face up in distaste. He turned back to Terion. "Anyway, I imagine you've got lots of questions. So how about we get to it."

Still reeling, both Terion and Avenrael nodded. They waited for Notyet to settle himself into a threadbare chair, where he sighed, leaned back, and then told his tale.

"It all started with Rayne," he began, looking sadly at Avenrael. "Might as well get this part out right off the bat. I know you're wanting to know."

"Is she...dead?" the Vi'Raaji asked in a pained whisper.

"Sixteen years ago, the answer was no," he answered. "We were able to track her down. Well, it was all Zarandrae really. She had the insight to know where to look after we found Shayene's keep in the Wraithlands deserted." Notyet then went on to tell them the entire story, cumulating in their confrontation with Kraegor and the demon succubus. He left out only the specifics where the demon, M'Zabareth, was acting as Rayne's surrogate mother, wanting to spare Avenrael the anguish of knowing that something had replaced her. "We didn't stand a chance," he admitted helplessly. "He sent everything he had at us and, by the time we got to the chamber where we found them, we were practically dying. Unfortunately, even if we hadn't been, we could not have stood against the combined might of both a corrupted dragon and a demon lord."

"What happened?" Terion asked.

"Kraegor attacked Zarandrae with his magic," Notyet replied quietly, his face growing darker. "Tried stealing her soul. I honestly don't remember much myself because of that damned succubus, but I was conscious enough to know that Zara began to transform and, when that happened, Rayne woke up." He looked at Avenrael again. "From what Terion told me about what happened to you, it sounds like it happened pretty much the same way to us. Rayne woke up and sparked a portal that sucked us in. We ended up here, on this world," he finished, looking around again. "Been here ever since."

"So Rayne is truly lost to us," Avenrael breathed, deeply sad. It had been sixteen long years without any knowledge of what had happened to her other daughter and, while this new knowledge wasn't easy to accept, she had long ago understood she would likely never see her child again.

"No way to tell," Notyet replied honestly, "but I would guess she's probably still alive. Kraegor laid claim to her as her father. He told us exactly that. I know that's difficult to hear, but I don't think he would kill her, if he took the time to kidnap her."

Avenrael was silent, sorrow evident in her eyes. Fyre walked over to her and knelt, laying her head on her mother's lap, her young face stricken. She had as much of a stake in Rayne's fate as anyone, and the knowledge of what had happened, or might have happened, to her twin sister was not easy for her to accept. Avenrael stroked her daughter's hair and leaned forward to gently kiss her cheek.

Behind them, Zarandrae walked into the room, drying her hands on a piece of cloth. She had been listening while she worked on Branson. "We would have given our lives to either save your child or spare her a life living under the hand of Kraegor," she said softly, directly to Avenrael. "But the portal sent us away before we could do anything. For that, I am truly sorry."

Avenrael looked up and studied the woman. She had never had any direct contact with Zarandrae in the past, but she understood very clearly what the woman would have gone through to go from an enemy to an ally. It was the very same journey she had undertaken with Terion. The fact that Zarandrae was a dragon likely made it even more difficult for her.

"How's Branson doing?" Terion asked Zarandrae hopefully.

"Your friend will live," she answered, tossing the towel onto a stack of gear. "The worst of his wounds was the one at his neck, but luckily, his carotid artery was not severed. He lost some blood, but not enough to kill him. I was able to sew it up before Zak brought him back. He'll be weak for some time, but he should be okay."

"He won't turn?" Terion asked carefully.

"They only turn completely if they feed and, unfortunately, most do," she answered. "We have learned over the years that if they are bitten, but die before feeding, the sickness in them dies as well. They can then be brought back as human with the right measures, providing you get to them immediately."

"That makes sense," Terion said softly, looking at Avenrael and remembering the terrible time he had thought that he had lost her the same way. "That's what happened to Avenrael when we first found her. She was already turning when Shayene killed her, but Dorsey, our friend, brought her back. He called it CPR."

"We have learned that, too," Zarandrae agreed. "At one time, we had a physician from this world with us, and he taught us that electricity was the best way to restart a silent heart. As you can see," she added, nodding toward her son. "Zak is rather adept at that."

"What happened to the doctor?"

"Same thing that happens to most people," Notyet answered, his voice low. "They die or get killed. Sometimes, they want to go off on their own. Too many of them crave being with their own kind, so they end up trying to join up with larger groups and that never works out."

"We've dealt with the same," Terion nodded, thinking back to their near disaster far to the south.

"Can I ask you a question?" Avenrael asked, looking at Zarandrae.

"Sure," she answered warmly, seating herself on a battered stool next to Avenrael. The woman was tall and imposing, but there was a kindness that seemed to radiate from her.

"If it's not too personal, how did you end up with Notyet?" Avenrael asked, needing something to hold back her own raw emotions concerning Rayne.

"He came to me and asked me to help him," Zarandrae replied, turning and smiling warmly at the scarred warrior. "He trusted me, when no one else would."

"Is it difficult, being a dragon and so much more long-lived than us?"

At that, Zarandrae's smile disappeared, replaced with sadness. "I don't really know," she began to explain and then faltered.

"She lost her powers," Notyet took over the explanation while looking at his wife with concern. "When we found Rayne, we also found that Kraegor had become strong in ways we didn't quite expect or understand. Trying to steal the dragon out of Zara was something we could never have guessed he could do."

"And he succeeded," Avenrael guessed.

"He did," Notyet replied. "But before he did, Zarandrae attempted one last transformation and it looked like she was going to be able to pull it off. Then Rayne woke up and sparked the portal."

"And you cannot do it anymore?"

"No," Zarandrae answered. "I don't know whether Kraegor actually succeeded or whether it's just a part of me being on this world rather than my own. But I can no longer become my true self."

"What about Zak?" Terion asked, looking at the young man, who was now sitting with his back in the corner, his eyes gazing at Fyre with something between curiosity and affection.

"He is the son of a dragon and a human—our son," Notyet answered. "Truthfully, we didn't know what would happen when Zarandrae told me she was with child. But Zak's birth was normal, if you can consider a baby being born in this forsaken world, normal."

"His ability to transform is remarkable," Terion said. "It reminds me of what happened with Arianna before she died."

"Don't I know it," Notyet agreed, touching his throat and wincing at the memory of having it torn out by a reaver. Arianna had been the one to save him.

"So when did you find out about Zak?"

"He was about six, I guess. We had been on the run for a while, but a group of trackers found us. They tried taking us themselves and might have succeeded if not for Zak. One of them got a shot on Zarandrae and all of a sudden, Zak wasn't quite Zak anymore."

"What happened?"

"He got pissed off and changed. Tore them to bits," Notyet shrugged and looked at his son proudly. "Saved our lives. When it was over, he transformed back like it was nothing and Zarandrae started working with him, helping him control his dragon essence."

"Well, I saw what he did in the tunnel," Terion said. "He's rather effective at fighting the vampires."

"That he is," Notyet agreed proudly. "What's more, he has immunity to them, too, so they can't turn him."

"Really? How'd you find that out?"

"He likes to hunt them, and he's been bitten more times than I can count," Notyet chuckled. "We definitely sleep a little better at night. But more importantly, because of who he is, I have to believe that Kraegor didn't succeed when he attacked Zarandrae, and that somewhere deep inside her, she's still got that dragon piece intact. I mean, it's part of her and she deserves to have it back."

"But in the meantime, I grow older as a human," Zarandrae added, looking fondly at Notyet. "It is not something that I am accustomed to, but perhaps that is how it is meant to be. If I can grow old with my husband, then I am content. I will have lived the journey my kind has always desired."

"Who knows, maybe one of these days we can find a place to settle in for a spell," Notyet added. "It would be nice to stop running."

There were murmurs of agreement from the others and Terion watched as Fyre got up and sat next to Zak. They began talking quietly together and Terion smiled, knowing how true Notyet's words were. To live in a world without having to run anymore—wasn't that what they were all looking for?

"What about your story?" Notyet asked, catching Terion's attention. "Shame that Branson got tore up again. He's got enough scars that he doesn't need anymore."

"He's a good man," Terion said and then looked at Zarandrae. "You have my gratitude for saving him. Thank you."

Zarandrae offered him a smile.

"How did you end up blocking the tunnel entrance?" Notyet asked. "We knew it was locked and figured that would keep the bloodsuckers out. But we sawed off the lower ladder rungs in the hole, just in case."

"That almost got us killed, by the way," Terion pointed out.

"Well, I didn't exactly expect your kind of company to come knocking on our back door."

Terion chuckled and said, "We had a friend with us. Dorsey. Old guy that helped us rescue Avenrael and Fyre all those years ago. He'd been with us ever since."

"Did he die in the tunnel?" Notyet guessed.

"He was the one that blew it up," was the answer. "He died making sure we had a chance to escape."

"Tell me about him."

Terion did, filling in the last sixteen years of their lives, from the moment he and Branson stepped through the gateway into Dorsey's house. He told of their rescue of Avenrael and then Fyre and how Dorsey had saved their lives after Uncle had ported them away from certain death at the hands of Shayene.

"We've been on the run for sixteen years," Terion finished. "It's been a hard life, but I can't complain. I couldn't ask to be with better people. But it's going to be hard to let him go. He was family."

"I know the feeling, my friend. We've lost friends over the years, too," Notyet said, his eyes distant as he remembered others. "Living in this world is never easy, and it's even harder knowing that the world is dying around us."

"Shayene got what she wanted—a world completely devoted to her," Terion sighed, a look of bitterness crossing his face.

"She wants more than that," Zarandrae corrected. "She still wants our world. She only waits for the convergence, just as she did when she began all this madness. And the convergence would put her back there with an army of millions, again just as she planned."

"Assuming anyone survives."

"She is counting on many people living through it," Zarandrae went on. "So she hunts down survivors on this world to make her own, while continuing to look for all of us."

"Why?" Avenrael asked, a frown on her face. "She cannot know any of us are still alive, can she?"

"She does," Notyet confirmed. "She knows that there is dragon blood on this world and so she actively seeks us out. You don't honestly think this is a chance meeting between us, do you?"

"I guess…well, I hadn't given that any thought yet," Terion admitted.

"When we came through the gate, it didn't take us long to realize that we were on the same world that you were," Notyet explained. "It was a simple act of figuring out the common occurrence in what happened to us and what happened to you," he nodded toward Avenrael. "That, and Branson's descriptions of his world, convinced us we were here. So, Zarandrae started searching with her senses, seeking the essence of another dragon. Fyre has dragon blood in her and logically, probably has the same abilities that Zak has."

Both Terion and Avenrael looked up at their daughter, while Fyre looked surprised.

"She has shown no signs of that type of power," Avenrael said cautiously. "Is it truly possible?"

"I wouldn't see why not," Notyet shrugged. "Whether or not she does, though, doesn't mean she doesn't have that blood within her. And Zarandrae can sense it."

"So you knew we were in the cabin?" Terion asked incredulously.

"Actually, we've been close to finding you a couple of times over the years," he answered. "Zarandrae would pick up a faint sense of Fyre, but usually it disappeared before we could zero in. When you guys moved, you moved fast and far."

"Aye," Terion said in amazement.

"We found this place here a few weeks ago and Zarandrae only recently sensed Fyre again. As it got stronger, we realized you were moving in our direction, and were making plans to go out and find you. The luck was in you breaking into the tunnel and ending up at our back door instead. The rest you know."

"So Shayene is tracking us the same way?" Terion reasoned.

"She has been tracking all of us that way," Zarandrae replied. "She can sense Zak and probably me, as well as Fyre. And she is an Arcai, so her abilities far exceed mine. My guess is that she uses her vampires as extensions of her, so she is able to search greater areas for signs of us."

"That would explain why we can never settle down for any length of time."

"And the fact that so many of them came after you tonight, makes me think she's definitely zeroed in," Notyet added. "So we'll need to move out again quickly."

"Are you thinking about leaving tomorrow?" Terion asked.

"Probably, but we'll get a good night's sleep and decide in the morning," he answered. "You haven't been outside, but this place is pretty defensible. It sits right near the peak of the mountain and up against a sheer rock face. They'd have to throw a lot at us from one direction to have much of a chance of breaching the doors. I'm more worried about the tunnel, though. If there are any trackers running with the packs in the area, they could blow us up from below without ever having to approach from outside."

"Fair enough."

"The place is small," Notyet went on, directing his comments to all of them, "but it has a couple of rooms off to the side. It'll be cozy, but we can get a good night's sleep. There's plenty of blankets in the rooms, too, so no one will freeze."

The reunited friends talked for another couple hours, sharing tales of what had happened to them over the years, as well as insights into how they could avoid Shayene. While Uncle immersed himself in one of the books he had found and Zak and Fyre huddled in a corner, whispering to each other, the talk between the adults turned to their families and of what it was like trying to raise their children in such a dangerous world.

Eventually, as talking turned to yawning, Notyet ordered everyone to bed and then settled near the door, listening to the silence of the night.

A short time later, the decision to leave immediately was made for them.

He had been settled in on watch for an hour when the noises began; shuffling sounds outside the front door and voices echoing from the sealed tunnel. There was no doubt that trackers had breached the tunnel below and the fact that they were doing nothing to keep their voices hidden, meant they knew their prey was trapped.

"Everybody up," Notyet whispered, moving quickly through the darkened rooms and rousing all of them. "They've found us."

"No chance to escape?" Terion asked, immediately on the alert.

"No," Notyet shook his head as he picked up a large metal hammer from a pile of gear next to the fireplace. "Trackers have the tunnels covered. You can hear 'em through the trapdoor. We'll have to go out the front and deal with what's out there."

"That's probably what they want us to do," Terion pointed out.

"Maybe, but I don't see any way around it. If I knew the tunnels were clear, I'd be content to bunker down here and defend, knowing we could escape out the back door if needed. But with the tunnel breached, we're going to have to clear the front and leave that way."

"Want me to run the tunnel again, Pops?" Zak spoke up hopefully, looking toward the stairs leading down to the cellar.

"No," it was Zarandrae who replied. "Those are trackers down there, not vampires. Humans will have weapons."

"Your mom's right," Notyet added. "We'll do better outside."

"Can we hold the building at all?" Avenrael asked, her ear to the door as she listened to the shuffling sounds outside.

"Depends on how many are out there. Won't matter, though, if the trackers bring in heavy weapons. Like I said earlier, if they want, they can blow the tunnel and us along with it. We best be out of here before it comes to that."

"Shh!" Avenrael suddenly said, her features tight. Everyone was silent as she listened, her eyes closed in concentration. When she opened them, her face was lined with concern and she quickly moved away from the door. "Here they come!" she shouted.

Even as she said it, there was an unearthly howl from outside as the creatures began hurling themselves recklessly against the building. The walls shook and glass from behind boarded up windows could be heard shattering. The door frame began to shake as the creatures beat on it relentlessly, trying to break down the heavy wood.

"Terion, help me with this!" Notyet exclaimed, rushing over to a large chest of drawers. He pulled it away from the wall and started sliding it toward the door. Terion joined him and together they shoved it against the door just as the wood began to splinter.

"I thought you said this place was defensible!" Terion shouted over the pounding.

"Against a few, yes! Sounds like a bloody army out there!"

"Do you have any guns?"

"No ammo," Notyet replied, which was the same issue that Terion and his group had. Guns were still plentiful and could be found in a lot of places. Most ammunition in the world, though, was gone; used up or no longer viable.

A clawed hand punched through the door just above the edge of the dresser and Notyet smashed it flat with his hammer, leaving a black smear on the wood. The howls only got louder, and suddenly they were above them, too. Overhead, scrabbling feet and tearing claws accompanied the growing din.

"They're on the roof!" Uncle cried out, throwing his arms over his head as if that would protect him.

"We can't stay here!" Terion shouted desperately, looking at his old friend. "There has to be another way out!"

Near one corner of the main room, pieces of ceiling began to fall. The vampires had already torn through the worn shingles and were ripping at the wood. They would be through in moments. Above them, cracks appeared from the corner, spreading across the ceiling. Suddenly, the wood splintered and the first body came through. The creature hit the floor and leapt forward, only to be smashed down by Notyet's hammer. Another followed and then two more and suddenly, the battle was on. Zak took the brunt of the attack, his body morphing into his dragon form and he tore into the creatures with a defiant roar.

"To the basement," Notyet yelled.

"The trackers will be waiting for us if we try to escape through the tunnel," Zarandrae reminded him.

"We have no choice. There's too many of them to go out the

front. We'll have to take our chances with the trackers."

As they moved to the back room, Zak tore the head from one of the vampires and then leapt up through the hole, blasting a group of monsters from the roof.

"Zak, no!" Zarandrae shouted in anguish, rushing back toward the breach.

A moment later, everything stopped, and there was only silence.

"Zak!" Zarandrae yelled again, her voice unduly harsh in the sudden quiet.

A moment later, the boy dropped back down through the hole, his body shifting seamlessly back to human. Zarandrae threw her arms around him, but he pushed her back toward the stairs. "We gotta go, Mom," he said quietly, fear in his voice.

"What happened?" Terion asked.

"They left," the boy replied. "Just went back into the trees."

"Then what…"

"There's something else out there," he added. "Something really big. I could see it in the trees. But it was just standing there."

"But why would the vampires leave?" Terion wondered. "That's not how they usually act."

"They are being controlled," Avenrael said quietly, moving up to stand beside her husband. She placed a hand on his shoulder, her eyes haunted and for the first time in many years, Terion saw fear in her eyes. "She's here."

"Who's here?" Notyet asked.

"Shayene."

"Are you kidding me? How could she be way out here already?"

"It is the only explanation," Avenrael answered. "I have felt her power and I know the hunger those creatures feel. They will only stop at her command. Nothing else can control them like this."

Notyet walked back toward the hole in the ceiling, when Uncle grabbed his arm, stopping him.

"Wait! What's…that?" Uncle asked, his eyes locked on Notyet's weapon.

The big warrior lifted the battered hammer and showed it to him. "Skull crushers are better than blades in close quarters when fighting bloodsuckers, but we don't have time for a lesson right now."

"No, that," Uncle said, pointing to the thin battered necklace and pendant that were wrapped snugly around the haft above the warrior's hand.

"Oh," Notyet said quietly. "We found it in the Wraithlands near the skeleton of a child."

"I…know that pendant," Uncle said slowly, mesmerized as he gazed at the battered medallion. "I…I think…I remember."

Notyet looked at him in shock and Zarandrae spoke up. "You were once in Shayene's keep," she said breathlessly. "You were her prisoner! I remember Draven talking about you!"

Notyet gently unwound the necklace, which once was gold and now was tarnished, bent and battered. The tiny little pendant in the shape of a world still hung from it. He held it out to the man.

Uncle gently took it, letting it drape over his calloused hand. He sucked in his breath and suddenly, he did remember. The dam inside his head broke and he remembered it all. Everything Shayene had taken from him came roaring back. He recalled his father, forced to open the gate to the Nether and brutally murdered to give the gate permanence and hasten the weakening of the barrier. He remembered his mother and his siblings; how Shayene had tortured and killed them to force his father to do her bidding. "My sister," he whispered, tears springing to his eyes as he continued to stare at the pendant. "Kya. This was hers. She was…only four."

"Uncle," Terion said gently. He laid his hand on the man's shoulder. "You can take us home."

The man looked up, tears streaming down his cheek. "I can," he agreed, gripping the necklace tighter in his hand. He climbed to his feet as the howling began anew outside. "I can," he said again, his voice louder.

"Come!" Uncle shouted and he herded them into the back room where Branson still lay unconscious on the table. Gathering everyone around, he fell into his magic, willing it to come to life inside of him. For sixteen years, his true power had lain dormant with no connection to his own world. Now, with his sister's necklace in hand and the memories of her and his family reclaimed, it blossomed to life with power that made his hair stand on end.

A shuttering crash hit the door in the main room as something big slammed into it, shoving the heavy dresser back several inches.

Uncle ignored it, closing his eyes and pulling the magic from his core, letting it flow from his outstretched hands.

The door splintered from the next crash and the dresser began to tip over. Notyet and Terion rushed back into the front room and shoved their shoulders against it, wanting to give Uncle the precious seconds he needed to complete the spell.

He did and moments later, it bloomed into existence, a pulsing circle of energy. Darkness lay beyond it, but they all knew they had no choice. They had to flee.

"Go!" Terion yelled to the others, keeping his back to the dresser to hold against the onslaught. The next hit almost sent him sprawling. "Go! Get them out of here! I'm right behind you!" he yelled to Notyet. The others stepped through the portal and vanished. Notyet rushed into the back room, scooped Branson up in his arms and leapt through the gate, vanishing into blackness.

The creature hit the door a fourth and final time, sending the dresser and shards of wood flying into the room. Terion stumbled forward and hurried toward the pulsing gate. He never slowed, wrapping his arms around Uncle's waist and diving through the portal, taking them both through the gate.

The magic snapped shut behind them as the enemy breached the room, a massive form of raw power and pure hatred. It was huge, easily eight-feet tall, corded muscles defining its entire body. Huge slavering jaws opened and closed in expectation, exposing sharpened teeth that could tear limbs and crush bones. Once just a man, its creator had used her magic and a good bit of this world's remaining science over the years to carefully shape it into the thing that it was today. It was Shayene's greatest weapon; her greatest hunter. None could stand against it. It was a true killing machine and it obeyed her every command.

Shayene followed the monster into the small cabin and looked around. When she had known for certain that her prey had finally been located, she had personally come to reclaim the girl once and for all. She had planned to let her hunter kill Terion and any who stood with him.

But now?

She walked into the back room, pausing to run her fingers along the bloodied table where someone injured had recently laid. She sensed the residual gateway magic in the air and understood it completely. Her prey had been here and somehow, her gatekeeper had reclaimed his power. She wondered what had restored his memory, as she had carefully removed his entire past to make certain he could never use it to return home. But somehow, he had just done so and taken her enemies and the girl with him. Closing her eyes, she reached out with her senses, sending her magic through her nearby minions, seeking any sign of the fugitives, just to be certain. There was nothing.

Nothing except…

She opened her eyes as she felt the ground begin to rumble beneath her, a slight tremor that briefly shook the mountain before going still. She smiled. She understood. They had indeed escaped. They had gone home. But no matter. The gatekeeper's magic had plucked the last tenuous string holding the worlds apart and had finally snapped it. Now, nothing could hold the two worlds apart. The tremors would begin again and grow in frequency and strength. In time, two worlds would become one.

The convergence had begun.

The fall of the gods was finally at hand.

Epilogue

A chill wind blew through the cavernous chamber as Kraegor the Black turned slowly from the ravaged and dying body pinned to the stone wall behind him. The hulking form of a vicious reaver stood quietly nearby, waiting for another command from its master. A questioning "chuff" rumbled from its throat and the human-form dragon absently waved a hand in response. Black tendrils of dark magic leapt up from the floor, swirling about the monster until, with a sizzling pop, it vanished, leaving behind only a wisp of greasy smoke.

A low moan from the mangled victim turned Kraegor's attention back to the wall. He looked at her and flashed a smile filled with rotted teeth. His power had grown significantly over the years since his return from the Nether and there were none that could stand against him anymore. But his body was beginning to decay, something that even M'Zabareth could not reverse.

"I give you credit, my child," he rasped, leering wickedly at the dying girl on the wall. "Your tolerance for pain and your tenacity to cling to your miserable existence is somewhat...admirable."

The young girl attempted to mumble a response, but her words were indecipherable, blood bubbling from her ragged lips.

Kraegor stepped closer, peering into his charge's battered face, reading her thoughts. "You wish to die?" he questioned, his tone sour. "Surely you have not come this far to give up now." He tapped a long black fingernail against her forehead, emphasizing his point. "It would be a shame to let one so full of promise pass from this world." He turned away, feigning a sigh, but clearly enjoying his game.

Behind him, Rayne raised her head and fought to keep her eyes open. Darkness was swirling through her consciousness and she knew her time was close at hand. Part of her wished to die, forever this time, and to be free of the torment and agony she suffered. But something held on. It always held on, her will to live, always refusing to let go. It was that will that drove the single word from her blood-caked lips.

"Revenge."

Kraegor paused, savoring the pain and fear that emanated from her, and he longed to taste her dying blood, for he knew it would be rich indeed. But there was something far more important at stake than simply feasting on her life force, tempting as it was. The convergence had arrived. He had felt the rumblings of the earth and the discordant tones of magic, foretelling the coming cataclysm. Something had severed the last strand of the barrier and it was unraveling quickly now. Time was short.

But through Rayne, he could bring about something far greater than the destruction of two worlds. He could use her to bring about a cataclysm that would claim *all* worlds, leaving him to rule over every soul that had ever been created. Every person and creature that had ever lived on any world; every god and Arcai that had ever existed—all would eventually bow to him. Then, so great would be his power, that he would challenge the One Himself. And the One would fall, leaving only him. He would no longer be *just* a god. He would be *the* God.

He looked at Rayne as she hung from a metal spike protruding from the stone wall, impaled there by the reaver's attack. Daughter or not, the long years of torture she had suffered at his hands had been done to hone her hatred and turn her into the weapon that he knew he would need. He had built her, molded her until she possessed a driving will above anything that he had ever seen; a desire to embrace power, regardless of the consequences.

"M'Zabareth!" he called, watching dispassionately as a single tear rolled down the girl's bloody cheek.

The succubus appeared at his side immediately, stepping out of a swirl of purple smoke. She looked up at Rayne and then clucked her tongue in distaste. "Must you always be so brutal with her?" she asked, reaching up and placing a hand over the girl's heart as she felt for her life force. It was there. Faint and faltering, but there.

"It is the only way she will be prepared to face her sister," Kraegor replied without a trace of emotion. "She must hate her completely. She must desire to destroy her utterly, for Fyre is the only one who can thwart our plans."

"Well, she lives, at least," the demon said, sounding almost bored.

"Of course she lives," Kraegor snapped dismissively as he turned away. "See to it that she is healed."

M'Zabareth cast a long withering look at the dragon and then went to work on her adopted daughter, pulling her down from the killing spike that had pierced her chest. Blood poured from the wound and the demon felt the young girl begin to slip away, her heart slowing as death tried to claim her again. But M'Zabareth fell into her magic, weaving the wounds closed as she had done countless times before, once again driving death away.

As she carried the girl from the arena, she let her mind linger in Rayne's tortured consciousness, sampling the nightmares that plagued her, adding to them as only she could. She might deplore Kraegor's vicious brutality toward their daughter, but she understood that only this way, could they adequately prepare Rayne to meet her destiny. She would have to face her sister and kill her, if she was to accomplish her final task. The Nexus. For everything to come to pass as they had designed, the Nexus would have to be destroyed.

And Rayne would be the only one who could do it.

Rayne felt consciousness return, but she lay still in the darkness, allowing wakefulness to come slowly. Her thoughts were jumbled. She remembered the torturous *training*—a term her father used—and she vividly remembered nearly dying again, one of the hundreds of terrible ends she had endured at his behest. She had strength and power and was already an accomplished sorceress at sixteen, stronger than most. With her magical abilities, she could easily defeat the creatures that her father forced her to face. But in most cases, he expressly forbade her to use her magic, instead requiring her to rely on her human-side physical prowess and speed. Occasionally, she was able to evade her attackers long enough that Kraegor would call an end to the trial, if he didn't summon additional monsters to join in the attack. Most times, though, she would tire as more and more challengers were thrown at her. The outcome was always the same. She ended up either dead or dying, followed by rebirth or healing at the hands of her surrogate mother. Time and time again, M'Zabareth would bring her back, only to stand aside while her father tortured her into oblivion once more.

Rayne considered the demon and struggled with who and what the succubus was to her. M'Zabareth always professed her love for her adopted daughter and was generally kind to her. But Rayne knew better. She knew when the demon was in her mind, sifting through her thoughts. She knew about the nightmares, the loss, the betrayal, the rage; everything the succubus helped plant and nurture within her. And yet, despite the knowledge of these things, she was powerless to resist. When M'Zabareth commanded her to hate her real mother and her sister, she did so without question. As both the demon and the dragon continued to prepare her to kill her family, she knew she would do so without hesitation and would enjoy doing it.

But the real question was, when would this happen? When would she face the mother who had abandoned her to this horrible fate; the mother who preferred the sister she had never seen, over her?

"All in good time, little one," the dragon's voice cackled, reading her thoughts as he always did. "All in good time."

Rayne slowly opened her eyes to find Kraegor's now nightmarish visage leaning over her. His skin had rotted through in most places on his face, showing tendons and tatters of gangrenous flesh still stretched over bone. His transformation into the abomination before her had been gradual over the years, changing him from a handsome man into a rotted corpse. His true form as a dragon, something she had witnessed only twice, was even worse. Revulsion ran through her but she held it carefully in check. Her first words, however, gave little doubt to what was on her mind. "What next?"

Kraegor smiled that horrible smile again. "What? Not even a wish for water?" he chided. "After all, you haven't had a drink in days."

"Water is for the weak," she said emotionlessly.

"Very good, my child," Kraegor replied. "Still, you are mortal, and magic can sustain you for only so long. You are in need of sustenance."

Rayne slowly raised herself to her elbows, feeling her body move with no ill effects. She looked down at her chest, seeing no trace of the hole that had been driven through her by the spike on the wall. She traced a finger between her small breasts, marveling once again that the demon was able to heal her without even a hint of a scar. At least on the outside.

"Yes, yes," continued the dragon, his tone disinterested. "You are whole again. M'Zabareth does impeccable work." He turned away, chuckling to himself, and then pointed to the open chest near the foot of the bed she was laying on. "Clothe yourself. We have work to do."

The fact that she was naked bothered Rayne not at all. Modesty was for single-minded slave fodder, not her. Nevertheless, she slipped off the bed and padded over to the chest. She was mildly surprised to see the black silk robes folded neatly within. They were plain and unadorned, but very different from the rough wool tunics and breeches she was accustomed to wearing. More importantly, they signified something had changed. These were in good order and the fabric was cool and soothing as she slipped it over her newly-healed body.

"Now you look somewhat presentable," said Kraegor as he pointed through the adjoining doorway. "You will find food in the next room. However, you will also find several other items laid out on the table. Choose what you will and then meet me in the arena for your final test."

Rayne looked slightly confused. "What is there to choose from?"

Kraegor checked his patience. It was holding, but just barely. "What you choose will determine your destiny. Choose correctly and your power can be limitless. Choose incorrectly and your sister will kill you, if I don't kill you first." With that, he stalked out of the room.

Rayne watched him leave and then slipped out after him. As promised, there was bread and cheese, along with a bottle of wine on the table. But she ignored the food and gazed at the other items that lay spread out. Several daggers, a beautiful bow, swords, a shield, some pieces of armor, rings, wands—anything an adventurer could wish for. She realized that someone walking around with even half this plunder would be a force to be feared.

Looking over the treasure slowly, she allowed her thoughts to focus. Throughout her trials, she had wished and fought for power, and that power was now vastly arrayed before her, in many guises and forms. To others, the choice would be difficult. But to Rayne, her decision was easy and with that, she reached out for her new weapon.

Kraegor stood silently in the center of the arena, the same room where he had tortured the poor girl for so many years. He noted how her blood still stained the walls and the floors. He felt it added a nice touch. Allowing himself to savor the past taste of her fear and pain, he lost himself for a moment and only became aware of her presence a second before her magical lightning hit him between the shoulder blades, driving him awkwardly forward. A smile played at his lips as he straightened and slowly turned to face his protégé.

She had taken only one thing from the gifts he had offered. It was a small musty leather bag which now hung at her side, a pouch he knew to hold some moldy spell components and talismans, items used only to enhance magic. Perhaps there was more to this little girl than he had originally thought.

"Congratulations," he whispered, his face cracking in a most horrible grin. "You chose correctly."

His hands flew forward and sizzling dark power shot from his outstretched fingers, slamming directly into Rayne's chest. The force of the attack lifted her clear of the floor and slammed her backward into the wall, narrowly missing impaling her on one of the blood-crusted spikes again. As the magic faded, she slumped to the floor and was still.

Kraegor watched expectantly as the girl then slowly climbed to her feet, the front of her new silk robes burned away, their charred edges still glowing and her tender flesh blackened and burnt. She was oblivious to it and her eyes flashed dangerously as she drew herself up to her full height. Her face was twisted with rage and hate, and she spit contemptuously on the floor, her gaze never leaving the powerful master before her. The challenge was unmistakable.

The undead dragon grinned widely and chuckled. "Very good, child," he hissed. "You have passed your final test. Now, it is time to prepare you for the world."

"What do you wish of me?" she snarled, wishing only to kill him.

"Your sister has returned from her long exile," he answered, still smiling. "So has your mother."

"I am to kill them," Rayne stated flatly.

"In time," Kraegor replied. "Do what you will with your mother when you find her, but you may find use for your sister before the time comes to kill her."

"I do not understand."

"War is about to begin and your presence will be required on the battlefield," Kraegor explained. "I believe you will find that you and your sister will have a common enemy."

"I am to ally with her?" Rayne asked furiously.

"To attain the final prize, yes," Kraegor growled. "Remember who your master is, child. You will do exactly what I command you to do."

"And then?"

"Once we have dealt with our enemies, you may kill her at your leisure," he answered. "Then, you will face your greatest challenge, a task that only you can accomplish. You must bring about the end of the Nexus."

Rayne knew what the Nexus was, as Kraegor and M'Zabareth had spoken of it to her many times. She didn't know and didn't care why they wanted it destroyed, only that they expected her to do it—not that she had any intention of obeying when the time came. "How will I accomplish this task?"

"You will need to find a special man, a being of two worlds. He possesses the only power strong enough to destroy the magic of the Nexus. You will find him and force him to complete his destiny. Only you can do this."

Rayne bowed her head, folding her magically tattooed hands before her. "As you wish," she said emotionlessly and then turned away. As she walked out of the arena, she knew she meant nothing of the sort. All she cared about was killing her sister and her mother.

When she had obtained her vengeance for being abandoned, she had no intention of doing her father's further bidding. Instead, she would return and kill him, too, and then truly be free.

Have a care with your thoughts, daughter, M'Zabareth's voice sounded inside her head. *If you truly wish to be free of your father, you will need my help.*

And how will you do that? Rayne answered back in her mind, knowing her father would remain oblivious to their conversation. M'Zabareth existed in a small place inside her mind, a place that the demon had showed her how to lock away from anyone else but her. That was the place she housed her darkest desires, including her intent to kill her father. It was also where she and M'Zabareth had had many conversations in the past.

The Nexus must be destroyed as your father wishes, the demon replied sweetly. *But what he is not aware of is that, when it is destroyed, he will become vulnerable.*

Weak?

Mortal, was the answer. *And then you may kill him.*

Why do you want him dead?

Because I have a covenant that binds me to him forever, my dear—or at least as long as he lives. I wish for my freedom as much as you wish for your own.

You swear to help me?

I do, the demon answered sweetly. *I will help you capture this man of destiny and unlock his power. He is known as Rook.*

How do you know this?

Because I helped create him.

☙❧

Thousands of miles to the south, the ancient wizard shuffled out of his study and began slowly climbing the stairs to his personal chambers, pausing to steady himself against the stone wall while the tower rumbled beneath him. He had already been old when he had commanded Eric to send Terion and Branson through the portal back into Branson's world, with the slim hope of finding Fyre. Eric had been successful in bridging the two worlds, but he had died in the attempt—and the young man's death had haunted the wizard ever since. Since Eric's death, the past sixteen years had been lived in loneliness and now, well past a hundred, Loken was beyond tired of living. But he dared not give in to mortality. Not yet. Not if he wanted any chance of a peaceful existence after death. Besides, Benovan had charged him with a task, and that still lay unfinished before him.

So he had soldiered on and had used his magic non-stop, doing everything he could to divine what the future was bringing and to discover those secrets he did not yet know. He knew on the night of Eric's death what Benovan meant about restoring Varankyl. He knew where the artifact was. That was the easy part. The rest would test him like never before.

And now, against all odds, Fyre had finally returned to their world. Loken had felt the portal open between the worlds, had sensed her return just as certainly as if she stood before him. Varankyl had returned with her, a part of her, although the young woman knew nothing of the being within her. The other half of the sentient artifact resided within her sister, Rayne, who he knew to be alive in the northern lands, a pawn of her father, Kraegor.

They were the mirror—two sisters separated by cruel fate, one dark and corrupted, the other innocent and unspoiled—both destined to be reunited and, together, to either destroy the Nexus and ultimately the universe.

Or save it.

Fyre's return signified another major development, as well.

Whatever had brought her back to the world had brought about the beginning of the convergence. The wizard knew it would take some time to fully manifest itself—perhaps weeks, maybe months, but it had definitely arrived. He could feel the fabric of the magical barrier between worlds unraveling, and the occasional tremor that rocked his tower confirmed it. When the barrier was completely gone, its end would bring forth a cataclysm that would bring ruin to the entire world. Two worlds would literally become one. No one could imagine what that truly meant, but even as terrible as that was, it was purely insignificant to the safety of the Nexus.

His studies and divination over the years had told him the certainties of what they were facing. The Nexus was failing. The convergence of the two worlds was but a symptom of the greater problem. If the Nexus was destroyed, all would be destroyed with it. Only hell would remain.

The Nexus was the key.

Rayne would attempt to destroy it.

Fyre would have to save it.

Both would have to die.

With a heavy heart, he shuffled into his personal chambers and directly to the huge crystal that sat in the middle of the room. With a weary sigh, he placed his hand upon the cool surface and closed his eyes, then uttered a single word.

"Rook."

Coming Soon!

Godfall, the Earth War Saga, Book 3

The epic tale continues as the devastating convergence finally arrives, bringing both worlds together in a fiery cataclysm beyond the scope of anything anyone could have ever imagined. The lands are ravaged, entire cities are destroyed, and countless men, women, and children are killed. The destruction is so great and so complete, that even the very gods themselves are banished to the ruined earth.

War quickly descends upon the world's survivors as the fallen gods walk among them and great armies appear, vying for what little remains of the shattered world. Kraegor's armies of humans and demons are vast, but Shayene's horde of vampires are beyond count. Caught between them are the few remaining humans desperate to survive in a nightmare beyond compare.

The future of all humanity hangs on a razor when, in the end, the mirror finally comes together and the twins—Fyre and Rayne—face off to see who will live and who will die.

Available Now!

Renegades: The Judas War

The year is 2387 and the Confederation is threatened by a faceless entity bent on the destruction of everything they hold dear: exploration, equality, and freedom for all.

During a routine FleetCom training exercise, a secret cabal of high-ranking officials launches their first attack as they embark upon a mission that will fracture the very foundation of the Confederation and plunge the galaxy into a genocidal war.

In the middle of the conflict is Lexxa Singh, First Officer of the Icarus, FleetCom's newest destroyer. Plagued by nightmares of a life she never wanted, she finds herself betrayed at every turn as she fights a desperate battle to save a Confederation she's not even sure is worth saving.

www.ingramcontent.com/pod-product-compliance
Lightning Source LLC
Chambersburg PA
CBHW030343020726
47493CB00003B/657